Dirty
Little Secrets

By

L.A. Lewis

Edited by Chandra Sparks Taylor
Taylor Editing Service
www.cstedits.com

Cover picture by Amadi Phillips
Cover design by Gerren McNair and Eritrea Dorcely

Library of Congress Control Number: 2009909743

ISBN 978-0-615-32200-1

This book is dedicated in memory of two educators I've loved and lost

To my mother
Lorna Mae Cyprian
who was not only a great mother, but also
the best teacher I've ever known.
I will love you forever!!!

To my coworker and friend
Denise P.
who's life was taken way too soon.
Your smiling face is still greatly missed,
but your memory will live in our hearts forever!!!

Acknowledgements

So there are no hard feelings let me explain the purpose of the acknowledgements. These acknowledgements are to recognize those persons who assisted me with this book, not in life. There are many people who are near and dear to my heart who I could acknowledge for many different reasons, but that's not the purpose of this page. Now without further ado....

You know I have to always start with the Most High God. I truly believe He opened my eyes to writing so that other wonderful opportunities can follow. He allowed me to see the gift within myself and to share that gift with each of you. I thank God for all that I was, all that I am, and all that I aspire to be, and will be one day.

My husband Neil who tolerated me throughout this whole process. At times when most husbands would probably be upset or feel left out, mine continued to support and motivate. I can't remember a time when he made me doubt myself or my work. He's one of my biggest cheerleaders and I love him more and more each day.

Our beautiful children AJ and Kirsten. I believe they are more proud of me than anyone else. They never miss an opportunity to tell people that their mom is an author. I don't know if they'll ever realize how much that means to me. Everything that I am is because of my babies.

My father who is another one of my biggest cheerleaders. He supports me through every hare-brained idea I've ever had. He's another one who tells everyone about his baby, the author. I honestly don't know what I would do without the man who I call Daddy.

To my three member fan club: Rose, Denise, and Sharmayne. These are what I call "die hard" fans because they read all 200 plus pages of my book from their computer screens. The funny thing is they kept asking for more. Without them I probably would've never finished this book. They critiqued each part and gave me their honest opinions and I love them and thank them so much for that. I also have to thank my Aunt Pat and Sharmayne, again, who supported me in other ways that they and I both know about (smile).

To the best editor in the world Chandra Sparks Taylor. Words cannot describe how thankful I am to her. I believe in my writing abilities, but Chandra allowed me to take it to the next level. She challenged me for more and I tried my best to do it, I just hope she's pleased.

To my book cover Photographer Amadi Phillips thanks for a wonderful picture. To my Graphic Designers Gerren McNair and Eritrea Dorcely, who worked wonders on making my cover perfect. To Carey Domino, bestselling author of “Sideline Ho” and “Who Does She Think She Is”; C.J. Peters, and Rhonda Peters, thank you all so much for helping to guide me through in one way or another. Words cannot express how much you guys are appreciated.

Chapter 1

I jump straight up when my phone rings at 3:00 A.M. I'm not afraid of bad news or anything because I've gone through this every night this week. I pick up the phone and hold it to my ear. No greeting is needed.

"Bitch!" *Click.* I unplug the phone, which has become my nightly routine. I hate doing this because I'm always so afraid of missing important phone calls, but it's a chance I have to take for my sanity. I am so sick of this. I don't know what else to do. I've called the police—no help. I've called the operator who directed me to the phone company who was absolutely no help at all. Instead of a number showing up on the caller ID, it shows up private caller. The phone company claims they can't give out information on anyone who's chosen a private number.

"I'm sorry, ma'am, I simply cannot give out that information," the operator, who had the deepest southern accent I've ever heard, informed me. I was so fed up, I even went as far as to request the police put a tap on my phone, but apparently they don't do that for this type of harassment case. The last officer I spoke with informed me that no crime has been committed. The person never threatened me. They're just being annoying as hell. I've seen enough movies to know that I should never take anything for granted. This person is obviously disturbed and who knows? This could just be the beginning. At any time he or she could decide it's time to go a step farther, whatever that may be. I guess once this sicko kidnaps me or my husband Mark then the authorities will finally take them seriously.

I've known Mark for eighteen years; we've been married for fourteen of them. I can't imagine my life without him, so the thought of someone hurting him makes me angry, and I know he feels the same way. I just don't understand why innocent people have to go through being harassed and no one seems to have a problem with it. I swear the law can be so backward at times. Wouldn't it make more sense to handle this psycho now before things go too far and someone gets hurt—or worse, killed?

"Another hang up?" Mark asks as he turns over to face me.

"Yeah. Go back to sleep." I wish I could, but my mind won't allow it. I just can't figure out who could be doing this to me. The only person I can think of is Ms. Davis, my problem student's mother. She and I have had several run-ins these last few weeks. I've been teaching at Greenwood Elementary for ten years, ever since I graduated from Southern University, here in Baton Rouge. In all my years of teaching, I've never had to deal with a parent as outrageous as this one. This is truly your parent from hell. She's obviously not happy with me being her child's teacher, but from what I hear she's not happy with any of his teachers. I've never heard any of them complaining about being harassed though. This just doesn't make sense to me.

Like every morning before I get out the bed I take a few minutes to gaze at my husband as he sleeps. Sometimes I still can't believe the life Mark and I have built together. I look at him knowing he could've had any girl he wanted in high school, but for some reason he chose me. Dating Mark wasn't always easy for me. He's always been very athletic and has the body to prove it. Mark stands every bit of six feet tall with broad shoulders and a stomach most men only dream of. When we were in high school, the girls use to go crazy when he'd walk in the room. All of a sudden they all had a little more twist in their walk and oh my God, I thought they would break their back trying to stick their chest out. Even now I notice women eyeing him whenever we're out together. I can only imagine what happens when he's alone. Mark's always been the most handsome man I know. He reminds me a lot of Denzel Washington. Not that they look alike or anything, but to me they both are average-looking men with above-average sex appeal. Mark isn't Shemar Moore handsome, but he can definitely hold his own. I guess that's why I never really understood why he was so crazy about me.

I'm the exact opposite of Mark. I don't have an athletic bone in my body, and if I didn't work out I would surely fall into the obese category. My weight has always been a big issue for me. Mark never says anything when I do put on a few pounds, but I always feel like he looks at me differently. That's what I mean when I say being with him has never been easy. I always feel like I have to compete with all those supermodel-looking women in order to keep my husband interested in me. Up until now I've never felt that Mark's given me a reason to believe he would step out of our marriage, but now there's just something different about him. I continue to watch him as a slow grin spreads across his face. I wonder what he's dreaming about and if that smile has anything to do with his sudden mood change. I can't allow my thoughts to go there right now. My walk down memory lane has lit a fire in me that only my husband can extinguish.

I reach under the cover and grab for Mr. Richard, which is Mark's code name for his manhood. Mr. Richard is an inside joke because of the nickname for Richard "Dick." Using it as a code name when we're around friends is so hilarious. In the middle of dinner, out of nowhere he'll say, "So Holly, I spoke with Mr. Richard, and he really wants to come visit tonight" or something crazy like that. I have to try with everything in me not to burst out laughing. I don't think anyone would've understood why that statement was so funny.

I stroke Mr. Richard and try with everything I have to wake him up. All of my efforts seem to go unnoticed.

"What you doing?" Mark asks groggily.

"Trying to visit with Mr. Richard before I leave," I answer in my most seductive voice.

"No, babe. Not now. Mr. Richard's very tired."

"You know what? Mr. Richard is always tired lately. Well how about you give him a message from me. Tell Mr. Richard I'm not going to keep trying, and he can keep playing with me if he wants, but don't get pissed when I'm suddenly never in the mood."

I get out of bed, angry, and go straight to the shower. I hear him coming in to take his morning pee. I wait for him to open the shower curtain. I just know he's going to try to come in and redeem himself. I get the shock of my life because he flushes, washes his hands, and leaves. Mark is the most horny man I know. He would have sex every day all day if he could. I remember about a year ago he begged me to take a week off work because he needed his fix, as he said. I think we may have left the bed once out of the whole week. We didn't leave the house at all. That's how high his sex drive is. For him to go from needing it all the time to barely wanting it at all makes me think something is definitely wrong, but what?

I'm out the house by 6:30 each morning. My commute to work is about thirty minutes. It's taking me some time to get use to this drive. Mark and I bought our dream house a year ago. As soon as we drove into the gated community with our realtor, I knew that this is where I was meant to be. I always describe the houses in my community as mini mansions. My two-story, three thousand square foot house is everything I've ever wished for. Mark and I bought the house brand new so there was no need for any upgrades. My mom always says that our house is way too big for just the two of us, but that's her opinion. Mark and I are big entertainers, and we love having so much space and such a huge backyard for our family cookouts. This house is why I didn't mind sacrificing my morning sleep in order to get to work on time. I have to get up an hour earlier now, but to be able to drive through my neighborhood with all the perfectly landscaped yards with the knowledge I actually live here is well worth it.

I've started a new morning routine, which isn't good but it's become a habit now. I can't seem to get my day started now without stopping by Starbucks to get my morning coffee. Mark has told me over and over that I'm throwing my money away. "Why would you want to make the rich man richer?" he asks. Mark thinks I should just make my coffee at home before I leave, but he doesn't get it, and I guess I don't either. It's just something about coming here that makes me feel good. These days even if I didn't want the coffee I would stop anyway just to aggravate him.

After leaving Starbucks, I put in my favorite CD and begin listening to my inspirational music. I need all the inspiring I can get today, and no one inspires me more than Yolanda Adams. I've seen a lot of her interviews, and just knowing her struggle and seeing where she is now is enough to inspire anyone. She makes me feel like there's nothing I will encounter that I can't handle. As I listen I try to clear my mind from all negativity and only allow the positive things in life to invade my thoughts.

I don't know how I went from positive thinking to Tyler Davis. That's usually what happens when I'm determined to think good things. I know it's the devil trying to bring me down because I'm listening to my good gospel music, and unfortunately I'm feeding right into it. I swear I can't get that little boy out of my head. I wish I could say it's because he's so sweet and I just love thinking about him. Wrong! He is everything but sweet—is there any word worse than *horrible*? If so that's the word I would use to describe him. He's truly a chip off the old block. It's no wonder he behaves the way he does because his mother truly isn't a good example for him. I'm trying hard to prepare myself to deal with him today, but obviously it's not working.

I arrive at work and sign in. I'm usually one of the first ones here besides the custodians.

"Morning, Mr. Jack," I say as I open my room door. Mr. Jack is the lead custodian. He's very sweet, but I do warn all the young teachers around here to watch him. I see him looking when he thinks no one is watching him. Mr. Jack is probably old enough to be their great-grandfather, but that doesn't stop him from trying.

"Good morning, Mrs. James. How's it going this morning?"

"Well, Mr. Jack, I could complain, but why? What good would that do?"

"You're right about that," he responds.

I go in my classroom and try to mentally prepare for the day. It's funny how walking into my room always changes my mood. I chose a tropical theme for my room this year and the kids and I both love it. I painted the walls a bluish-green, which reminds me of the ocean. I read somewhere it's supposed to be a very calming color. The decorations are all tropical things like the fish on the walls and the big palm tree in the corner, which we use as our reading center. Of course it's not a real palm tree, just one I made from colored paper and a big carpet roll. The response when the kids walked in the room on the first day was priceless. I could tell by their expressions they really loved their new classroom; that, on top of the excitement of now being in the third grade. I can remember that day so well; it's hard to believe we are at the halfway point already. Once we come back from Christmas break, the rest of the year is going to fly by. I sit at my desk thinking about nothing in particular when I hear Smith unlocking her door. She's the other third-grade teacher along with Jones and Myers. I often wonder if teachers are the only people who refer to each other by their last names. Even if we don't put a proper title in front, we still only use last names. However, there are certain unspoken rules to the name thing. We do add titles in the presence of students and parents, and for some reason the office and custodial staff missed the no-title memo because we tend to add titles to their names and vice versa. I guess it's a teacher thing.

This is my first year working with Smith, and we've become really close. That's probably because we have two things in common: Tyler and his mom. Smith had the unfortunate opportunity to be his teacher last year.

"Good morning," she says as she peeps her head in my door.

"Good morning, yourself. My, don't you look nice today." I say admiring her black wrap dress and silver accessories.

"Thanks. It's really the only thing in my closet I didn't have to iron, so I threw it on."

"Oh, I've had those days," I respond.

"So, did you get in touch with Tyler's parents yesterday?"

"Unfortunately, I tried to talk with his mother, but as usual, she wasn't very cooperative. I still think she's the one making those obscene phone calls every morning."

"Did you report those? This has been going on long enough."

"I did, but there's nothing the police, the operator, or the phone company can do because right now it's just speculation. I have no proof that it's her."

"I just don't understand why she would harass you. I mean she and I had some pretty heated discussions last year, but it never got to this point. She just doesn't seem like the type to hide behind a phone. She tells you upfront what she has to say."

"I know. That's why I'm not one hundred percent sure it's her, but she's the only person I can think of. She has no reason to be upset with me—I'm just trying to help her out. The fact is her child is terrible, and she needs to get him under control now before he's too far gone."

"What about his dad? Have you tried talking to him about his behavior?"

"His emergency card didn't have a number for his dad."

"I think they separated last year. From my understanding it's a big mess. He's Tyler's stepdad so she probably didn't put it on purpose. It's too bad because he believes in disciplining him. Last year I had to stop him from trying to whip him in class. Now you know I really wanted to turn my head and act like I didn't see a thing, but I decided to do the right thing."

"I know exactly what you mean. If Tyler was anything like he is now I don't blame you. I see why you only agreed to move up with your class if they removed him."

"Girl, I could not go through another year like last year."

"I can say now that I completely understand. Tyler makes it very hard for anyone to like him." Immediately when the words left my mouth I wished I could take them back. I know I shouldn't be telling this teacher I didn't like this child, but her response made me feel a little better.

"I know. I use to cringe when I saw him walk through the door. I had to make myself put on a front for this child. It's truly sad to feel this way about a child, but I just can't help it."

Smith and I talk for a while longer, then finish preparing for the arrival of our students. Even though my classroom is the very last one on the hall, I can still tell when they are coming. They sound like wild horses running down the hall. I hear teachers hollering, "No running. Go back to the door and walk, mister." My students began to flow in all jolly and eager to start learning. Well, a teacher can dream, can't she? I do my morning greetings to each of the students. Everyone is here except Tyler. I know he'll be here shortly, so I go ahead and start class.

"Okay, boys and girls," I begin, "let's take our seats and get ready to do our journal for today." I call on a student to read the journal prompt and tell them all to get busy. As they're writing I proceed to call roll and take up lunch money. With all the inventions in the world, you would think someone could invent an easier way for teachers to start their morning.

The beginning of my day runs very smooth, maybe because my star student still isn't here. I know it's too good to think he could be absent all day, but I have to admit it is a good thought—take that back, it's a great thought.. As I began introducing my reading lesson for the day, I have an interruption.

"Mrs. James," Mrs. Craig, the secretary calls over the intercom.

"Yes," I respond.

"Mr. McNair asks if you can get someone to watch your class. He needs to see you in the office."

"Okay," I say. What I really want to ask is where am I suppose to get this mystery person to come in and watch my class. Is there a person on campus he keeps on standby, and if so why is he hiding them from us? I go next door and ask Smith if she can listen out for my class because I've been summoned to the office. I quickly give them an assignment and am on my way. Most of the teachers here absolutely hate being called to the office, probably more than the students. Mr. McNair, the principal, usually has a complaint about something you were doing, had done, or that he dreamed last night you might do. He is so annoying in every way imaginable.

As I walk in the office I see Tyler and his mom sitting there, obviously waiting for me to arrive. "Hello," I say when I enter the room.

I receive nothing in response. I so do not feel like going through this drama with her today. Hoping that Tyler had gone home and confessed what a terror he'd been on yesterday and she was here to make him apologize to me was just wishful thinking. She should be upset because she's dealing with an out-of-control child. For some reason she just doesn't see that.

"Mrs. James," Mr. McNair says, interrupting my thoughts, "please have a seat so we can get started."

"Okay. What's going on?" I ask. My curiosity is really getting the best of me.

"Mrs. James, Tyler informed his mom an incident happened yesterday and you pushed him out of the class."

"Excuse me?" I say. "Please repeat that again." He did as I asked, and hearing the words again did not make me feel any better. I'm shocked and for a few seconds at a loss for words.

"Mr. McNair," I begin, "let me assure you I did not push Tyler—at least not the way he's making it seem."

"Okay, then how did you push him?" Mrs. Davis finally speaks, "because obviously you put your hands on him some kind of way, and you better believe if you did he'll be the last child you put your hands on."

"I will be more than happy to explain what happened yesterday, but what I will not tolerate is you sitting here threatening me." I have to let her know she can't talk to me any kind of way and think I'm just going to sit here and take it. What she needs to do is chastise her child and maybe we wouldn't need to have these little meetings.

"Ladies, please," Mr. McNair finally steps in. "Let's remember we are the adults here, and there is a child in the room."

"I'm sorry," Ms. Davis responds, still obviously aggravated, "but I don't allow anyone to put their hands on my child, and that's just the bottom line. If he's acting up then you call me and I'll handle him myself. Tyler has one momma, and that's me. If this little—"

"Okay," Mr. McNair interrupts again, obviously knowing that the next word out of her mouth isn't going to be a good one. "Ms. Davis you are completely out of line. I thought we could all sit down and get to the problem at hand, but obviously not. Maybe it would be best if I spoke with you two alone and then make a decision from there."

"Ms. Davis," I begin explaining, totally ignoring Mr. McNair's suggestion, mainly because I don't want to deal with this foolishness any more after today, "yesterday Tyler was completely out of control. I asked him to go across the hall to Ms. Smith's class until he could cool off. He refused to move. Since it was obvious he was going to be outright disrespectful, I asked another student to come to the office to get Mr. McNair. When Tyler heard this he decided to go on his own. He walked as far as the door, then stopped. I asked him again to go. He did not move. At this point I took his hand and brought him to Ms. Smith's class. At no point did I push him or anything else."

Ms. Davis looks at Tyler and asks, "Is she telling the truth?"

I cannot believe my ears. Never in all of my years of teaching have I had a parent to question what I said. I would think if I was so abusive some parent would've come forward before now. I've been here for ten years. Why would I wait until now to start mistreating children? Apparently I'm the only one who sees how ridiculous this whole situation is. I cannot believe I've been summoned from my classroom wasting valuable teaching time to sit here for this nonsense. Tyler sits there quiet for a few seconds before he finally responds.

"I was sitting at my desk," he began, sounding like he's about to cry at any minute. "I asked if I could go to the bathroom and Mrs. James said no."

"What did you do after she told you no?" Mr. McNair asks.

"I started doing my work and that's when Chris started teasing me."

"What did you do then?" Mr. McNair asks again.

"I tried to tell Mrs. James but she wouldn't listen to me."

"Okay, so let's get to the part where Mrs. James said you were being disruptive. How were you disrupting the class?"

"I don't know," he says. I'm sitting here speechless. I cannot believe this child is sitting here lying the way he is. I know they can tell he's lying. They have to be able to see through this.

"Tyler, tell them the truth," I demand.

"There you go again trying to call my child a liar," Ms. Davis interjects.

"You cannot tell me that you believe this," I say almost pleading with her to open her eyes and see her child is lying.

"Mr. McNair, I'm sorry. I'm not going to sit here another minute and subject my child to this kind of treatment. It's obvious Mrs. Davis has already made up her mind Tyler is a troublemaker and the least little thing he does, she's going to blow it up and make it more than it really is," Ms. Davis says as she stands to leave.

I'm sitting here still dumbfound by this whole ordeal. I have no idea what's going to happen next. I know putting your hands on a student is a very serious offense. I don't know what to do to make them believe me. Right now it's my word against his. If I could throw this child over my lap and wear his tail out, I would, but of course that's against the rules in public school. I will not lose my job over this little liar.

I decide to try one more time to get him to come clean and tell the truth. "Tyler, you know I never pushed you out the door," I say, obviously upset by these accusations. He just stands there next to his mom like he is the most innocent child in the world. I wonder where's the child I had yesterday, the one who refused to do as I told him, the one who told another student he doesn't care what I say he's not leaving. Where is that child? He's definitely not the little boy who's sitting before me today. I want to suggest that Mr. McNair talk with the students because obviously they saw the whole thing, but I'm not sure if I should chance bringing them into this. Most of the students are so afraid of Tyler that they will probably go out of their way to defend him and apologize to me later. I don't know what he does to them, but I do know that they are definitely afraid of him. I've even had some kids who were almost suspended because they were taking the rap for something Tyler did. They didn't care that they would have to go home and deal with upset parents. In their world dealing with the parents is a lot better than dealing with Tyler. I would love to think they would risk everything and back me up, but I simply can't take that chance and I can't put them in that position. This is a battle I'll have to fight alone.

Mr. McNair assures Mrs. Davis, who's even more upset by now, that he will investigate the situation. When they leave he tells me he will definitely go to bat for me, but for now he has no choice but to put me on leave while he continues to get to the bottom of this mess. I ask how long I'll be on leave and when it starts. Imagine my shock when he says I'll be on leave about two days and it starts immediately. He then tells me to go to my room and prepare for a substitute to come in, and then I'm to leave to go down to human resources. They will continue looking into the situation.

I can't get out of this building fast enough. I call my union from my cell phone, and a representative is meeting me at the school board office. He informs me the situation will be taken care of and assures me I'll return to work soon. I feel better after talking with him, but still can't believe I'm going through this. People say it's a first time for everything, but this is something I can live without experiencing.

After meeting with human resources and my union representative, I head home. It seems like the longest drive ever. I want nothing more than to run into my husband's arms and have a good cry. I'm so preoccupied that entering my neighborhood does nothing for my mood. Usually I can be having the worst day and once I arrive here my troubles all of a sudden seem minute. I guess I didn't know a real bad day until today. Teaching is what I love the most. I can't imagine doing anything else. I don't want to imagine doing anything else.

I enter my house to find it looking and smelling fresh and clean, which tells me one thing, Ms. Laura, the cleaning lady, came by today. My mom thinks we're living way above our means because we hired Ms. Laura. When we moved here I knew it was too much house for Mark and me to keep clean by ourselves, especially with our busy schedules. Sometimes I think she forgets that Mark is an accountant—well was an accountant. He manages our money very well, not to mention the good investments we've made over the years. We wouldn't have hired a housekeeper if we didn't know we could afford her. I must admit I'm rather spoiled to having her now. My mom and everyone else can say what they want, I love having Ms. Laura, and I'm not giving her up anytime soon.

I walk down the hall and there's Mark sitting at the computer working. Mark started doing medical billing, which allows him to work from home. I was actually shocked when he told me he was thinking of quitting his job to do medical billing. While accounting never sounded very interesting to me, he always seemed to enjoy it. Mark's been doing medical billing for about a year now. I was sure he would try it for a few months before he realized he wasn't meant to be home all day. To my surprise he actually loves working from home. I must admit some days I'm rather jealous, especially those days when it's rainy or cold. Lucky for me we haven't had any real winters here in Louisiana.

"Hey," he says. "What are you doing home?"

When I lift my head and he sees the tears streaming down my face he really becomes concerned.

"Honey, what happened to you?" he asks worriedly. "Did you make it to work?"

I pull myself together long enough to tell Mark the whole story. After I finish I'm like a running faucet. The tears just keep coming. I'm thinking I'm surely going to dehydrate, but thankfully I don't. Mark must be thinking the same thing because he gets up to get me some water.

"Here," he says. "Drink this." He hands me the glass. "So what are your plans? Surely you're not going back to that place. This is utterly ridiculous. Is that what the world has come to? I remember when I was in school, you didn't dare go home and call yourself telling on the teacher. You were likely to get two whippings—one for telling and another one for causing the teacher to have to fuss. I can't believe the parents now. It's because they're young and can't take care of themselves, more or less trying to raise a child. They think they can be these kids' friends and not their parent."

Mark goes on and on about the problems with the kids and parents in today's society. I have to admit I agree with a lot of what he's saying, but I'm still too emotionally disturbed to have this conversation with him now. Even though his argument is right, it doesn't apply to my situation. Ms. Davis only looks to be a couple years younger than I am, so I wouldn't put her in the young and dumb category. I attribute her behavior to ignorance and nothing else. She's ignorant to the fact that her child is terrible and that she's only making him act worse.

I excuse myself from the living room and go to our bedroom to be alone. I decide a good hot soak may help to relax my tense muscles. I lay in the tub and replay the events of the day in my head. Each time I think about it, I cry. I don't know how I'll be able to face my colleagues when I do return to work. Surely, the word has spread around the school by now. I remember when Coach left early one day. By the time I'd heard the story the version had completely changed. I was told he left because a neighbor called and said there was a suspicious car in front of his house and that his wife was possibly having an affair with the car's owner. Come to find out his neighbor did call, but to tell him his security system was going off. I can only imagine what they're saying about me. I'm sure from their accounts I had to leave because I beat a student and put him in the hospital. I probably had to be escorted off the campus by the police. It won't shock me one bit if this is the story they concoct.

I try to keep myself busy the rest of the day. I even volunteer to help Mark put in some information, and he knows how much I hate being on that computer. Mark has so much work stuff on the computer that it's difficult to do simple tasks like check your emails. I usually handle all my business before I leave school so I won't have to worry with his computer. I left today in such a haste, checking emails was the last thing on my mind. Before I begin working I decide to check and read my inspirational message for the day, which our church, Mt. Olive Baptist, emails to all the members. It really helps me to focus on it throughout the day. Right now I need inspiration. The pastor's message on let God fight your battles is encouraging. Reading this does make me feel better, but it's also one of those things that's easier said than done. I vowed I was not going to stress, that I was going to do just as the message instructed, but I still have those moments where my mind starts to think the worse. Each time the phone rings I think it's Mr. McNair calling to tell me I've been fired. I don't know if I can handle that kind of news at the moment. I'm trying to be strong, but I feel like I'm fighting a losing battle.

I refocus myself and close out my email when a message pops up on the computer.

Each time Mark receives a new email the sender's name and title of the message pops up on the screen. I start to click ignore when I notice the subject says: It's me. I want to press ignore, but something tells me I may want to read this one for myself. Even as I'm opening the message I tell myself this is just junk mail or some type of advertisement. So why can't I shake this feeling? Other than Mark being a little distant lately, he really hasn't given me any reason to believe he's doing anything wrong. I know he's not cheating, so he's probably just going through a midlife crisis a little early.

I open the email and it's definitely not an advertisement. My mouth is hanging open as I read the words on the screen. It's sad because I remember the words verbatim. It says, "Hey, Hon, it's me. Give me a call at your earliest convenience." I can literally feel my heart fall as I read these words over and over. I'm still staring at the screen when Mark walks back in the room.

"You got it?" he asks.

"Yeah, I definitely got it," I respond sarcastically.

"Good," he says as he comes closer to get a few files off the table.

"What's that?"

"That's what the hell I want to know."

"Excuse me?"

"You heard me. What's this? You don't remember it? Well let me refresh your memory: *Hey, Hon, it's me. Give me a call at your earliest convenience.* Does that jog your memory?"

"Oh, that?" he says, laughing.

"Yes, that, and I don't see what's so damn funny."

"Look, I know you're upset but you have to calm down and stop jumping to conclusions without having all the facts. For your information that's an email from Janet Foster. You remember she's the one who first introduced me to the medical billing business?"

"And when did she forget your name and start calling you Hon?"
"That's just Janet. She calls everybody hon. I know you aren't jealous," he says halfway laughing again.

"I'm sorry, but when another woman gets more attention from my husband than I do, then yes I may tend to be a little jealous."

"What are you talking about? You're just upset because of today? Why don't you go relax for a while and I'll fix dinner?"

I decide I should go, but not because I need it, but because if I stay in here any longer listening to him flat out lie to me, I will probably do something I'm positive I won't regret later. I don't know why, but for some reason I'm just not buying the Janet story. A few months ago I probably would've believed him without any doubts, but as of lately he's just been acting so differently. I guess I'm paranoid about everything these days.

I serve my two days and return to work. The school board decided there simply isn't enough evidence to suggest I abused this child in any way. Up until now I've had a clean record, not one unhappy parent, and I think that's something to be proud of. I decide I will walk around with my head held high. I know I didn't do anything wrong. I know I will never do anything to hurt a child. That's not me. I'm a nurturer—that's what I do. Surprisingly enough everyone is normal. No one says a word, not even a dirty look. I'm sure they discussed it among their cliques, but like everything else, I'm now old news.

"Hey. Welcome back," Smith says as she sees me opening my door.

"Hey. Thanks," I say, happy to be back.

"So, did you enjoy your vacation?"

"I wish it was a vacation. I made myself sick because I was so busy worrying about what the outcome would be and what everyone would think of me."

"I can believe that. I've never been in that situation, but I can believe it isn't fun."

"You know, when all of this first happened I was so angry. I couldn't believe Tyler would flat-out lie about what happened that day. The more I thought of it I concluded he was probably too afraid to tell the truth."

"You think so, but what would he be afraid of?"

"Afraid of his mom. I know I was, and I'm grown. Have you met the lady?" I ask, laughing. Smith laughs too because she has met Mrs. Davis on more occasions than she cares to remember.

"Hello, ladies," Mr. McNair says as he enters the room. "Mrs. James, may I have a word with you?"

"Sure," I reply.

"If you two will excuse me, I have to go and get prepared," Smith says as she makes her exit from my room.

"What can I do for you, Mr. McNair?"

"I just wanted to check on you and make sure you understand that I did what I had to do. The handbook clearly states that—"

"Mr. McNair, I'm well aware of what the handbook says. I understand your position. You did what you thought was best, and I have no choice but to respect that."

"Well, good," he says. "I also wanted you to know that Mrs. Davis requested that Tyler be removed from your class."

"Oh really?" is my only response.

"I hope you understand. I have to respect her wishes. I'm moving him to Ms. Jones' class today. If you would, please start getting his things together so his move is a smooth one."

"Yes, sir," I respond. It still felt funny calling him sir being that we're probably the same age if he's not younger. I grew up during the time where no matter the age you always respect those in the position of authority. Mr. McNair heads for the door. Before he leaves he turns around to extend his apologies to me again. He has no idea that right now I could care less about anything that happened. The result of all of this is that Tyler Davis is now out of my class. I don't know if I want to jump up and down or run down the hall shouting for joy. I settle on going across the hall and sharing my news with Smith. I can't believe it. I'm not going to have to deal with Tyler Davis again.

Today could've been a very good day if it wasn't for our dreaded weekly faculty meeting. No one ever understood the purpose behind them. The things we discuss can easily be discussed during our grade-level planning meetings. We've come to the conclusion this is just another way for Mr. McNair to torture us. We sit there listening to him ramble on about absolutely nothing. Eventually, he's tired of hearing himself talk and finally allows us to leave. We're getting out of there like we've all just been released from prison. I swear the parking lot clears in a matter of minutes. Well, except for those Goody Two-shoes who always feel the need to do a little extra at the end of the day. Honestly, I just can't think of enough to do that will keep me in my classroom until 6:00 P.M. I guess there are things I could do, but why would I want to? Right now all I want to do is go home and relax.

The next few weeks at school are great. I hate to think it's because of Tyler being removed from my class, but a part of me did believe that. It's amazing to me how one child can change the whole dynamic of a classroom. The class is completely different. I'm able to actually teach without hearing "Mrs. James, Tyler hit me," or "Mrs. James, Tyler took my pencil." Everyone is getting along and working in their cooperative groups the way it was designed to be worked—cooperatively.

I wish I can say my personal life is just as good. I'm still receiving those harassing phone calls that wake me up every morning. I'm tired of getting the runaround with the police. I keep getting the same answer, "We're sorry, ma'am. There's nothing we can do. You may want to think of getting a private number." I've thought about it, but having to go through the trouble of giving all our friends and family the new number is just too much. On top of that Mark just hasn't been himself lately. He's so distant and quite moody. I'm usually too tired from work to even pay much attention to his attitude, but it is starting to get very old very fast.

Chapter 2

Saturday, a teacher's best friend. I decide to do something I haven't done in a long time, finally spend some girl time with my best friend, Janelle Donaldson. Janelle and I have been friends since our days at Southern University, or SU as we so loving refer to our alma mater. Janelle dropped out during our sophomore year. After winter break she simply decided that she couldn't do the school thing anymore, at least that's what she told me. I tried hard to convince her to stay. I even offered to write her papers for her because I knew that was always a struggle for her. We were roommates our freshman year and by the next year we were best friends. I knew a lot about her by that time. I always felt like dropping out would be a decision she would regret over time, and it seems like the time has come. I don't agree with her lifestyle, but apparently it works for her.

Janelle has always been a very beautiful lady to me. When she first walked in our room I was mesmerized by her beauty. She's the type that all the guys fall over with her chocolate brown skin and jet-black shoulder-length hair that drives all the men wild. I think the thing that caught my attention first is her eyes. Janelle has hazel-brown eyes, which I could've sworn were colored contacts. I finally worked up the nerve to ask her one day and she had to practically poke her eyes out to prove me wrong. Once I met her family I knew where she got her beautiful eyes from. Almost everyone in her family has light eyes with the exception of her sister. Janelle said she use to always tease her sister and tell her she was adopted because her eyes are different. Janelle still finds that story funny, although her sister, Robin, doesn't seem to get the humor from it. After all these years it still affects her that she's somewhat different from the rest of her family.

It was always difficult to be in a committed relationship and have a friend like Janelle. When we were in college she used to have a date every night. That wasn't a problem, but when the dude she was seeing had a friend who needed to be hooked up, then that's when we would have our disagreements. Janelle felt I was being stupid for not dating other people. "I bet Mark's not sitting home thinking about you," she would say. I use to hate when she would say stuff like that, but I could never let her know. I always felt like Janelle was the strong one and I was the wimpy one. If I let her know she hurt my feelings, to me that would have just confirmed I really was the weak one. I did let her convince me to go out on a few dates that meant absolutely nothing to me. To this day, Mark still has no idea about any of those. I use to feel bad, but Janelle finally made me believe Mark had a few skeletons in his closet too. She told me a little mystery is good for the relationship. I don't understand that logic, but for some reason it made sense back then. I guess that's where the term *young and dumb* comes from.

Janelle and I haven't spent much time together because lately my time is divided between Mark, my parents, work, and church. That's why today is very special for both of us. We have the whole day planned. We're looking forward to shopping, eating, and just enjoying each other's company.

"Hey you," Janelle greets me as she walks in the spa. It's funny because after all these years my friend hasn't aged a bit—still as beautiful as ever. I finally convinced her to cut her hair in an inverted bob. She was very reluctant because the shortest she's ever gone is to her shoulders. Once she cut it, she immediately fell in love. She all of a sudden got a whole new swagger in her walk.

"Hey. You have no idea how bad I need this massage today," I say as she leans down to embrace me before sitting.

"You look tired. Are you still getting those phone calls?" she asks.

"Every morning like clockwork."

"Girl, you need to handle that."

"Okay, what am I suppose to do? I don't know if it's Ms. Davis, but she's where I would put all my money, if I were a gambling woman."

"Well, like I said, handle that. Give her one good beat down and she'll leave you alone."

"Okay, so I just beat the woman up, and what if it's not her?"

"Then you say, 'Oops, my bad.'" Hell, I'm sure she deserves a good one anyway, even if it's not her. She's given you enough hell this year."

We both fall out laughing. That's what I love about Janelle; she's everything I'm not. I'm more passive-aggressive, and she's just plain aggressive. Janelle is a no-nonsense sista. She takes nothing from no one. Last year she was fired because she cussed her boss out. He accused her of something, and she completely went off. From what I heard, it was bad. The police was called and everything. That little white man almost had a nervous breakdown because of Janelle. This is only one incident from a whole list of Janelle-isms. This is what I call crazy things she does because no one I know but Janelle, would act so outrageous.

"Mrs. James, we're ready for you," the massage therapist says, escorting Janelle and me to the back.

After our massages, we go to lunch. I haven't been out in so long, I suggest we go to my favorite restaurant of all times Olive Garden. Janelle and I are seated and immediately order a pitcher of sangria. I'm not usually a drinker, but I decide to mix things up a little today. It's sad this day is probably the most relaxed I've been in a really long time. It feels really good.

"So, how's Mr. James doing these days?" Janelle asks.

Oh well, there goes my good mood. "Girl, Mark's fine, I guess." I just got to the place where I'm comfortable telling Janelle about problems between Mark and me. In the past she really wasn't too fond of Mark. She always felt like he was holding me back from having fun. I guess that's why she's so close to my parents because that's one area where they all agree.

"You guess? Don't you live with the man?"

"We share a house. That's about it."

"Did something happen? Please don't tell me you and Mark are having problems. You two are the only reason I still believe in true love. You know I live vicariously through your marriage," Janelle says, smiling.

"I'm sure I'm just over exaggerating. He just seems different."

"Different? Different how?"

"I don't know, just not as attentive as usual. He doesn't come to bed until I'm good and sleep. I guess I'm just not use to that. Mark use to make sure we went to bed together. No matter what he was doing as soon as I said I'm going to bed he was right there with me."

"Maybe he's busier now. You did say his business is really taking off."

"That's probably it. I'm sure it's nothing. That's why I didn't bother mentioning it to you earlier." The truth is I didn't mention it because I'm too embarrassed to tell anyone that my husband is no longer interested in me. I was sure that Janelle would jump on the bandwagon and immediately agree that he's probably lost interest. I guess her feelings for him really have changed over the years. A few years ago this conversation would be a lot different. She would probably be trying to drive me home to pack my clothes by now.

Janelle and I eat and head straight to the mall. Janelle did most of the buying. I'm still wondering how in the world she can afford to shop as much as she does. Now it's true I'm a teacher and make a little more than nothing, but I do have a steady job. Janelle seems to have a new job every week, which would be fine if they were good jobs. I never bother to ask about her income, mainly because I don't want to know whose husband is taking care of her for the month. It's true that Janelle and I are best friends, but that's one thing about her I don't like. Janelle does not mind who she dates—he can be married, crippled, or gay—as long as he's a man, she'll date him. I never understood, but it's not for my understanding. Besides, I have enough going on in my own life.

Today is so relaxing. I can't remember the last time I did something just for me. I always promise myself I'm going to take more me time and do things like this more often, but it never happens—well not as often as I would like.

I arrive home and just sit in my car for a while. I don't want this feeling to end. I know when I walk in the house, I will immediately feel depressed because then I won't have a choice but to face the fact that my home life is not what I would like it to be. I wish Mark and I were as close as we once were, but that changed quite some time ago. I'm determined to end this night as good as it started. I will go in, take a nice hot bath, get a good night sleep, and start again tomorrow.

I'm really hoping Mark and I can spend Sunday together—take a ride or something before I have to start on my lesson plans for the week. That's wishful thinking. Mark claims he can't leave because he has too much work to do. I tell him I'll do my work while he does his and afterward maybe we can catch a movie or something. He still turns down my invitation. I am so not use to this rejection from him. He's usually the one dying to spend time with me, and unlike him, I always make time. It's funny how now he's too busy for me.

I decide tonight I'll wait up for Mark so we can talk. I know it may not help, but it doesn't hurt to try. I hear him getting out of the shower, so I turn off the television and sit up in bed.

"You still up?" he asks as he steps out the bathroom.

"Yeah. I think we need to talk."

"Okay, shoot. What's on your mind?"

"Us."

"Us? What about us?" he asks.

"I'm just not happy with the way things are between us these days. We never spend any time together."

"Well, you know that's because I'm busy. Isn't this what we've been praying for, a financial blessing?"

"It is, but not at this expense."

"At what expense? I'm here every night."

"But you're not spending time with me. Being here is good, but what about quality time with your wife?"

"Holly, you're really making a big deal out of nothing," Mark tries to assure me.

"But it's a big deal to me. Can't you understand that?"

"I'm sorry, baby. I didn't realize you still felt this way. I promise I'll be more attentive." "You say that now and you will be more attentive, but that'll only last a little while then we're right back to square one again."

"It won't be that way, I promise."

I wish I could say his promises are golden, and it's sad because they use to be to me. Mark could tell me anything and I'd believe him. I guess a part of me still does. I know in my mind that Mark is feeding me bull these days, but my heart believes he's being sincere. I guess only time will tell. If Mark is doing anything wrong eventually I'll find out. I'm a firm believer of what's done in the dark will come to light. I don't have time to look through his cell phone, search his pockets, or snoop through his things. For his sake he better pray he's walking a straight line because I don't know what I'll do if I ever find out otherwise.

"That's all I ask," I say. For the first time in a long while I feel a lot better. Well, I do up until 3:00 A.M. when my phone rings. I pick up the phone and lay it on the end table. I can hear someone talking on the other end, but can't make out what they're saying. The more I think about it, it probably is a good idea to go ahead and get a private number. I cannot continue to go through this.

Chapter 3

I arrive at work early as usual. Mr. McNair is already there. I'm not completely surprised because our school is being observed today. Mr. McNair was a basket case on Friday, making sure our rooms were in order and that we have current student work displayed. I never understood why he is so nervous because we always do what we're supposed to. He really does have a good staff. I just wish he could recognize that and give us the appreciation we deserve. I walk in the office and find him sitting behind the secretary Mrs. Craig's desk talking on the phone.

"Good morning," I whisper. He waves. I can tell the call must be an important one. I walk to my room and begin preparing for the day. I'm writing my journal prompt on the board when I check my watch. It's now 7:45 and Smith hasn't made it here yet. That's a shock because she's usually right behind me. I assume she's still in the office or out front talking to someone. Eight o'clock comes and the students begin coming to class. Smith still hasn't made it, so I have her students to sit in the hall until she arrives. At 8:15 I send one of her students to the office to ask if someone can come open Smith's door and to see if she called in. Before the student can make it to the door, Mr. Jacobs the P.E. teacher comes walking down the hall to get her class.

"Ms. Davis, Mr. McNair wants to know if you've talked to Ms. Smith this morning," Mr. Jacobs asks.

"I haven't heard from her," I respond. I ask if he can also listen out for my class while I walk to the office to see what's going on. No one in the office has heard from her, and she didn't schedule a substitute for today. "Maybe she's just running late and for some reason can't call," I tell them. I go back to my class and wait on her to arrive.

One of the observers decides to visit my room this morning. I'm in the middle of my lesson when Ms. Craig calls my room and asks Mrs. Jackson, the observer, to come to the office. The next call is an all call over the loudspeaker. This is when someone from the office wants to send a message to the entire school. I hate these interruptions, but it comes with the territory I guess.

"Teachers, please take your students to the auditorium and report to the library for a short meeting," Mr. McNair says.

"I wonder what that's all about," Jones says.

"I have no idea," I answer.

We all do as we're told and wait in the library for Mr. McNair to come. We all can't help but to be a little nervous. We've never had to interrupt our classes to report anywhere, unless it was a fire drill. This whole situation is very strange.

"Does anyone know what's going on?" one of the fifth-grade teachers finally asks. Everyone shakes their head.

"I really don't like this," another teacher says.

"Where's Smith?" Jones ask.

"She hasn't made it yet," I respond.

"Oh, God, I'm not getting a good feeling about this at all," Jones says.

We all know something is terribly wrong when Mrs. Louis, the guidance counselor, comes in with a hand full of Kleenex boxes. As soon as we see the tissue, eyes begin to water. No one really knows why they're crying, but we know that something is terribly wrong. We wait maybe a minute later, but it seems like forever for Mr. McNair to arrive.

"I'm sure you know that something has happened. There's really no easy way to say this so I'm just going to say it. Ms. Smith was murdered last night."

I hear the words and I see his mouth still moving, but I have no idea what he's saying next. The only thing I keep hearing in my head is "Ms. Smith was murdered last night." I see people crying hysterically, but for some reason I can't cry. I have absolutely no feelings at all. My whole body goes completely numb. I don't remember anything from that point on. I wake up in Mr. McNair's office with Jones sitting next to me. I look at her bloodshot red eyes and know that I'm not dreaming. What I think I heard is true. At this point I can't hold it in any longer. I cry until I feel I can't cry anymore.

"Do you want me to call your husband?" Jones asks.

"No, I'll be fine," I assure her.

"Mr. McNair said we can stay in here as long as we need to. There are counselors sitting with the students. They don't know what happened yet. Mr. McNair is calling to see how to handle this situation with the children. He doesn't know if we should tell them or if we should wait and let them find out once they get home."

"I hope he doesn't tell them. I don't know if they can handle that," I say. "I really think they need to be with their parents when they hear."

"I agree, but I think he's going to tell them anyway. The phones have already been ringing off the hook with concerned parents. They saw it on the news. He's afraid the students may hear it anyway so he wants it done right."

Today our campus is filled with parents and counselors. I decide I need to be in the room when they tell Smith's class. Those students really loved her. I know they're going to be devastated when they hear the news. I tell myself I'm not going to cry again, but hearing the counselors telling the students really gets to me. I leave out the room because I don't want them to see me crying. I pull myself together and go back in to help console her students. There's no doubt there is a dark cloud over our school. There is a silence that's speaking louder than words. No one has any words, just hugs.

I don't know why I torture myself by watching the news over and over. Everything is still so surreal to me. I see Smith's picture on the screen, and I hear the word *murdered,* but it still doesn't make sense to me. That night, Mark holds me while I cry again. I feel so safe in his arms; I don't want to leave them anytime soon. "The police say it was a home invasion," I inform Mark. "I just don't understand. They said she was shot in the back. I wonder if she was scared. I hope she didn't suffer." I can barely get the words out.

"Holly, don't do that to yourself. Don't think about that," he says, holding me tighter.

"How can I not think about it?" I snap. "I'm sorry, honey. I'm just so hurt and so angry right now. I can't believe this. I just talked to her last night. She called to see if I remembered to pick up treats for our class. She was in the store and was going to get them if I hadn't." I start to cry again. "That's just the type of person she was, you know? She always looked out for me, was always there when I needed her. What am I suppose to do now?" I ask, not really expecting an answer. I must've fallen asleep because I wake up in the bed. Mark isn't there, so I walk to the living room. I can hear him talking, but can't understand what he's saying. He hangs up the phone when I walk in the kitchen.

"Who was that?" I ask.

"Oh, honey you're up. Are you feeling better?"

"I'm okay. Who was that?" I ask again.

"That was Janelle. She was calling to check on you. I told her you had fallen asleep."

"Okay. I'll give her a call tomorrow."

I love Janelle to death and I know she just wants to make sure I'm doing well. Every since we met she's always taken on the position of being my protector. I guess that's what best friends are for. Even though I know her intentions are good, I'm not in the mood to talk tonight.

Surprisingly, I don't get a wake-up call at 3:00 A.M. I guess my harasser does have somewhat of a heart. I'm assuming that's the only reason I was spared tonight. It's not like they can wake me up being that I can't sleep anyway. Every time I close my eyes I see Smith's face. Each time she's smiling. I hope that's God's way of showing me that she's okay.

I drag myself out of bed that morning when the phone rings. "Hey, girl," I say to Janelle when I answer the phone. Caller ID takes all the mystery out of receiving phone calls. I wish it would help when I receive my other calls, but those all show up Private Caller. I knew if I didn't pick up the phone, Janelle would be knocking on my door in like fifteen minutes. She gets so worked up when she can't get in touch with me. Sometimes I feel she's taken on the mother role. I don't think my own mother worries about me as much as she does. It's funny sometimes and other times it's just plain annoying.

"Hey. How're you doing? I called you last night and Mark said you were sleeping."

"Girl, I'm okay. Still feel like I'm living in a dream and really ready to wake up."

"I know what you're going through. I still remember the day my sister died like it was yesterday. I think that's something you never forget." Janelle's oldest sister Sharon died as a result of a drunk driver when she was in high school. Janelle was in middle school at the time. Every once in a while she'll mention her, but for the most part I hardly ever hear her talk about her sister.

"I've never lost someone this close to me before. This pain is unlike anything I've ever experienced."

"Are you going to work today?

"Yeah. I'm getting ready now." I say as I put her on speakerphone. I try to get through my morning routine, but this morning it's very difficult. Curling my hair has never been a big deal, but today it seems like an endless task. I wish I would've taken Janelle's advice and cut it off a few months ago. I love short hair and seeing her new look makes me want to even more. Some days I would like to, but Mark would have a fit. He's old-fashioned when it comes to a woman's hair. It's easy for him to say keep it long because he doesn't have to deal with it every day. My hair now touches the middle of my back and I would love to donate it to Locks of Love or some charity that can appreciate it. I have a good mind to go get the scissors and chop it off myself, but I know I'm emotional and that may not be a very good idea at the moment.

"Why don't you take the day off? You need this time to rest and get yourself together emotionally," Janelle suggests.

"If it wasn't for the kids I would stay right in this bed all day."

"The dedicated teacher," she says, I'm sure trying to at least get a chuckle out of me, but I'm not in the mood for humor this morning.

"I try. Girl, let me go so I can get out of here. I'll call you this evening when I get home."

I hang up with Janelle and finish getting ready for work. It takes everything in me to go this morning. I dread walking down that hall, seeing Smith's room and knowing she won't be here today or any other day. I don't know who Mr. McNair will hire to replace her, but I already know I'm not going to like her. I know that's the wrong attitude to have, but I can't help it. I can't stand the thought of someone else coming in trying to take her place. There is only one Susan D. Smith, and she can never be replaced.

The next few days are very hard. Mr. McNair puts a substitute with Smith's class until he can find a permanent teacher. The class is very disruptive, but she understands they are all dealing with their teacher's death. I walk over a few times and talk with them. I tell them Smith would want them to be on their best behavior. She would want them to show this teacher what a good class she has. They all seem very receptive to what

I'm saying, and from my knowledge she doesn't have any more problems out of them. Smith really does have a good class. It's probably because she taught them in second and now third grade. They knew that she meant business. She was very strict, but very fair—the way a good teacher should be. She was a great teacher. I always told her I would want her to teach my children, if I had any.

Now that I think of it, it really didn't take much to amuse her. She was such an easygoing, loving person. It's tearing me up inside to know that someone so calm and so sweet had to die in such a violent way. I don't know who's the coward that took her life, but I can only hope the misery and pain Smith felt in her last moments are what they'll feel the rest of their life.

Chapter 4

Every since I was a child, Christmas has always been my most favorite time of the year. I remember going shopping with my mom to get gifts for all our family and friends. I love everything about Christmas—the colorful lights on the houses, and the cozy feeling inside with the smell of Mom's sweet potato pie, which I've perfected, drifting throughout the house. People seem to be just a little nicer around Christmastime. I think the holidays somehow have a magical effect on everybody. I'm angry because I feel like I've been robbed of that magical feeling this year. It's been almost two months since Smith's death, and even though things are finally starting to seem like normal again, I still have my days where I think of her all day, and of course that brings me down. It's not like she and I were best buddies outside of work, but her murder is just a constant reminder of how unfair life can be sometimes.

"Are you going to buy that or what?" Janelle asks, interrupting my thoughts. She and I decided to use today to do some last-minute shopping. I don't know why, but I always wait until the last minute to buy Mark's gift. I never know what to get him because to me he has everything. Mark is the type who buys whatever he wants. He never gives me time to buy things for him. He always says, "I wanted it so I just bought it." His philosophy is that life's too short and we should live for today and yada yada yada. I feel that way too, but I'm also more conservative when it comes to spending. That's funny being that he's the accountant. One would think he would be the conservative type. Mark handles all the finances. He wouldn't spend if we didn't have it.

"Um, hello. Is anybody home?" Janelle asks, trying to get my attention again.

"Oh, yeah I'm going to get this one," I say, holding up the shirt in my hand.

"Well can you get it so we can go? I'm starving."

"What's new, Janelle? You're always starving," I say as I head to the checkout counter.

After making my purchase we walk out the mall toward the food court. I have to admit I'm a little hungry myself. I try to be a little more conscious of my eating because, according to my scale, I'm up five pounds. I definitely don't want to put on any more weight before Christmas day. That's the day I really let loose and eat whatever I like. I pay for it later, but on that day working out and dieting are the last things on my mind.

"Hey, isn't that Mark?" Janelle asks.

"Where?" I look around, but don't see him anywhere.

"Right there in the toy store."

"Girl please. What would Mark be doing in a toy store?"

"I don't know, but I'm telling you that man looks like your husband."

I don't know who she sees, but I do know it can't be Mark. Janelle is one of those people who has to check everything out, so of course we turn around and go back into the toy store. We look all over and there's no sign of Mark anywhere. Just as we're heading out, I turn around to do one more check and there he is, standing in the middle aisle looking at toys. Of course my blood is boiling when I see him because I practically begged him to come shopping with me, but he was too busy. What made him come now, and why is he in a toy store? I guess there's only one way to find out.

"Well hello there," I say being sarcastic.

"Holly, um, hey," he says, sounding like he's just receiving the shock of his life. "What are you doing here, I thought you'd decided to go get your hair done instead?"

"I think a better question is what are you doing here, Mark. I thought you were too busy to go shopping today."

"Oh there you are. Girl, I turned around and you were gone," Janelle says as she approaches us. "I told you I saw Mark, I know I'm not crazy." She smiles.

"Hey, Janelle. What's up?" Mark asks, totally avoiding eye contact with me.

"Hey, Mark. What are you doing here?" she asks.

"Yeah, Mark, what are you doing here?"

"I just came by to pick up a little gift for Toys for Tots. They're doing a toy drive at the church you know?" he says, looking at me for confirmation.

"Yes, I know. I thought I told you I'd picked up a toy already."

"I must've missed that. Oh well no need to buy this one then," he says as he puts the truck back on the shelf. "So where are you ladies going now?"

"Straight to the food court," Janelle answers. "My stomach is about to cave in I'm so hungry. Would you like to accompany us?"

"No, no, I'm going to get out of here. I have a lot of work I need to catch up on at home. I'll see you when you get home, babe."

"Yeah, okay," is my only response. I don't know why, but I can't shake this feeling that Mark is lying to me. I know I told him I bought a toy for the church. As a matter of fact I'm sure of it because he asked if I needed him to drop it off when he went for board meeting. *Okay, Mark James, you're hiding something, and as God is my witness I will find out what it is.*

"Girl, what is wrong with you? You've been so distant today." Janelle says as she shoves a handful of french fries in her mouth.

"I have? I'm sorry. I just have a lot on my mind, I guess." I answer as I shove the lettuce around on my plate. Right now eating this salad is the last thing on my mind.

"Okay, so we're keeping secrets now? What's bothering you, and don't say it's nothing because you know I know you better than that."

"Janelle, I think Mark's cheating on me," I say, and that's the first time I ever let those words leave my mouth.

"Okay, Holly, now you're really trippin'. Now you know I don't trust any man—I guess it's hard to when most of the men I'm involved with are married— but in spite of all of that, I believe Mark would not do that to you. He loves you. You have to know that."

"I know that he loves me, but like Tina said, what's love gotta do with it?"

"Look, I don't know what's going on with you, but you need to get yourself together. Maybe you're still emotional over losing your coworker."

"I would like to think that you're right, but Mark's different, and he's starting to get a little sloppy with his lies. I told Mark that I bought a toy. I know I did, so why is he lying?"

"Maybe he just forgot. Just because he's forgetful doesn't make him a liar. Don't be so quick to always think the worse. Give the man the benefit of the doubt."

"Okay, alright, I'll leave it alone.

Janelle and I finish our food and continue our shopping, and as hard as I try to put my cheating thoughts about Mark out of my head, I'm just not successful. I'm so glad I had Janelle with me. Because of her I'm able to get the last of my gifts. Now I don't have to come back out tomorrow and deal with the Christmas Eve crowd.

I drop Janelle off and decide to take the scenic route home. I need some me time.

Okay, Holly, you can either fight to make your marriage work or just throw in the towel. Maybe it's you. Maybe your husband simply isn't attracted to you. You have put on weight. How's he suppose to look at all that and get turned on? Before I know it I feel the warm tears streaming down my face. I decide the only way to make this better is to go home and deal with my husband. It's time we had a real heart to heart. No fussing, no accusations, just real talk.

I walk in, and again Ms. Laura's presence greets me at the door. I swear my house never smells this good when I do decide to clean it myself. I step down into my den and take a few minutes to take in the neatness of my house. I look at my tan sectional sofa with every pillow neatly in place. Above the sofa is a poster-size picture of Mark and me on our wedding day. I've been telling Mark for years that it's time we take another picture to replace it. Mark hates taking pictures so that's always been a losing battle for me. Now, as I look at the two of us on the happiest day of my life, I wouldn't change it for anything. That picture is a reminder of the life we've built together. Mark and I went from living in a studio apartment to a three-bedroom house, and now we're in the house I've dreamed about my whole life. I know I wouldn't do anything to mess up the life we have together, and I can only hope Mark feels the same way.

Every since Mark and I have been married we've had our own little Christmas Eve tradition. We always spend Christmas with his family or mine, so Christmas Eve is our special time together. We turn off all the lights, with the exception of the Christmas tree lights, and we snuggle on the couch and watch all our favorite Christmas movies. We always begin with *It's a Wonderful Life* and end with *Scrooge.* I walk in excited, ready to spend a romantic night with my husband. I enter our room to find Mark fully dressed in the black Armani suit I splurged on last Christmas. All I can think is Mark's changing things up this year and we're possibly going to a Christmas party or something. I start to feel the excitement starting to stir up in me when Mark turns around and notices me standing in the doorway.

"Do we have plans tonight?" I say with a grin so big I can no longer keep it to myself.

"Hey Babe. No, actually I have to go meet with some prospective clients."

In the medical billing business, it's up to Mark to find doctors to become his clients. The more doctors he can obtain, the more money he makes. I never interfere when it comes to his job, but this is absolutely ridiculous.

"Holly, I really am sorry, but I have to meet with them tonight. It's now or never with them, honey. This man and his wife have several practices. Do you know what that could mean for our business?"

"Mark, I understand you have to work. I'll tell you what, how about I come with you?"

"Holly, I would love for you to come, but I don't have time for you to get ready, babe. Why don't you just stay here and get some rest? I promise when I get back I'll make it up to you—all night long," he whispers in my ear.

A chill goes down my spine that I haven't felt in a very long time. I decide not to argue with him. Instead I stay and get myself ready for a night of ecstasy with my husband. I run a hot tub of water and soak in my favorite Bath and Body Works scent. I've tried others, but I always go back to Sweet Pea. It's Mark's favorite too, so naturally I went with it that night. After a long soak, I put on a little makeup, and pin my hair up. Mark loves when I pull it up with a few strands hanging out. I call it the messy pin-up, and he just calls it sexy. After readying myself for my husband I lie in bed and await his arrival. I watch television until I can't take it anymore and give in to sleep.

I wake up and the clock shows twelve o'clock. Okay, I may not know a lot about obtaining clients, but I do know that most of them end before midnight. Just as I reach for the phone to call Mark, I hear the security alarm chiming.

"So that must've been some dinner," I say as I stand at the stair railing looking down at him.

"Why are you still up?" he asks.

"Because it's kind of hard for me to sleep when my husband is out all night," I say with much attitude.

"I was not out all night, Holly. Please don't start trippin'."

"Don't start trippin'? You leave here before seven o'clock for a dinner meeting, come in at midnight, and never bother to call and say anything, and I'm suppose to just be okay with that?"

"Yes, you are. It's not like I left here and you didn't know where I was going. I was having dinner with potential clients, and if I had to sit there the whole night to get that account then I would've."

"So where did you go eat?"

"What?"

"You heard me. Where did you go eat?"

"Why are you questioning me so much these days? Look, if you have something to say, just say it."

"So, was that enough time to think of another lie, or do you need more? I asked you a simple question, and instead of you just giving an answer, you go off. I'm trying really hard to be patient with you, but you aren't exactly making this easy."

"You're crazy, you know that? Most women would be happy that they have a husband who works as hard as I do to make sure they can live the way we're living now, but no, not you."

"Oh I'm so sorry, please forgive me, Mark. How dare I want to spend Christmas Eve with my husband? What in the hell was I thinking?" I say sarcastically. I turn around and go to the bedroom. I hear Mark turn on the television in the den. So much for our romantic night together. He's successfully ruined that—again.

Chapter 5

It's been six months since Christmas and things still aren't the same at home. School, however, is great. Summer break is coming, and boy, do I need a break. I haven't received any more phone calls. I don't know what happened. I just thank God they stopped. I still really feel that it was Tyler's mom. I don't know why, but for some unknown reason she's made up in her mind I am public enemy number one. From day one she seemed to have it in for me. I assume it's because she's had a problem with each one of Tyler's teachers. Whatever the reason, there's no mistaking she cannot stand me.

I'm packing up my bag to go home when I look up to find one of Smith's students standing at my door. "Brittney, what happened? Did you miss the bus?" I ask worriedly.

"No, ma'am," she speaks softly. "I didn't want to ride the bus today."

"Well, how are you getting home? Did you call your mom yet?"

"No, ma'am." She again speaks very softly.

"Baby, we have to call her. She'll be worried sick about you."

"My mom's still at work," she informs me.

"Okay. Well, who's at your house?"

"My grandpa."

"Okay, then let's call your grandpa and let him know you're here. Do you think he'll be able to come pick you up?" The next thing I know Brittney turns and runs out the classroom. I immediately jump up and run behind her. "Brittney! Brittney! Please stop!" I yell as I run a few feet behind her. She runs to the end of the hall and stops at the door. She turns around and I see tears streaming down her face.

"Brittney, what's wrong? Please tell me. That's the only way I'll be able to help you," I say as I breathe harder than I should. I really need to get back in the gym.

"I don't want to go home," she says between sobs.

"Does something happen to you at home?" I ask. I really hope she won't get scared and decide not to tell me or worse, take off running again. I put my hands on her shoulders to ensure that doesn't happen.

"Yes," is her only response.

"Do you want to tell me what happens to you?"

"No," she answers again.

I try to figure out how to handle this situation delicately. I don't want to say the wrong thing and scare her off. I have to get her to trust me. "Brittney, please let me help you. You remember that day you came in to show me your bracelet?" She nods. "Well, I knew you were coming. Ms. Smith wanted me to look at your arm because she was very worried about you. She cared about you a lot, you know. She cared about all of her students. More than anything she wanted you to be safe. I know she would be very happy to know you came to me, and she would be even happier if you let me help you." I guess that makes her feel better because she starts talking.

"My mom works at night, and she's usually gone by the time I get home from school. My grandfather stays at our house to keep me while mom is working. After mom leaves he does things that I don't like."

"What kind of things, honey?"

"He touches me in my private area. He makes me do things to him that I don't want to do. I want to holler at him and tell him no, but I'm too afraid. One time I did and he got angry and he hit me. Sometimes I have to sleep in the bed with him at night. He always puts me in my bed before my mom gets off work. Once he fell asleep and didn't wake up in time, and my mom came home and found me in the bed with him. He told my mom we were watching a scary movie and that I was too afraid to sleep alone so he let me sleep with him," she says as she begins to cry again. "I should've told her then, but I didn't know if she would believe me."

I'm getting chills when she tells me all of this. I want to go to her house and beat this son of a bitch myself. How could someone do this to a child, his own grandchild? I explain to Brittney that I have to call Child Protective Services and tell them what's going on. She isn't happy about this at all.

"No!" she screams. "You don't understand. He said if I told he would kill me and Mommy." She begins to cry again.

"Brittney, I assure you he's not going to do anything to you or your mom. He told you this because he knows if you tell, then he'll be punished. Please understand the only way to protect you and your mom is to call the proper authorities."

After explaining everything to her, she finally starts to feel better and agrees to come with me to make the call. When they arrive she tells them everything she's told me. I really didn't want to hear this again, but I promised her I wouldn't leave her alone.

Ms. Foster, Brittney's mom, comes to pick her up. The representative from Child Protective Services tells her everything Brittney told them. She's crying hysterically. She is obviously torn apart by what she's hearing. I guess it's not easy to hear your father is molesting your daughter. I stay there a while longer trying to console Ms. Foster and calm her down. I think if we allowed her to leave she probably would've killed her father. Luckily, the police are notified and sent to their house to pick him up.

I feel sick to my stomach the whole weekend. I can't get Brittney out of my mind. Hearing about child molestation, unfortunately, isn't uncommon, but I've never had to deal with it so close and personal. I see this child every day, and while I knew she was going through something, I had no idea it was this bad. "Well, Smith, I know you're smiling down on us, especially, now that Brittney's safe." I find myself still talking to her periodically. Some may think I'm crazy, but it's my comfort, and I know she's listening just as she did when she was here.

Chapter 6

I turn over to look at the clock: 3:00 A.M. "Oh no," I mumble, "not again." I reluctantly pick up the phone.

"Please, don't think I forgot about you." *Click.*

Okay, I've finally decided enough is enough. If the police don't want to help me then I have no choice but to take care of the situation myself. First thing in the morning I'm calling and getting an unlisted number.

It dawns on me, while I am lying in bed struggling to get back to sleep, that Mark doesn't seem concerned at all about these calls. He just shrugs them off as a kid playing on the phone. I really don't believe very many kids are up every morning at three o'clock. I really hate to extend my list of things that are bothering me about Mark, but this really is starting to get to me. The talk we had a few months ago helped for about a week, and then it was back to normal. I'm so tired of discussing the same thing over and over with him. If he's not happy in this marriage I wish he would just tell me and leave me alone. He's just so distant. He pays little to no attention to me. I could leave for a week and he'll never know. I can't deal with that right now. My priority is putting a stop to this phone madness. I hate to get an unlisted number, but I guess I really have no choice.

The first thing I do the next morning is to call and get an unlisted number. I feel a lot better once I get this finalized. I still, however, have the tremendous task of contacting all of our family and giving them our new number. Because I don't know who is actually calling, I decide to only give the number to immediate family and really close friends, which is only Janelle for me. I explain to Mark we can't give the number out to everyone. He socializes with quite a few guys, and to him they're all considered close friends. I hope he listens and understands we have to be extra careful now at least until we find out who the culprit is. We simply can't take any chances.

This weekend, like most of them, passes too quickly. I think everyone arrives to work early on Monday. It's the last week of school, and we can't be happier. We all spend the day clearing the rooms out for summer. They tell us to teach until the last bell sounds on the last day of school, but honestly that never happens. After the last set of grades is turned in, the students become helpers. They help take down bulletin boards, clean desks, pack boxes, wipe down shelves, and anything else we need done by the end of the day. It's amazing because this is probably the only time of year teachers don't have to fuss all day. Students love being helpers, at school that is. Many parents tell me they wish their kids would clean at home the way they love to at school.

When I leave school I feel so good. I have so many wonderful plans for the summer. Besides sleeping late, I also want to take an art class. I love using my hands and think this will be the perfect hobby for me. I'm on cloud nine.

Before going home I decide to stop by Wal-Mart for a few items. I haven't cooked in a while, so I'm thinking maybe I will cook dinner and Mark and I can share a good homemade meal together. I don't know how receptive he's going to be, but it doesn't hurt to try. Mark is still a very busy man, according to him anyway. The business is doing very well; meanwhile, his marriage is falling completely apart.

I finish shopping, check out and head to my car. My cell phone rings as I walk out the store. "Hell-o," I answer cheerfully.

"Hey, girl," Janelle says.

"Hey. What's…" I pause because as I make it to my car I cannot believe my eyes. All four of my tires are flat. I look around the parking lot and run back in the store. I completely forget I'm on the phone with Janelle. Once I remember I tell her what's happened and that I have to call her back.

I wait inside the store until the police arrive. They talk with several people, but no one saw anything. In the midst of everything going on I completely forget to call Mark. I call the house and he doesn't answer, so I try his cell phone. After a few rings he picks up.

"Hey, babe, what's up?' he says, sounding very strange. It's hard to describe, but his tone is somewhat distant like he is distracted or very busy.

"Mark, someone slashed my tires," I tell him, still feeling something wrong with his tone.

"They did what?" he hollers in the phone.

"They slashed my tires," I say, this time beginning to cry.

"Holly, calm down. Where are you?" he asks.

"I'm at Wal-Mart," I say in between sniffles.

"You need to call the police. I'm on my way. Are you at the Wal-Mart near the house?"

"Yes. I've called the police already. Just hurry up and get here please." I don't realize how shaken up I am until I talk to him. Mark has always been my rock, and just having him near makes everything better.

A few more minutes pass and Janelle arrives before Mark. I tell her she didn't have to come, but I am glad she's here. My heart is still racing because this whole situation has gotten completely out of hand. It doesn't take long before I spot Mark walking through the door. I run to him and hold on as tight as I can. I can feel my whole body trembling.

"Mark, this has got to stop. I can't keep going through this. Why are they doing this to me? What did I do?" I say, crying uncontrollably. Mark talks with the officers for a while longer. We leave after the officers reassure us they will do all they can to find the person or persons harassing me. I'm so paranoid walking to the car. I'm constantly looking behind me to make sure no one is following us. For all we know that crazy person could still be here, just watching and laughing. How can a day that started out so great, end so terribly?

I barely slept a wink last night. I am still so shaken up. A part of me still feels it was Ms. Davis, which I mentioned to the police, but another part of me feels this has to be someone else, but who? I don't know anyone else who could be this upset with me. I'm a very quiet person, and besides Janelle, I have no friends. I've always kept my circle of friends very small.

Every thought imaginable is running through my head. I even thought that Smith's murderer and my harasser could be the same person. I'm wracking my brain trying to figure out who we have in common. Again, the only person I can think of is Ms. Davis. Both Smith and I have had several very heated conferences with her, but nothing that should make her react like this.

"Good morning," Mark says as he enters the kitchen.

"Morning," I greet him back, because there sure isn't anything good about it. "Would you like some breakfast?" Now that I'm home I feel somewhat obligated to make sure he eats a good breakfast, lunch, and dinner. I'm a very old-fashioned woman. I believe in cooking and serving your man. That's what my mom always used to tell me. Whenever my dad would come home from work, she'd have his bath water ready and his food piping hot. All he had to do was sit and wait to be served. When I was young, I vowed I would never serve a man like that. My mom looked like a maid to me. It wasn't until I met Mark that I realized having a good man will make you want to serve him, especially when he constantly shows you how much he appreciates you. Up until now I've felt appreciated. I guess I've become accustomed to having Mark's undivided attention. Maybe it's the job. Maybe I'm just being overly sensitive these days. From now on I'm going to chill out and stop being such a nag. I'm lucky because Mark has always been very easygoing, so even on those days I don't feel like cooking, he never complains.

"No, I'll just grab a bowl of cereal," he answers.

"Are you sure? It's no problem," I assure him.

"I really don't feel like a big breakfast. I'll just eat cereal."

Mark never said anything, but I think this whole thing has shaken him up as well. He plays cool, but deep down I know it has to bother him too. Besides, the person isn't just calling my house, they're calling *our* house and vandalizing *our* vehicle. I would think it would have some effect on him. I start to feel bad because I never bothered to ask how he was doing.

"Honey, are you okay? I know all of this is a lot to deal with," I say.

"Oh, I'm fine. I just want you to be okay. I'll feel a lot better when they find out who this person is," he says, obviously very concerned. Mark never really talks about the phone calls, but I guess he feels like I do, that this person has taken harassment to a whole new level. The phone calls we can handle, but now they're actually damaging our property.

Mark sits at the kitchen table, clearly very distant. He has a blank stare. I have to call his name three times before he finally answers.

"What?" he answers.

"Is something wrong?"

"Uh, no, just thinking about this whole incident. I'm just happy you didn't walk up on this person. Who knows what she would've done?"

"I know. I thought about all that last night. I'm truly thankful that God protected me and the situation wasn't worse than it was. Do you really think it's a woman? "

Again, no response from Mark. He's acting a lot stranger than usual. I'm use to the silence, but not like this. This isn't just "I'm working" silence. This was "my mind is very full" silence. I just conclude he has a lot going on and try not to make a big deal out of it. "Mark." I call him again.

"Huh?" he answers, sounding very distant.

"I asked do you think it's a woman."

"I don't know. I guess I do because you keep mentioning that parent."

He's right. I do bring her name up a lot. As crazy as it sound, I like thinking that it's her because at least I know who to watch out for. The thought of it being some random person scares the shit out of me.

"Holly," he finally says.

"Yes," I answer.

"You know I love you, right?"

"Yes, of course." I'm not happy with the way things are between us, but I never doubted his love for me. I know he loves me. What I don't know is if he's still *in love* with me. "Mark, you're really scaring me. Did something else happen?" I ask, starting to get very nervous.

"No. I just felt I haven't told you in a while. This whole incident just scared me. I don't know what I would do if something happened to you."

Did he say scared him? Something actually scared him. This is what I want to say, but decide now isn't the time.

"I know, babe. This whole situation is scary. We both need to be very careful. This person is obviously very crazy."

"Yeah," he agrees. Mark and I sit in silence for the next few minutes. Our silence speaks volumes. We're both preoccupied, but everything in me is telling me we're not thinking about the same thing. I don't know why, but Mark's behavior is really tapping at my intuition, and the feeling I'm getting isn't good at all.

Chapter 7

Mark told me he's going to be extremely busy today. He finally heard from the husband and wife doctor team, and they agreed to contract him to do the medical billing for all three of their practices. Mark's excited and nervous all at the same time. Taking on all of their practices is really going to have him working some serious overtime. He mentioned he's going to use today to get some files organized and he may start looking for an assistant to help him out. I'm all for expanding the business, but I don't know how excited I am to have my husband working all day with some strange person in our house. Let me be honest. I don't know how comfortable I am having some strange woman in our house with my husband. I would like to believe he would be good. He's never given me a real reason to believe otherwise, but why tempt him?

I decide today will be a good day to get out the house and have lunch with Janelle. I haven't heard any Janelle-isms in a while, and Lord knows I can use some right about now.

"Are you sure you're okay?" Janelle asks for the hundredth time.

"Yes, Janelle, I'm sure. I'm still a little shaken up, but I'm not going to let that keep me in hiding all summer. Besides, it's the middle of the day. I'm sure I'm safe right now."

Just as I'm about to order my drink, my cell phone vibrates on the table. It's a private caller. "Hello," I answer.

"Having fun?" the caller says.

"Who's this?" I ask.

"Your worst nightmare, bitch." My heart drops and so does the phone.

"Holly, what's wrong? Who was that?" Janelle asks, obviously very worried.

"I don't know," is all I can say.

"Well, what did they say?" she asks.

"That they're my worst nightmare." This person is making it their mission to make my life miserable, but why? What did I do to her...or him? I can never tell because the voice is always very distorted. The sad thing is they really are becoming my worst nightmare.

"You know what? This is ridiculous. We are going to the police station, and if I have to stand on the table and yell at the top of my lungs I will, but we are not leaving there until someone does something about this psycho," Janelle says, obviously very upset.

I can't even argue with her. Right now, if that's what it takes for all of this to stop, then I'm all for it.

We arrive at the police station, and I ask for Detective Brown. He's the one handling my case.

"He's out right now, but he should be back shortly," says the officer behind the desk. "Would you like to wait for him?"

"Yes, we would," Janelle says.

"Then take a seat and I'll call you when he comes in."

We sit for about fifteen minutes before Detective Brown comes to the waiting area where we are.

"Hello, ladies. If you would follow me," he directs.

I hate police stations. They all look so dark and dreary, especially with that awful green paint on the walls. I guess it's not supposed to be warm and inviting considering it is a place for criminals. Just being here makes me sick. Why should I have to spend part of my summer vacation dealing with this? I'm suppose to be having an enjoyable day with my friend, but instead I'm allowing this person to take more of my precious time. I swear if the police don't do something and fast, I don't know what I'll do because each day I feel like I'm ready to snap. Why does this person have to remain anonymous and hide behind a distorted voice? If they're so bad, why can't they make their identity known so we can deal with it like adults. I guess that's what's pissing me off the most. It's easy to be bad when no one knows who you are, but can they back all that talk up in person? I've never had a fight in my life, but today I feel like I have a lot of fight in me.

We go into his office and are only halfway in when Janelle starts talking.

"Officer Brown, this makes no sense. Why is she still being harassed? Surely, there's something you or someone can do to put an end to all of this," Janelle says, obviously very disturbed.

"It's Detective Brown, Now Mrs. James did you get another call?" Detective Brown asks me.

"Yes. She just got one about thirty minutes ago," Janelle answers, quite upset, but I know it's because he corrected her, not because I'm still being harassed.

"Did they call your house?"

"No. They called her cell phone," she answers for me again.

"Ms…." Detective Brown says, looking at Janelle.

"Phillips," Janelle responds.

"Ms. Phillips, do you mind if I talk to Mrs. James?"

"Okay, but she's very upset," Janelle says.

Now it's true this whole situation does have me on edge; however, I am still quite capable of speaking for myself. Once again, I love Janelle to death, but she always feels the need to protect me. Sometimes I want to tell her I'm grown and quite capable of taking care of myself, but why bother? It's not like she'll listen.

"Yes, detective, I just got a call on my cell phone about thirty minutes ago, as Ms. Phillips stated," I finally respond.

"Mrs. James, you do understand it's very hard for us to protect you from phone calls. We're still investigating the incident from last night. The most we can hope is that we get some type of clue from that. I'm sure you feel as I do, that the person who slashed your tires is the same one making these calls. Have you given any more thought to getting an unlisted number?" he asks.

"I did get an unlisted home number, but this is the first time I've received a call to my cell phone."

"I know you don't want to hear this, but you may have to change that number as well," he advises.

"That's it, that's all you can tell her is to get an unlisted cell phone number? This is complete madness. I cannot believe the police, the people who took an oath to protect and serve, cannot seem to do either of those things for my friend. What has to happen before you can do something? So when she's shot down somewhere, can you do something then? Huh, Detective Brown?" Janelle says with a lot of emphasis on the detective part.

"Ms. Phillips, I'm going to strongly advise you to calm down before you really cross the line," Detective Brown warns.

"I'm sorry, detective, please forgive my friend. She's just emotional. This whole thing has taken a toll on us," I try to explain.

"Don't apologize to him. You should be upset too. Some crazy person is calling you, making your life miserable, and all he can say is get an unlisted number. How's that protection?" Janelle continues.

I finally drag Janelle out of there without being arrested. When she gets started it's hard for her to calm down. Janelle has absolutely no respect for authority. Janelle's quiet so I know something's wrong.

"So you're just going to say nothing?" I finally ask.

"I think I've said enough. I'm tired of saying something while you sit back and let people run all over you." I detect a lot of attitude.

"Janelle, what in the hell was I suppose to do?"

"You were suppose to tell that dumb good-for-nothing officer off."

"He's a detective." I correct her because I have nothing else to say.

"What the hell ever, Holly. I can give a rat's tail who he is. He's good for nothing, and he's going to continue giving you the run-around as long as you sit back and accept it."

"Please forgive me, Janelle. How crazy of me to think it's unacceptable to disrespect an officer of the law. What was I thinking?"

"Say what you want, Holly, but you're going to have to learn to stand up for yourself and stop letting people run all over you. That's probably why this person is harassing you. If they know you, then they know you're an easy target. Get some backbone and grow the hell up. You keep saying you can handle your own. Don't you think it's time you start doing that?"

The rest of the ride is spent in complete silence. Janelle's words totally ripped me apart, but it'll be a cold day in hell before I let it show. So on top of dealing with a psychotic harasser and an inattentive husband, now I can add a disgruntled best friend to the list. Could my life get any better? I mean really, what else could possibly go wrong?

Janelle and I run a few more errands before I take her to her car. My drive home is miserable. Janelle's never been so upset with me. We barely say two words to each other the rest of the day. I asked what else could go wrong, but now I'm regretting that question. I've always been told to never ask that question because things could always be worse.

I arrive home and walk in. I go in the computer room looking for Mark and surprisingly he isn't in there. I call his name a few times, but he doesn't answer. I walk to the bedroom and hear him talking. I peep in and see him on the phone. His back is to me so I decide to listen in. I hate that I don't trust him, but I have to get to the bottom of what's going on with him. I can only hear his side of the conversation, but what I hear lets me know he is obviously upset.

"What do you want?" he asks. He holds the phone for a moment, listening to the person on the other end. "You know that's not going to happen. You know what? I'm tired of having this same conversation with you over and over. You really need to grow up!" He slams the phone down and turns to walk out when he sees me standing at the door.

"Who was that?" I ask, very disturbed by what I heard.

"I don't know, someone playing on the phone," he answers. Men are the worst liars in the world. It was evident from the conversation he knew exactly who he was talking to.

"So, you don't know who it was?" I ask again, trying to give him a chance to come clean.

"Didn't I say I don't know? Why are you interrogating me?" he asks, directing his anger at me.

"I'm asking you again because I find it hard to believe you would actually sit and hold a conversation like that with a total stranger. You know who was on that phone, but for some reason you're hiding it from me. I swear, Mark, if I find out you're cheating on me…"

"What are you talking about? When do I have time to cheat on you? I'm always home with you." He tries to give me the line that all men give, like I'm so naïve, I don't know that if he wanted to cheat, he would definitely find the time.

"You know what, Mark? I'm not going to sit here and listen to you tell me anymore lies. I don't need to stress or worry about this anymore. Just know that if you are cheating, I will find out. Cheaters don't stay in the dark forever," I say and leave the room.

Chapter 8

My car is still being investigated so I have to get a rental car. I'm glad I did because the last thing I want is to have to ask Mark to use his car. I decide to go and register for a pottery class. I am so excited when I see all the ladies and one gentleman sitting in the class working. This will be just the thing for me. I observe a while longer and pay my fees. The receptionist informs me I can start as early as the next day. I assure her I will be back.

As I walk to my rental, I can tell something is sitting on the hood of the car, but I'm too far away to see exactly what it is. I cautiously walk a little closer and see it's a bouquet of flowers. They are probably from Mark, I think. We haven't spoken since our argument three days ago. I guess he's ready to call a truce. While I appreciate the effort, it still doesn't erase the fact that he's lying to me. I pick up the flowers and read the card.

I bet you thought these were from your husband. I'm the only person he sends flowers to these days. I just wanted to see the disappointment on your face when you realized they weren't from him.

The person signed the card, "The Real Mrs. Mark James." I look around to see if anyone is there, but the parking lot is empty, except for a few cars. I throw the flowers on the ground, keep the card, and head home. I think of going to the police again, but there's only one person who can put an end to this madness, and he lives with me.

Everything I want to say and do to Mark is running through my mind. I've felt for quite some time he is cheating, but I didn't have proof. I'm determined I'm not going to cry, but just as the thought enters my head, I feel my eyes burning. I don't want to believe he would actually do this to me—to us. We've been through so much together.

Mark and I were high school sweethearts, if you can call it that. I was a freshman in high school and he was a senior. My parents were totally against our relationship. Just going into high school they felt my focus should be on academics and not boys, as my mother would often say. We met the summer before I started high school. He was at the community park playing basketball with a few other guys from the neighborhood. That was my first time ever seeing him there, and I soon found out why. Mark didn't live in our neighborhood, but his best friend, Larry, did. It's no surprise that I never saw him being that I was a true homebody back then. My mom use to have to make me go outside and play.

"You need some sunlight," she would say.

Well this particular day I left out for sunlight, but came back with a lot more. Mark stirred up feeling in me I didn't even know I had.

Even though my parents weren't exactly thrilled about our relationship, they didn't do much to fight it. My mom warned me he was too old and would surely forget about me once he went away to college. Mark assured me what he felt for me was real, and no other woman could ever take my place. I guess that's what I loved about him. While everyone else was still treating me like a kid, he saw me as a woman. That's a big deal when you're in high school.

After Mark graduated and left for college we only saw each other on weekends. I always felt like I just existed during the week and really came alive on weekends when I was with him. It's funny that so much time had passed and my mom still felt what we were experiencing was puppy love and he was still going to break my heart. Imagine her shock when Mark came to our house on my eighteenth birthday to ask for my hand in marriage. My dad was against it, but after a very long, drawn-out conference with my mom, he decided it was pointless to argue the issue any longer. She told him I was eighteen and I was either going to do it with their permission or without it. She felt it would be best to just give their consent. I'm an only child, so the last thing my mom wanted was to risk losing our relationship.

Mark and I were married for five years before we started discussing having a family. We both agreed we should wait until I graduated from college and had taught at least a year before we started having kids. Once we felt the time was right we tried for six months to get pregnant with no success. Each month was like an emotional roller coaster for both of us. We tried not to get our hopes up, but of course, we're human. It was hard not to. We eventually decided to try alternate routes. Nothing worked. We knew something was not right, but just couldn't figure out what. After many months of trying to conceive, I believe my doctor was just as frustrated as we were. Dr. Lee decided she needed to run a few tests to see just what was going on. Mark and I were poked and prodded over and over before we finally had an answer.

I was finally diagnosed with having fibroids, which meant my chances of ever getting pregnant were very slim. My doctor was very skeptical to say it would never happen, because she said it could, but it would be best for me to prepare myself for the possibility of never getting pregnant. I decided to take on the attitude that I would prepare for the worst, but pray for the best. My pastor didn't really agree with my attitude because he said if I was preparing for the worse, then I didn't have faith in my prayers. I tried to explain to him that for my own sanity, I had to do it this way. I know that God does not always give you what you want, and that's not a bad thing. I figured if for some reason it wasn't meant for Mark and me to have our own child, then we would find another way. I had no doubt we would make great parents. We just had to figure out which road we would take to get there.

The drive home is longer than it needs to be. I decide to slow down and take the alternate route while I take my trip down memory lane. A part of me is still holding on to hope this is all one big misunderstanding. I can only hope this crazy person has her people mixed up. Maybe there is another Mark James and she confused him with my husband. I really want to believe that I, and our marriage, mean too much to him to risk losing, but obviously not.

I make it home and dread going inside. I really don't feel like facing this. I literally feel I'm about to walk in this house to end my marriage. At this moment I'm more angry than hurt, and that can be very dangerous. I don't want to hear anymore lies; I promise I cannot be held accountable for what will happen to him if I do. I walk in to find Mark away from his usual spot. This time he's sitting at the kitchen table with a very far-away expression. He must be deep in thought because he jumps when he sees me standing at the entryway.

"Hey," he says.

I don't feel like small talk. I want to get right to the matter at hand. "Care to explain this?" I say as I hand him the card that accompanied my lovely arrangement of flowers. He reads the card and looks at me. I can tell by the look in his eyes he isn't the least bit surprised.

"Sit down. We need to talk."

"No, thank you. I prefer to stand," I state firmly.

"Holly." He calls my name and says nothing else. The silence says it all.

"Just tell me why," I say, starting to cry again. He sits there for the longest time, then puts his head in his hands. The one thing Mark can't stand is to see me cry.

"I messed up," he whispers more to himself than to me. "I wish I could give you the answers you're looking for but I can't. I've asked myself this same question over and over and still can't come up with an answer that makes sense."

"Maybe because it doesn't make sense," I state.

"I know. I really messed up," he says again, but this time he's definitely talking to me.

So many thoughts are running through my head. I don't want to have this conversation because a small part of me really doesn't want it to be true. I can't ignore his confession. I can no longer make myself believe I'm just overreacting. Now I have no choice but to accept this is reality.

"How long?" I ask, very afraid of the answer, but I need to know how many months I've been stupid.

"Nine years, off and on," is the answer I receive.

"Excuse me?" I ask because surely I did not hear him correctly. "We've been married for fourteen years, so basically you're telling me for over half of our marriage you've been screwing someone else." My calmness scares me. I don't understand why I haven't introduced my fist to his face yet. Maybe because deep down I already knew, but once again denial has become my best friend.

"It wasn't nine years consistently."

I know he does not call himself trying to reassure me. Is this supposed to make me feel better?

"Is that supposed to make this better?" I ask.

"I know it doesn't make it better. I just want you to know."

"So why now? Why are you coming clean now? I've been asking you for quite some time if you were cheating, and each time you said no, so why now? What makes today so different?"

"She called and told me she sent you the flowers. I guess I could've lied, but I'm tired of lying. I'm tired of seeing you hurt and knowing I'm the one causing it. I just want to get it out so we can deal with it and move on with our lives."

Surely, he has lost his mind. He actually thinks it will be that simple. In his mind that's how the scenario will go: He'd confess, I'd be upset, then we would "deal with it" as he said and move on. He can't be serious.

"No, you weren't tired of lying you were just busted, and there's a big difference. Is she the one who has been harassing me all this time?" It finally dawns on me this would make perfect sense. It never really registered to me why Ms. Davis would be that upset, but it does make sense that a mistress would be.

"Yeah," he answers.

"So, you allowed me to go through all this drama when you could've stopped it a long time ago?" I ask in disbelief.

"I tried to stop it. I tried when it first started. Do you really think I enjoyed this? This was miserable for me as well."

"Oh, really? I can't tell. You two were probably getting a good laugh at my expense. I'm running crazy, going to the police thinking someone is out to kill me—or you too for that matter—and all along you were just sitting back taking it all in," I say now in tears.

"Holly, don't be ridiculous. This wasn't fun for me. I love you. I—"

"Don't you dare tell me you love me. Don't you ever tell me you love me again. I'm sick of the lies. This whole marriage was a lie, and why? Why did you have to do this to me? What did I do to deserve this?"

"You didn't do anything, honey. That's just it. That's why this is so difficult for me. I never intended to hurt you, and despite what you may think right now, I do love you. This had nothing to do with you."

"Well, that's obvious. Not once did you think of me and my feelings, but why should you? You were too busy enjoying life with…" I remember I never even bothered to ask who this mystery woman is who destroyed my marriage, or helped to destroy my marriage. “Who is she? What’s her name?”

“Holly, who she is isn’t important. What’s important to me right now is you—and us.”

“Oh, so now I’m important? Now this marriage means so much to you? I wonder where were those feelings when you were in bed with her! That’s when you should have been concerned about me and our marriage because as far as I’m concerned, now is too late.”

“Holly, don’t say that.”

“Don’t say what? The truth? See, unlike you I don’t believe in lying to the people I love. I’ve been nothing but good to you. I’ve spent the last eighteen years of my life dedicated to you. Not once, not once have I ever even thought of cheating on you, and please don’t think the opportunity hasn’t presented itself numerous times.”

“You’re a beautiful woman. Any man would be happy to have you. Don’t think I don’t know what a wonderful woman you are. You have to believe I didn’t do this to hurt you. Please, just please, tell me what to do to make this better.”

“Can’t you understand there is no making this better? I don’t trust you. I can’t stand to even look at you. All I want is for you to tell me who she is.”

“I don’t understand why that’s so important.”

“You don’t understand why I would want to know who the woman is who’s been harassing me and sleeping with my husband? You can’t understand why I want to know that?”

“I just don’t think we need to bring her in this right now. We need to deal with this ourselves. This is our marriage.”

“Which you allowed another woman to come into. The bottom line is, if you can’t tell me who she is then we have nothing else to discuss. Get your stuff and go.”

“Why does anyone have to leave? This house is big enough for both of us.”

“You just don’t get it, do you? I cannot stay in this house with you. Right now I need to be as far away from you as possible. I thought you would love to hear that. That just gives you another opportunity to go spend time with your woman.”

"She's not my woman."

"Oh, really? Well maybe you should tell her that. I can't really blame her though. Hell, after nine years, I would assume I'm your woman too. "

"She knows that. That's why she's doing all this. I told her I can't see her anymore, that I can't keep doing this, and she got mad. She told me she would not make my leaving that easy, so that's when she started harassing you."

"Was that her you were on the phone with the night I was with Janelle? When I walked in on what was apparently a very heated conversation? You remember, the wrong number lie you told me?"

"Yeah" was all he was able to say because now all the lies are starting to come out.

"Okay, so what was that about, because you were obviously upset?"

"She was giving me one last chance to leave you. She said if I didn't, she would tell you everything. I knew it was just a matter of time. I just didn't know when."

"So common sense didn't tell you to come clean while you had the chance?"

"I guess I was still holding out hope she wouldn't tell."

"And I could continue playing the fool. Still believing that you love me? Is that what you were hoping for?"

"You were not playing the fool, and you know I love you."

"Each time you say that, I just want to reach out and slap you. So why didn't you do it?"

"Why didn't I do what?"

"Why didn't you leave me for her?"

"What do you mean why? I didn't leave because I don't love her."

"So after nine years of seeing her, you can honestly say it all meant nothing to you?"

"No. It was sex, that's it. I know that doesn't make it right, but I'm trying to be honest. "

"Then you're more stupid than I thought. You gave up our marriage for sex, something you could've gotten from me whenever you wanted."

"I didn't give up our marriage. You're giving up our marriage."

"No! You gave up our marriage the first time you stepped out of it. I can't do this anymore. I feel sick." I run to the bathroom and hurl, barely making it to the toilet. Mark comes in to see about me, but the first opportunity I get, I push him out and lock the door. I must've stayed in there for hours crying uncontrollably. He tries to get me out, but after about an hour he decides to stop trying. I hear the front door close. I leave the bathroom and go to the bedroom to lie down. I see a letter on the bed. I know it's from him. I want to tear it up, but I can't. I can barely see through my tears, but I manage to read it. It says:

Dear Holly,

I know you're upset with me right now. You probably even hate me, and I can't blame you because I hate myself. I never meant to hurt you. All I can say is that I made a stupid mistake, and if I could change the past I would, but I can't. If you would give me the chance I will spend the rest of my life making this up to you. You didn't deserve this. Holly, you've been the love of my life for eighteen years, and I want nothing more than to spend many more years with you. Please pray about it before you make any decisions. I'm going to Larry's tonight. Call me if you need me.

Love Always,
Mark

He just doesn't get it. I probably would've forgiven him if he'd cheated on me once. Okay, I would've forgiven him. Before our talk I knew in my heart I wasn't ready to end our marriage, but when I found out this has been going on for nine years, that's just too much. Mark said he didn't have feelings for this woman, but after nine years, he has to feel something. Not only that, but I don't trust him. He lied to me for nine whole years, so what's going to stop him from doing it again? I just can't take that chance.

Mark was my first real boyfriend. Actually, he was my first everything. The thought of losing him is devastating. I've never experienced pain like this before. It's not even describable—it just hurts so badly.

Chapter 9

I must've fallen asleep because the phone woke me up. I look at the clock and see its 2:30 A.M. I am so not in the mood for this right now. I start to ignore it, but I think maybe she can tell me something that Mark couldn't: who she is.

"Look," I answer, "Mark told me everything so—"

"Holly honey, is that you?"

"Mom?" I say. Once I realize it's her then I become nervous. "Mom, what's wrong?"

"It's your dad, baby. He's had a heart attack."

"Oh my God. Where is he? Is he okay? Mom, please tell me he's okay."

"We're at the hospital. The doctor said he's had a mild heart attack. They're expecting him to pull through, but he's not out of the woods yet. I wasn't going to call you, but I thought you should be notified."

"Mom, what hospital? I'm putting on my clothes now."

"We're at St. Mary's, but Holly, don't come out here by yourself. You need to wake Mark up and bring him with you. You don't need to drive alone."

"I will, Mom."

The last thing on this earth I want to do is call Mark, but I have no choice. I'm not ready for my parents to know that we're separated. They really don't need this right now. All of our focus needs to be on getting my father better and out of that hospital.

"Hello," Mark answers groggily.

"Mark, it's me."

"Holly, what's wrong? Are you okay?" he asks.

"Mom called and said Dad had a mild heart attack. They're at St. Mary's and I need you to go with me."

"Oh God, Holly. Okay. Do you need me to come pick you up?"

"No. I'm already dressed, so I'll come pick you up. You're at Larry's, right?"

"Of course I'm at Larry's," he says with a hint of attitude.

I decide to hang up in an effort to avoid an argument. Once I pick him up we drive to the hospital in complete silence. I have no words for him. When he gets in the car I make it perfectly clear the only reason I called is so my parents wouldn't be worried. If I was a better liar I would've told my mom Mark was out of town or something, but it was always hard for me to lie to her. I always felt like she would know I was lying and then I would get into more trouble, so to avoid all of that, I just stuck with telling the truth. I know all of that would change this morning. I have to lie if for some reason she asks anything about Mark and me because as far as I'm concerned there is no Mark and me, but I can't tell her that—not yet anyway.

Mark and I make it to the hospital in ten minutes flat. I guess the fact that I was going well over the speed limit helped.

"Hi. I'm looking for Mr. Fred Moore's room please," I tell the receptionist.

"Fred Moore?" she asks as she looks at her computer screen.

"Yes, ma'am."

"Okay. He's in ICU. Go straight down this hall, and take a left." she points.

"Okay, thanks."

Mark and I follow her directions, and as soon as I turn the corner I see Mom sitting in the waiting area. I run to her because I really need to be in her arms at the moment. It's funny how Mom's arms still feel like the safest place on earth. I hug her and cry. I cry because my dad is sick, I cry because my marriage is over, and I cry because it just feels like the right thing to do. I feel Mark rubbing my back as I hold my mom. I wish I can tell him politely to get his damn hands off me, but that will probably alert Mom that something is wrong, so I keep quiet.

As Mom and I are finally turning each other loose, the doctor walks in. Mom rushes to him to get an update on Dad's condition. The doctor says it is still touch and go, but he feels positive about the outcome. He can't guarantee he will pull through, but his words make us feel better. This time Mom and I hug and shed tears of joy. We hold hands and pray, and I don't mind Mark touching me because my dad needs all the prayers he can get.

It's funny how things can go from bad to worse in a matter of minutes. Just when I think things couldn't get any worse, this happens. I felt like life was over earlier today as I listened to Mark telling me his dirty little secret. Being here in this hospital waiting to find out my dad's fate is reminding me that life truly is precious. It's sad because that reminder should inspire me in some kind of way, but it doesn't. No matter what, life for me will never be the same again.

The days after my dad's heart attack is like one long roller-coaster ride. Each time the phone rings I expect bad news, but thanks to God my dad makes it through He stays in the hospital for a week before he's finally discharged. I spend every day at the hospital with him and Mom. Being an only child I feel it's my responsibility to take care of my parents. I dread being around them these days because periodically they ask about Mark, and I quickly think of something pressing he had to do to explain why he hadn't been over to check on my dad. I realize I'm getting real good with lying to my parents. This makes me hate Mark even more. I wouldn't have to lie to them if he'd kept his penis to himself. The thought of it makes me nauseous all over again. And he wonders why I can't look at him. Just the thought of him makes me sick.

Janelle begs me to go away with her in a couple weeks. Her sister is getting married in the Bahamas. I tell her I will think about it, but in my mind I know I probably won't go. A part of me wants to, but I feel too guilty going away while Mom is taking care of Dad by herself. I know she really needs my help, although she'd never admit it. I swear sometimes my mom thinks she's Superwoman. She still has to be in charge of everything, and it seems the older she gets, the more in charge she wants to be. I ask her often if she can ever just rest and allow someone else to handle things for a while. I always get the same response: no.

I always pray for a lot of things, but tonight I also pray for guidance. I don't know what direction to go in. My head is telling me to leave Mark and never look back, but my heart says differently. I ask God to show me what to do next, if anything.

I don't receive my usual call this morning. I wonder if it's because my husband is with her. I guess there's really no need to harass me if you've got what you want. I hate feeling this way. I hate thinking about him possibly being there with her playing house while I sit here alone and miserable. The phone rings, interrupting my thoughts for the moment.

"Hello," I answer.

"Hi, honey. It's Mom."

"Hi, Mom. How's it going? Is Dad okay?"

"Oh yes, he's fine. He's sitting up here eating his second helping of grits and eggs. I would say he's doing better than me these days. I think he just likes the attention."

"That's because you spoil him," I respond.

"I sure do. That's my baby," she says, laughing.

"Oh, Mom please," I respond. She knows that grosses me out. Why? I don't know because of course I know what goes on between a husband and wife, but they're old people.

"Listen, your cousin Ann just called and she's coming down to stay with us a while. She said she needed a break from work and really wants to spend some time with your dad and me."

"Oh, that's nice of her. When is she coming?"

"She should be here next weekend."

"I can't wait to see her. It's been what, three or four years now?"

"Yes. It's been about four years I would say. It's too bad you won't be able to spend much time with her."

"I'm on summer break. I have time."

"I was thinking now that Ann's coming you should go on and go with Janelle to the Bahamas."

"I don't know, Mom. I still don't feel right leaving you right now."

"Holly, please go and have fun. Your dad and I will be fine, and I'll call and check on Mark for you, make sure he's behaving himself," she says with a laugh.

I laugh too, but not because it was funny, but because if I didn't she would know something is wrong. I want to tell her he needed someone to keep check on him nine years ago. My mom would die if she knew what Mark's done. She often refers to him as the son she never had. My dad loves Mark, but as a son-in-law. I don't think he ever really saw him as a true son. I don't think my dad ever really got a good vibe from Mark, and now I know why.

Chapter 10

It takes a little convincing, but my mom finally gets me to agree to accompany Janelle to the Bahamas. The plane ride is rather rough, but once we arrive, all of that seems like a distant memory. I don't know if I've ever seen a more beautiful place before in my life. Our suite looks bigger than the whole first floor of my house. The view from the balcony is breathtaking. I can't get enough of the white sandy beach and miles and miles of nothing but deep blue water. It looks like a scene from a calendar or something. For someone who's never left Louisiana, this is simply amazing to me.

"Aren't you going to unpack?" Janelle asks as she walks into the living room.

"Yeah," is my response because I'm still taking in all the beauty that's surrounding me.

"I was thinking maybe we could get changed and go downstairs to the restaurant and grab a bite to eat."

"Yeah," I answer again, still in awe.

"Holly, are you listening to me?" she finally asks.

"What?"

"Did you hear anything I just said?"

"I'm sorry, Janelle. I'm just so overwhelmed by all of this. I can't believe I'm actually here. I went online and looked up this place and they had pictures, but to actually see it in person is just amazing."

"I know. It's beautiful, isn't it? That's why I wanted you to come with me.

"I'm glad I came. I was just worried about leaving my parents, and I didn't want to be a drag on your sister's special day. You know I'm not really feeling the love thing these days."

"Girl, please. You and Mark will be back together in no time."

"I doubt that. What would I look like taking him back after all he did to me? Nine years, Janelle. Nine whole years. It's not like he made a mistake and ended it. No he let it go on for nine years. How in the hell am I suppose to forgive that?"

"Look, I know it's a lot to deal with, but there is an advantage to keeping your husband."

"Excuse me? An advantage? Please do share because I can't wait to hear these words of wisdom."

"Well, at least you know what you're working with when it comes to Mark. Try dating again and see how you like that. The pickings are very slim out there, trust me. If it were me, I would definitely make him suffer. I'm not saying go running back now, but eventually I would go back."

This is definitely a different side of Janelle. She's never been the sensitive type. This is the first time she's ever alluded to the fact that single life isn't that great. She always seems so happy to live the life that she does. It was never the lifestyle for me, but we're very different in many ways. I've always been the wifey type. I love everything about being a wife: taking care of my husband and tending to his needs, cooking his favorite meals, and spending time with him, and even if we don't talk, just being in his presence. That's why I always say I was born to be a wife. On the other hand, Janelle is always content with being kept. She would always say she gets the benefits without the headache. I'm starting to realize now that was just her way of dealing with it. Obviously she's not happy being the other woman.

"It's your life though. I'd never tell you what to do, but I do think you need to think about it before you just throw in the towel. Now, that's my advice of the day, and it didn't even cost you anything. Can we go eat now, please?"

"You know, you have to be the greediest person I know. Janelle gives me a look that I know all too well. We've been friends long enough now that no words are needed. I can read her thoughts. Her face is saying loud and clear, *Girl, if you don't hurry up.* I do know not to push it with her though. Janelle does not play, especially when it comes to her food.

"Fine. Give me a minute to freshen up and we can go." While in the bathroom it hits me that here I am on this gorgeous island with Janelle. I love Janelle to death, but I should be here with my husband. This could've been the honeymoon we never had. Mark and I were too broke to go away, so we created our own escape in our little apartment. Mark decorated the living room to look like a beach, complete with beach chairs and the works. We sipped on frozen coconut drinks and fed each other fruit. My eyes began to water when I thought about how happy we were back then.

Okay, Holly, you will not do this to yourself this weekend. You have plenty of time to sulk over Mark, but right now you are going to pull yourself together and enjoy this wonderful island getaway. I have to have these little pep talks with myself from time to time.

"Holly, come on. My folks are waiting for us downstairs!" Janelle hollers from the front room.

"Coming." I quickly wash my face and apply more makeup. Just because I'm a mess on the inside doesn't mean I have to advertise it on the outside.

Janelle and I go downstairs where her parents, her sister, and her sister's fiancé, and some unknown gentleman were waiting for us to arrive. I hug her parents and her sister and speak to the other gentleman. The unknown man is introduced as Janelle's cousin Dexter.

We decide to try the restaurant inside the hotel. No one really feels like going anywhere else.

"So, what do you ladies have up for tonight?" Janelle's dad asks.

"We haven't decided yet, but you know we have to do something. We definitely can't just sit in the room all night. I did not come all the way down here to sit around doing nothing," Janelle responds.

Little does she know, I'm looking forward to doing nothing. I've already made up my mind I will open the balcony up and listen to the waves from the ocean while lying in my bed. I don't want to hear a television or a radio, just the soothing sounds of nature. I guess I have to change those plans. I don't want Janelle to regret bringing me along; however, I know Janelle well enough to know she's going to do what she wants, with or without me.

"We should go check out one of the clubs. I heard some of the locals telling these other people about them. It sounds like it could be fun," her cousin Dexter suggests.

"Oh, I am so there," Janelle says with pure excitement.

Great, Janelle will go with Dexter, and I can escape to the bedroom, I think.

"Holly, how does that sound to you?" Janelle asks.

"Um, well actually…" I begin

"Don't even try it, Holly. You are coming with us. I never pressure you to go out with me at home, but we're not at home, and it's time you live a little," she so lovingly tells me.

"Janelle, I don't have anything to wear out. I think it'll be best if you and Dexter just go on, and I'll stay here. Really, I don't mind."

"The last time I checked we are the same size, so there, problem solved. You're going."

I see I'm not going to get out of this very easy, so I may as well give in and go out with them. Who knows? I may accidentally have fun. I try to psych myself into believing I will anyway.

"So, Holly is it? What do you do?" Dexter asks.

"I'm a third-grade teacher."

"Really? A teacher. That's great. We need more teachers out there."

"Yes, we do. I don't know what's going on with the education system these days. For some reason, it's hard to find good teachers. Back in my day we had real teachers who looked like teachers. No disrespect, Holly, and I'm not referring to you, but I see these teachers on the news for sleeping with their students and all that foolishness. We didn't have any of that, and our teachers surely didn't look like those teachers do. The teachers I had were all old. Definitely no one I would want to sleep with. That's what's wrong with the world today—too much sex. Teachers can't even teach from thinking about sex. Don't get me wrong, it doesn't stop there. Sex scandals are now coming out in the churches. I almost died when all this stuff starting coming out about the priests sleeping with little boys. That one really blew me away. I don't believe in playing around with God, and that's just what those priests are doing if you ask me. Just the thought of it disgusts me," Janelle's dad says.

"Yeah, times sure have changed," Janelle's mom adds.

We finish our meal and our enlightening conversation about the education system and how it's shot to hell—her dad's words, not mine—then we head upstairs to prepare for our night on the town.

Chapter 11

I don't remember the last time I danced so much. I don't know if I've ever danced so much. I've always been the wallflower, the one who watched the purses while all my friends went out on the floor and danced. I think that's why they always wanted me to come along, so I could babysit the purses and drinks. Tonight that person does not exist. I dance more than anyone else, well except Janelle of course.

Janelle danced with majority of the people there, men and women. She is always the life of the party. I find myself at one point dancing alone. I don't care. I'm so caught up in the music that I don't even notice Dexter has come to join me. I feel very uncomfortable, why I don't know because all we're doing is dancing and there's like a mile between us. I guess because Mark's the only man I've ever danced with, both slow and fast. Now that I think over my life, I realize how sheltered I've been. I never really experienced much in life. I went straight from high school to being Mark's wife. Sure, I went to college, but I wasn't the traditional college student. I lived on campus, but only attended a couple of the fraternity or sorority parties that Janelle dragged me to. Even though I missed all the others, I still had the pleasure of hearing about them on Mondays in class, but that's about it. It's funny because I could tell my peers were having the time of their lives, but I never envied them. I always felt I was living the life I wanted to live. I was content being with Mark on weekends. We were married, and it was bad enough we weren't living together. No way was I about to give up our weekends. Now that I know about Mark's affair it makes me feel really stupid. Just thinking about the life I gave up in order to be with him. I can't look back and tell about any wild times I had during my college years. My walk down memory lane would be quite boring. Janelle provided the excitement by telling me about all the crazy things she did. Now that I'm thinking about it I'm starting to feel very envious of the life I gave up becoming a wife so early.

"Is something wrong?" I hear Dexter holler over the music.

I didn't realize I'd stopped dancing. He must think I'm out of my mind standing there looking like a fool on the dance floor.

"Oh, no I'm sorry. I was just deep in thought."

"What?" he hollers, barely able to hear.

"I said…never mind."

We Cupid Shuffle and do the Cha Cha Slide until my feet start burning. Damn Janelle and these three-inch heels. Once I hear Luther's "Here and Now" I know that's my cue to take a seat. *Why on earth would they play this old song tonight? It's simply to torture me.* This is the song Mark and I had our first dance to as husband and wife. I try to play it cool when Dexter asks me to dance. I guess my emotions get the best of me because before I knew it I'm running outside. I'm such a mess when he finally catches up to me.

"Holly, are you okay?" He turns me around to look at him. "You're crying. What's wrong?"

I am such an idiot. I can't believe I'm out here crying like a baby about someone who doesn't deserve my tears. "I'm sorry, Dexter. That song just brought back memories for me."

"An old boyfriend, I assume," he says, obviously very concerned.

Because I don't want to get into the whole sordid tale that had become my life, I simply nod. Mainly because it's none of his business and because I'm too embarrassed to tell him my husband had a whole other relationship while I played the fool at home.

"Hey, how about we ditch this place and go somewhere for drinks?" he offers.

"No, thanks. I think I'll go back to the hotel and get some rest," I respond.

"Oh, come on. The night's still young. Just one drink and I'll be happy to walk you back to the hotel."

I really don't feel like going to the hotel. I know the night will end with me crying myself to sleep, which has become my routine this last month. I also don't feel comfortable having drinks with this man. I finally convince myself it's just drinks. Why not?

We walk down the strip to the bar on the beach. The night air feels great against my skin. I borrowed a dress that left nothing for the imagination from Janelle. I'm addicted to working out, so I thought it was about time I show everyone what I'm really working with. Of course Janelle still had to convince me to put it on. By the way Dexter is looking at me, I can tell he's noticed.

I should feel ashamed because I have to admit I'm noticing him too. From the time we sat at the table for dinner, it took everything in me not to stare. I have to admit I am somewhat prejudice to skin color. I've never been attracted to light-skinned men, maybe because I'm light-skinned. Paula Abdul did say that opposites attract. So why do I find this man so attractive? He's everything I dislike: light-skinned, curly hair, light eyes, which I see run deep in Janelle's family. One thing I can't take away from him though is his body. He looks to be around Mark's height, give or take an inch or two. I can tell he hits the gym often and it's really working for him.

Oh my God Holly, get a grip. You are a married woman—well sort of. Try to focus and stop drooling over this man, I tell myself. I've always been a very stubborn woman. No matter what, this is just drinks, and I have no reason to feel ashamed.

"He's a fool, you know?" says obviously noticing my distant look.

"Who?" I ask, bringing myself back to reality.

"Your boyfriend or ex-boyfriend. I don't know what he did, but I know it was bad enough to make you cry."

"Thanks," is all I could say. I am starting to feel very uncomfortable. I'm not use to getting this much attention anymore. Mark barely knows I exist most of the time. I can parade around butt naked and he wouldn't notice.

"I'm sorry. Did I offend you?" Dexter asks.

I guess my quietness tells it all. "No, it's okay. I just don't want to talk about it, if you don't mind."

"Not at all. So, Holly, what do you do for fun?"

That's hilarious. Should I tell him how I do lesson plans, cook meals, clean the house or just sit around watching HGTV most of the time? Instead I decide to make my life sound a little more exciting. "I like going to the movies," I respond. *Oh what a nerd, going to the movies. Is that suppose to be exciting? I'm pathetic.*

"Oh, really? So have you seen any good movies lately?"

I can tell the poor guy is trying to keep this conversation going, but I'm not giving him much to work with. "No. Time hasn't allowed me to go lately, but anyway, enough about me. How about you? Tell me about yourself."

"Well, there's really not much to tell. I'm a banker from Atlanta. I'm single, no kids, no baby mama drama, and all that good stuff."

"And what do you do for fun?" I can't believe I'm actually sitting here having a real conversation with this guy. It feels good—really good.

"Let's see, when I'm not bogged down in work, I like to travel."

"Really? So have you been able to travel lately?"

"You mean other than being in the Bahamas?" he says, smiling.

"Obviously."

"Well, like you, time hasn't allowed for many leisure trips, but I did get to Italy last summer."

"Wow, Italy. That's impressive."

"It was fun—you know, something to do."

"That's it? Just something to do? Must be nice. My idea of just something to do is walking around Wal-Mart."

Dexter laughs but I'm very serious. He talks about going to Italy like he's going around the corner or something. Maybe he's just use to traveling, and it's not a big deal to him anymore, or maybe he's trying to be a show off. If he is showing off, that's not a very attractive quality, not that I'm attracted to him. I can't be attracted to him. I'm a married woman—well sort of.

"So, are you ready to head back to the hotel now?" Dexter asks.

"Yeah, it's getting late. I'm sure Janelle's worried crazy right about now." I guess I just need something to say because knowing Janelle she's not nearly finished partying. I'll be lucky to see her anymore tonight. She always says, "I only have one life, and I want to have so much fun that one is all I need."

Dexter and I finish our drinks and stroll back to the hotel. I'm in no hurry because the warm ocean breeze feels really good against my skin. I pull my hair clamp out and allow my hair to fall. I love the feel of it blowing in the wind. Being here surrounded by all this beauty is almost orgasmic. It's been a long time since I've felt so good. I decide to put all of my problems aside and really take the time to enjoy myself while I'm here. One thing's for sure, my problems will definitely be there when I get home. I'll worry about them then. For now it's nothing but food, fun, and all the drinks I can stand.

Chapter 12

Janelle spends the next few days helping her sister and her mom get ready for the upcoming nuptials. I spend the next few days spending time with Dexter. I do feel bad for not being of more assistance with the wedding, but if I'm going to have fun, then I can't consume myself with the wedding. That would be depression waiting to happen. I try to avoid it at all cost, and in the meantime I've come to realize Dexter's really good company and quite interesting. I love hearing all about his traveling expeditions. Today he convinces me to go snorkeling. I've seen it done on television before, but never had the desire to do it myself. I really love water, but from a distance. The closer we get to our destination the more I feel myself tensing up.

"You okay?" Dexter asks, obviously sensing my mood change.

"No, not really," I answer nervously.

"I'm telling you, it's nothing to it. Diving off the boat is the hardest part. Once you get underwater, the beauty is so captivating you'll forget all about being scared."

Something about him makes me trust him. However, I did make that mistake before. Dexter isn't my husband, so being disappointed by him isn't such a big deal. He says I'll love it, so I'm going to believe he knows what he's talking about. We arrive at the boats in about ten minutes. We go through our training and we're ready to go. I whisper a little prayer before I do anything. I've heard a lot about vacations that went terribly wrong. I don't want to be the one people are reading about.

"You ready?" he asks.

"Do I have a choice?"

"You always have a choice, but I believe if you don't do this you'll regret it."

"I'm going to do it. I just have a bad case of the jitters."

"Just try to relax," he says as he starts massaging my shoulders.

I pull away because his touch sends a sensation through my body I haven't felt in a long time. I'm really starting to scare myself. I shouldn't feel this way simply because he touches me. I realize I have to be extra careful because the last thing I want is to be caught in a situation I can't get out of.

"I'm sorry, Holly. I didn't mean to overstep my boundaries. I just wanted to help you relax a little."

"No, it's not you. I guess I'm just more nervous than I thought," I lie, trying to cover up the fact that I'm making a big deal out of nothing.

We get to the deep part of the ocean and prepare to make our entrance in the water. I'm so nervous, scared, and all these other negative emotions, but to my surprise I actually do it. I'm so glad because Dexter is absolutely right. Being underwater is such an enchanting experience. I feel so light and free. It's hard to be in any negative mood in this scenery. The beauty is unbelievable. I see fish of all colors swimming right in front of my face. The colors are awesome. I'm so glad Dexter told me to bring my disposable waterproof camera because this is definitely an experience I want to capture on film.

On the way back to the hotel, the mood is a lot different. I can't even describe how great I feel. Being on this trip is opening my eyes to all that life has to offer. I've truly been so sheltered going to work and coming home each and every day. Mark's and my idea of going on vacation is going to Varnado to stay with his grandmother. Varnado is a small town about two hours east of Baton Rouge. The population may be four hundred people, maybe, being the operative word. I love Mark's family and I love going there to visit, but it's definitely not your ideal vacation spot. I would love to experience snorkeling and being in this tropical paradise with him, but thanks to him that may never happen.

"Is that a no?" Dexter asks, interrupting my thoughts.

"I'm sorry, what was that?" I have to ask because I don't hear a thing he says.

"I said would you like to have dinner with me?"

"I would love to, but Janelle and I are hanging out tonight."

"That's too bad," he says, looking at me, trying to make puppy dog eyes.

"Oh, please, you know you're happy to be rid of me. Now you can stop babysitting and go really have fun."

"Babysitting. Why would you say that? I've really enjoyed spending time with you."

“Okay, whatever. All I know is you’re a single man, and I’m sure there’s a single lady here who’s already caught your eyes.”

“Oh, you have no idea.”

“See, that’s why you need to go out and have fun with her. We’re only here two more days.”

“You really don’t know, do you?”

“Know what?”

“Never mind. Well, have fun with Janelle, and I’ll try to entertain myself somehow,” he says, smiling.

“I’m sure you will,” I respond.

We arrive back at our hotel. I walk in the room to find Janelle, her mom, and sister sitting in the middle of a floor full of wedding favors.

“Hey,” I greet them as I walk in.

“Hey yourself. Did you have fun?” Janelle asks with a smirk.

“Yes,” I answer slowly mainly because I am confused by the silly look on her face. “What are you guys doing?”

“In here trying to get these favors together,” their mom answers. “But I’m glad you’re here, baby ’cause I need to go check on your dad,” she says, looking at her daughters.

I help Mrs. Phillips up and walk her to the door. “Oh, well, let me shower and change and I’ll help,” I say as I walk back in the room.

“Shower? Why do you have to shower? What have you been doing?” Janelle asks.

I don’t like the accusing sound of her voice, because I know what she’s implying and she knows me better than that.

“Don’t even go there, Janelle. Dexter and I went snorkeling,” I reply, giving her the evil eye.

“Oh, touchy, I’m just playing. You know I know you didn’t do anything, not Miss Goody Goody,” she says, laughing.

Again, I must say I love Janelle to death, but sometimes she gets on my nerves when she’s around her family. For some reason she always feels the need to pick on me. I never understood it, I just tolerate it. After showering I make my exit from the bathroom and deliver on my promise to help. We do wedding favors, laugh, and talk for about an hour. It feels really good, and for the first time in a long while, I don’t even think about Mark.

Chapter 13

Robin, Janelle's sister, looks just like the brides in the magazine walking down the beach. She's wearing a beautiful princess-cut white gown with sparkles everywhere. Her makeup and hair are flawless. The day is perfect for a wedding. They decide to have an evening wedding, which means just as they are exchanging their vows, the sun is setting behind them. Seeing the sun set on the ocean and these two beautiful people vowing to love each other eternally is just too much. I try to put on a brave face, but before I know it the tears are falling. Luckily, everyone thinks they are tears of joy for the happy couple. Little do they know these tears have very little to do with them.

I love the ceremony, but I'm happy when it's over. I just can't take much more. I've been avoiding these emotions all week, and I don't want to stir them up now. If it wouldn't be so rude I would excuse myself and make my way back to the room, but I decide it's my last day here so I'm going to make myself enjoy it. Once I get on the plane Sunday morning, then I can let the tears freely flow, but I refuse to release any more of them today.

I'm sitting at a table looking out at the water when someone touches my shoulder. I know who it is even before I turn around because I experience that chill again—the one that goes straight down my spine.

"Hey, beautiful," Dexter says as he sits beside me.

"Oh please," I respond.

"Please what? You don't think you're beautiful? Girl, you are killing them in that dress. Did I tell you white's my favorite color," he says, smiling.

"No, I must've missed that memo."

"Well, it is, and that dress looks magnificent on you."

"Thanks," I say, laughing. Funny thing though, Dexter isn't laughing. In fact he looks very serious. "What?" I finally ask.

"I just think it's really sad when women don't see in themselves what everyone else sees in them. I've been watching you, and I've noticed several men checking you out. It's obvious to them you're beautiful, so why don't you see it?"

That's a really good question. Why don't I see my own beauty? Once upon a time I use to think I was beautiful, but over the years that's changed. I guess when your husband finds comfort with another woman you tend to question yourself. I find myself doing that a lot lately, but I honestly don't realize I'm doing it until now.

"I don't know," I finally speak. "I mean I don't think I'm the ugliest woman in the world, but I just think beautiful is pushing it a little."

"Oh, he really did a number on you."

"Who?"

"Your ex. I'm assuming he's the reason you don't see yourself for what you are."

I need to think fast because I'm really tired of this whole conversation. "So, did you enjoy the wedding?" I finally ask.

"Okay, I can take a hint, and yes, I thought the wedding was really nice."

"I agree," I say as I take another glass of champagne from the waiter who's walking around.

"Are you sure you can handle that? It seems you've had quite a bit already." he says.

"You're monitoring my alcohol intake too? Just how long were you watching me?"

"I didn't have to watch you to know that," he says, pointing to my empty glasses on the table.

"Oh," is all I can say.

"So, why are we sitting here? Let's join the party."

Surprisingly, I don't resist when he pulls me out on the makeshift dance floor. Again, we dance and dance. I don't know if it's the alcohol or just me finally letting loose, but I even agree to a slow dance. Immediately once our bodies touch I regret agreeing to this. *I should not be this close to another man. Oh, but his touch feels so good. No! No! No! I can't think about another man touching me. So why can't I stop? Okay, it's fine. I mean we're dancing. It's not like we're making love.*

Chapter 14

Oh, please tell me I'm dreaming. Tell me I'm going to open my eyes and I'll be in this bed alone. Okay, here goes. Oh no! How did I let this happen? How did I end up in bed with Dexter?

"Well good morning, beautiful," he says as he turns over to face me.

I'm speechless for a minute, but I finally tell myself I have to speak or he'll think I'm an idiot.

"Good morning" is all I'm able to say. What I want to say is, "What the hell did you do to me? Why am I in this bed, and with you?"

I vaguely remember last night. I remember us dancing for a long time. I also remember him offering to walk me back to the room. After that I'm drawing a complete blank. I vow to never touch champagne again. I must've been out of my mind to think I could handle all those glasses. For someone who rarely drinks, one would've been more than enough.

"So, you hungry? I can order room service if you would like breakfast in bed," he says.

"Um, no, no thank you. I'm just going to go back to my room now."

"Are you okay? Listen, what happened last night can remain between the two of us if you're worried about what Janelle will say."

"No, that's not it. I just can't believe I allowed myself to do that, that's all."

"Do what? We're two single, consensual adults who are on vacation having a good time."

"That's just it, only one of us is single."

"But I thought you said you and your boyfriend broke up."

"Well, I never really said it was a boyfriend who broke my heart, I just let you believe that it was."

"So you're married?"

"Well, sort of."

"What do you mean, sort of? There's no sort of, either you're married or you're not."

"I'm married, but we're separated."

"Are you divorced?" he asks with a little attitude.

"No, not yet."

"Okay then if you're not divorced, then you're married," he says as if he is schooling me on the rules of separation.

"Look, I really don't want to talk about this right now. All I want is to get my clothes and get out of here."

"So when would you like to talk about it? I can tell you when I would've liked to have talked about it, before you allowed me to sleep with a married woman," he says obviously very disturbed.

"Will you please stop saying that?"

"Stop saying what?"

"That we slept together."

"What are you, twelve? We did sleep together, woman."

"Look, I'm sorry, okay, but I did not expect this to happen. I'm still very confused on how all of this happened."

"What do you mean you're confused? You're married, surely you know what goes on in the bed between a man and a woman."

Being that nothing's been going on in my bed for quite some time, maybe I did forget what goes on. "Yes, I'm well aware of what goes on in the bed. What I'm confused about is how I got here."

"Well, I offered to walk you back to your room and you agreed. When we got to the elevator I guess all the alcohol had its toll on you because you fell out in my arms. I took you to your room, but Janelle was still downstairs and I couldn't find your keys, so I brought you to my room and laid you in the bed."

"So you took advantage of a drunk woman? That's sick," I tell him.

"I didn't take advantage of you. You're the one who woke up in the middle of the night undressing me. I asked you over and over if you were sure, and each time you said yes. How was I supposed to know you were still drunk?"

"Because I would never come on to another man, that's how you should've known."

"I've known you all of a week. How am I supposed to know your character?"

"You cannot be serious. Do I seem like the type who would just sleep with anybody? Surely you could've picked that up in a week," I say, getting very agitated by this whole situation.

"Holly, look, I promise you I did not intend to take advantage of you, but you have to be fair. What man do you know is going to have a beautiful, fine woman in his bed who's coming on to him and turn her down? If he does, I promise you he's gay."

I hear him talking, but I can't understand what he's saying because I'm in shock. I can't believe I came on to him. I've never been the assertive type. Even when it came to Mark, he was usually the one who initiated sex. Could I be that desperate that I allowed myself to totally lose control? I must admit Dexter is a very attractive man, but I thought I was able to at least have some self-control around him. Obviously, that was wrong. Okay, I need to get out of here and fast.

"Do you mind turning around while I get dressed?" I finally ask.

He sits there wearing a ridiculous smile. "What?" I ask.

"I just think it's funny that now you don't want me to see you naked. Don't you think I've seen you already? What do you have to hide now?"

"Could you please just turn around?" I ask again.

"I'll do you one better. I have to visit the boy's room so I'll go and you can change."

"Thank you."

He gets up, and oh my God! *Okay, I'm not going to look. I'm not going to look. Why can't I stop looking?* Dexter has a body that would put any man to shame. Those abs…Oh, I'm a sucker for abs. I'm at the gym a lot and I see a lot of fine men, but nothing I've seen can come close to what I'm seeing now. Mark has great abs, too, but Dexter has him beat.

"Like what you see?" he asks, laughing.

"No," I lie.

While he's in the bathroom I quickly put my clothes on and head to my room. I can only hope that Janelle's still asleep and I won't have to deal with this at the moment.

I enter our room and it sounds like the coast is clear. I don't hear anything so I assume she's still asleep. I peep my head in her room and to my surprise she's not even there. Where could she be? Just as that thought enters my head I hear her turning the lock. I run to my room and lock the bathroom door. I can't let her see me in the same clothes from yesterday. She'll really know something isn't right.

"Holly," I hear her shouting outside my bathroom door. She has to shout because I turned on the shower. I pretend I can't hear. I'll talk with her later. At the moment, I just need time to think. I knew my trip to the Bahamas would be a memorable one. I just didn't think it would be quite this memorable.

Chapter 15

The ride home is very quiet. Surprisingly Janelle has very little to say. Naturally, I start to feel guilty. I just know she knows I slept with her cousin, which is wrong on so many levels. I decide to probe her to see what she knows.

"Did you have fun last night?" I ask her.

"I did. It was really nice," is all she gives in response. This is different from the Janelle I know. The Janelle I know is always willing and ready to talk about her latest escapes. For some reason she isn't giving up much information about last night.

"Are you okay? You're awfully quiet today," I just have to say.

"Holly, what does love feel like?"

Wow, what a question. How do I answer that?

"I really can't describe it, Janelle."

"Well how did you know you were in love with Mark?"

"I knew because he's all I thought about. I was my happiest when I was in his presence. I felt safe with him, like being with him would protect me from anything." That's funny now that I've said it because I never would've thought he was the one I would end up needing protection from. "Why are you asking me this?" *Oh no, she knows,* I think. Why else would she want to remind me of the time I was happy and in love?

"Because I actually psyched myself into believing that I could be in love. Isn't that ridiculous?" she says, laughing.

"What?" So this whole conversation has nothing to do with me. I breathe a sigh of relief and now I'm finally able to give her my undivided attention.

"You think you're in love, with whom?" I ask.

"I said I wasn't going to say anything because you would think I'm crazy. I spent a lot of time with this guy named Derrick. We had the best time together. We laughed and talked and the first time it wasn't just about sex. You know, like all my other relationships."

"Janelle, that's sweet, but I don't know if you can say that it's love. Not right now anyway, it's way too early.

"I know, and that's exactly why I wasn't going to say anything because I know you're one of those people who believe you have to date forever and a day to know if you're in love or not."

"Maybe not forever and a day, but definitely longer than a week. You don't even know much about him. You can't in only a week's time. You need time to get to know a person to decide if you love them or not."

"Well, you dated Mark for four years and look how that turned out," she says.

I can tell she regrets saying it once she sees the hurt on my face. I can't believe she would throw that in my face now.

"Holly, I'm sorry. What I was trying to say is it really doesn't matter how long you date because you never really know the person. I would think that as the years pass you constantly learn new things about them, and that's not a bad thing. That's what makes the relationship exciting."

I still can't believe she said that, but I decide for now to just let it go for now, but we will discuss it again.

"Janelle, you're right. You may never know all there is to know about a person, but shouldn't you know the basics, like what's his last name? What are his parents' names? What does he do? Where's he from originally, like where was he born? Does he have any bad habits? Any criminal background? Those are some things you should know before you decide if you're in love or not."

"All I know is for the last few nights we've stayed on the beach talking all night. You know I believe in getting my sleep, but our conversations are so interesting that sleep was the last thing on my mind. Anyway, it's over. I know I'm not one for doing long distant relationships. Especially when the distance is this long." she says with a faraway look on her face. No doubt replaying her time with Derrick in her mind.

"Well, I'm certainly not the one to be giving relationship advice. Like you said, I dated Mark a long time and look what happened.."

"I apologized already, and anyway I still feel you and Mark will find your way back to each other, eventually."

I don't even know if I can go back to Mark. I'm unsure when he cheated, but now that I've done the same thing, I don't know how our relationship will be able to stand all of this. I do know this getaway has shown me that I'm not completely ready to have him out of my life. As much as I hate to admit it, I really miss him. Maybe that's how I ended up with Dexter. Maybe being inebriated clouded my sense of reality. Maybe it was Mark I thought I was making love to last night. That's the only explanation that makes sense to me.

"I've decided to call him when we get home. I think it's time we sit down and talk like two mature adults," I tell Janelle.

"That'll be really good. Hopefully you'll be able to figure out how to put the pieces back together and move on together. Life's too short to be without the person you love. We all make mistakes. It's the lesson we learn from them that's important."

Boy, have I learned my lesson. I don't want to see another bottle or glass of champagne as long as I live.

"He's going to be too shocked when he finds out I've been to the Bahamas."

"Um, you didn't tell him?" she asks.

"No, I would have to talk to him to tell him that. You know I wasn't trying to have any type of conversation with him."

"Oh, well I may have messed up," she says nervously.

"Janelle, what did you do?" I ask accusingly.

"I tried to get your attention, but you didn't hear me," she begins.

"When? What are you talking about?"

"This morning when you were in the shower, your phone started vibrating and I saw it was Mark."

"He's been calling all weekend. I hope you hit the ignore button like I've been doing," I say already knowing the answer.

"Holly, I couldn't ignore him. I'm glad a didn't because he sounded so worried about you."

"Good. He needs to worry."

"Well, he may not be too worried anymore."

"You told him I was in the Bahamas, didn't you?"

"Yes, and—"

"And? And what?"

"I sort of told him that you would be home tonight," she says as she looks toward the floor.

"Well why didn't you just give him my flight information, no need leaving anything out," I say very aggravated.

"Oh good, so you're okay that I gave him the flight information?" she says, smiling.

"Janelle, I swear you have the biggest mouth in Baton Rouge. Now I remember why I keep some things to myself," I say as I turn my back to her.

"Oh, come on, Holly. Don't be like that," she says as she pokes me in my arm. "You forgive me," she asks as she makes the most pitiful face I've ever seen.

"I don't know, let me think about it." I look at her, and we both burst out laughing. I'm not happy she felt the need to give him all my information, but it's not enough for me to be angry with her. I know in her heart she feels she's helping. For someone who couldn't stand Mark, once upon a time, she sure is his biggest fan now. We talk for a while longer before I finally succumb to sleep. In my dreams I'm back in the Bahamas. I'm having a great time on the beach, sipping on my fruity drink. Next thing I know I'm making love with someone I assume to be Mark. He holds his head up and I see that it's Dexter. I jump so hard I almost hit Janelle.

"Girl, what is your problem? Are you having a nightmare?"

"I guess it should be, but—"

Janelle looks at me very confused. I ignore her, lay back, and drift off into dreamland. I allow my dreams to take me wherever they desire.

Chapter 16

The cab pulls up to my house. I really enjoyed myself, but there's truly no place like home. I am so ready to get in and get to my bed and bathe in my tub. Janelle and I say our good-byes and I go inside.

I am not prepared for what's waiting for me inside. My whole living room looks like an island. There are fake palm trees, lounge chairs, frozen drinks and even sand in a kiddie pool. What in the world is going on here? I think.

"Welcome home," he says, coming out of the kitchen.

"What's all this?" I ask.

"It doesn't look familiar to you? Remember our honeymoon night?"

I actually do remember, but I can't make this easy for him. I can't give him that satisfaction. "Oh," I respond with absolutely no enthusiasm.

"Holly, look, I know I messed up big time, but I promise you I've learned my lesson. Just as I told you in the letter, I will spend the rest of my life making this up to you. I'll do whatever you want me to do. If you want to go to counseling I'm open to that too. Just don't leave me, please, Holly."

Then he does something I've never seen him do before. He starts crying. Mark never cries, not in front of me anyway. His mom died last year after battling cancer for six months, and I never saw him shed a tear. Before I know it we're both holding each other crying.

We talk for most of the night. We reminisce about some fun times we've shared. Mark holds my hand tight, like he's scared to let go. I'm still very angry with him, but I'm also still very in love with him too. Our night ends with us making love in the middle of our homemade island. I know I shouldn't be doing this, especially after last night with Dexter. The difference between now and then is that I know exactly what I'm doing and exactly why I'm doing it. I haven't been with him in so long and right now I really need to feel him next to me. Call me selfish because tonight has more to do with me and my needs than his. I put all negative thoughts behind and I allow Mark to take me to a place I hadn't been in a long time. It almost feels like we're making love to each other for the first time. His touch has become so foreign to me, but I guess it's just like riding a bike, you never forget. Mark touches me in all the right places, and I simply can't control myself. My whole body shudders and the tears begin to flow. Now I remember, now I feel like I'm home again, and home feels really good.

I know this is going to sound really strange, but even after last night I'm still not ready for Mark to move back in yet. I still need time to myself to think and really sort out my feelings. I'm still dealing with the fact that not only did Mark cheat, but so did I. Now I'm questioning myself and my ability to commit if I allowed myself to go there with Dexter. I'm so torn up on the inside because now I'm the one with the dirty little secret. I tore Mark down for giving his body to another woman and I turn around and do the exact same thing. I stepped out of my marriage, and even though I don't remember a thing, it doesn't excuse the fact that it happened.

The phone rings and thankfully puts a halt to my thoughts. I know I'm making myself depressed sitting here thinking about the web of deception Mark and I have created. It's probably Mark. He had an early meeting so he was up and gone by the time I dragged myself out of bed.

"Hello," I finally answer.

"Hey, how's it going?" Mark asks.

"Okay. I'm just sitting here.

"Oh. Listen, I was thinking if you're not busy I could come by and pick you up, and maybe we can go get something to cook together."

"That sounds nice," I tell him.

"Great. I'll call when I'm on my way."

"Sounds good." I'll use this time to find something extra cute and skimpy to put on, I want to look extra good now. I want him to see exactly what he had all along.

I'm actually looking forward to tonight. It amazes me after all we've been through, I still get very excited to see Mark. I guess those feelings just don't go away no matter what. Love is a funny thing. I'll never understand how one thing can make you feel like you're on top of the world one minute and like your world is coming to an end the next minute. All in the name of love. I call Janelle and try convince her to meet me at the gym. I never met anyone who eats as much as she does, hates to work out, and still stays so small. According to her she only sweats for one reason and it's not from working out. "My exercise is done in private, well sometimes depending on my mood," she likes to joke. At least I hope she's joking.

Mark calls, while I'm putting the finishing touches on my makeup, to inform me he's turning into the subdivision. Some would think I'm crazy for putting so much effort into going to the grocery store. No one understands this goes a lot deeper than the grocery store. I want to make him drool over me. I want it to be a job just for him to keep his hands off me, which is why I chose my nice low-cut sundress. The twins, which I so lovingly call my breasts, are behaving very well today. For some reason they seem a little perkier than usual. That's enough to drive Mark crazy. He's a breast man. I hear his car door close as I put on my strappy sandals.

The doorbell rings, and Mark greets me at the door with a bouquet of a dozen pink roses. He's really pulling out all the stops these days.

"Thank you," I say. "Let me put these in water and I'll be ready to go. I have to, of course, give him a chance to check out the view from the back."

"Okay," is all he manages to say.

I find a vase and meet him at the door. "Ready?" I ask.

"Uh, yeah. Holly, are we changing our plans," he asks, sounding somewhat confused.

"No. Why?"

"You're just… You look really nice, and I wanted to make sure we were still going to the grocery store."

"Am I suppose to go out looking raggedy?" I ask, knowing this is not the attire I would've ever chosen for the grocery store.

"No, not at all. You look really good by the way."

"Thanks. Shall we go?"

"Certainly."

Unlike our last car experience together the night of my dad's heart attack, this time Mark and I talk nonstop to the grocery store. It's amazing after all these years we still have so much to talk about. Most of our conversations are about his friend Larry who is truly a character. Let's just say he's a male version of Janelle. I tell her often I'm going to hook them up because they deserve each other. She always laughs because Larry is so not her type. This surprised me because I didn't know Janelle had a particular type. I've seen her with men of all heights, weights, and color. This leads me to believe that she's just not into the single type.

We arrive at the store and prepare to get our items. Mark decides we should have steak, baked potatoes, green beans, and strawberry cheesecake for dessert. We got everything and are just about to leave when I spot Ms. Davis and Tyler. Oh no, the last thing I want to deal with is an unruly child and an out-of-control mother. I only have a few weeks left of my summer vacation. These are the last people I want to see while on vacation, especially since because of her and her lying child, I could've been out of a job. I make up my mind when we pass each other to be cordial and speak, even if she doesn't speak back. All of that, to me, is water under the bridge.

I'm about to point her out to Mark, who isn't paying attention at all. Just as I get his attention I hear Tyler enthusiastically holler, "Daddy." I turn around hoping to finally see his dad, but no one is there. Just as I turn back around Tyler is wrapped around Mark.

"Tyler baby, what're doing?" I ask, confused.

"I'm hugging my dad," he responds.

"This isn't your dad, honey. This is my husband, Mr. James," I inform him.

"AKA Tyler's father," says his mother who is now standing right by us.

"You are really sick," I tell her. "Are there any limits to how low you'll stoop to call yourself hurting Tyler's teachers?"

"Bitch, please, this has nothing to do with you. I really don't know why you're even here because see this?" she says, pointing to the three of them. "This is a family."

When I hear the word *bitch* I immediately know I've finally come face to face with my harasser. I've heard it way too many times not to recognize it.

"This is her? This is the person you stepped out of our marriage for?" I ask Mark all while holding back tears because I would never give her the satisfaction of seeing me cry.

"Holly, let me explain," he begins.

"Mark, you've already explained, and I completely understand why you wouldn't want me to know it was her, especially given our history. It's okay. We'll work this out. Let's just go," I say and we walk away. We buy our groceries and load them in the car. Once inside Mark feels he needs to feel me out to see if I'm okay.

"So, are you really okay with this or was that just—?"

"A damn lie? Yes, the same thing I've been getting from you. Have you lost your mind? Hell no, I'm not okay with this. I wasn't about to stand there and give her the satisfaction of thinking she'd ruined our marriage, but as far as I'm concerned we're right back where we started. You're still lying to me, and you constantly ask me to trust you, but not one time while you were doing all of that confessing did you mention that you had a son, and that he's the little brat I told you about."

"How was I suppose to tell you that, Holly?"

"You open your mouth and say it. You'd already hurt me, so what was one more thing? At least I could've dealt with all of this at the same time, but now I have to try and deal with this too. So what was the plan? You would just raise him with her and I would never find out, was that the plan, Mark?"

"No. I told her that I would help her out financially but nothing other than that. I tried to step back and allow her husband to be Tyler's father, but after their divorce she started calling me again."

"Okay, so basically not only are you a cheater but you're also a deadbeat dad. Oh, please continue talking because now I'm seeing the person I really married. You are not the man I thought you were. The man I thought you were would jump over mountains to take care of his responsibility, not run away from it."

"At the time I thought I was doing the right thing."

"Really? The right thing? You know, it's no wonder that poor child is the way he is. Look at who he has for parents."

"Holly, that's not fair."

"No, this situation you created is not fair. You know what? I'm done. Just take me home, and please don't bother to get out."

"Holly, we can't keep running from our problems. We need to talk this out."

"I agree, we do need to talk this out, but not today. I have too much to think about today. I'll let you know when I'm ready to talk."

"Will you call me?" he asks.

"I said I'll let you know when I'm ready to talk."

"Okay, fine," he says, sounding very defeated.

All of this is just too much for me to handle right now. I'm still finding it very hard to believe that Mark is Tyler's father. All this time I've been talking about this child and his crazy mama and he said nothing. I really thought Mark and I could work our marriage out, but now I don't know. I just don't know.

Chapter 17

The next few weeks seem to pass by way too fast. Other than leaving to decorate and organize my classroom for Monday, the first day of school, I probably would've turned myself into a hermit and stayed in the house all day. I'm just not comfortable facing the outside world. I'm trying to pull myself together because the last thing the kids need is to be greeted Monday by a messed-up teacher. I haven't told anyone about the incident in the store with Tyler, not even Janelle. I can only hope to avoid him and his mother this school year. That may be asking a lot, but if I never see them again, I will not be mad. The thought of that whole situation makes me angry all over again. I pray with everything in me no one finds out, especially at work. The last thing I need is for everyone to look at me in pity. I know people will find out eventually, but I'm not ready to deal with it just yet.

I'm staying in bed all day, but it's not by choice. Even though my classroom is ninety-eight percent ready, there are still a few loose ends I need to tie up. I was hoping to go Monday with everything complete, but that's not going to happen. I couldn't leave out today if I wanted to. I feel absolutely horrible. I'm waiting on Janelle to come bring me some broth because I can't seem to keep anything else on my stomach. I always feel horrible when my sinuses drain. I absolutely hate going through this. Just as I'm about to make my way to the bathroom, I hear the doorbell ring. Janelle would come just as I'm about to pee all over myself.

"Coming," I holler from the bedroom. "Hey, come on in," I'm about to tell Janelle, only it isn't her. It's Mark.

"Mark, what are you doing here?" I ask, halfway pissed he has the nerve to show up.

"I'm sorry to bother you, Holly, but I really need to pick up some folders."

"Okay, whatever," I say as I turn to go to the bedroom. I hear him call my name but decide to ignore him, one because I don't feel like conversing, not with him anyway, and two because I really have to get to the bathroom.

After handling my business I decide to go back up front to get this conversation over with so he can leave. I walk in the living room only to find that he's left. "Good," I say to myself, now if I can only make myself believe it. Every part of me wants to hurt Mark very bad. If I could only get rid of the other part that still longs to be with him.

I feel myself getting weak, so I quickly sit on the couch. I know it's because I'm dealing with so many emotions. Most days I don't know if I'm coming or going. At the moment going sounds really good. I would love to go far away from here.

The doorbell rings again and this time it better be Janelle.

"Hey, girl," I greet her as I open the door.

"Hey. How're you feeling? Um, because you look awful" she asks as she walks in.

This time she gets the, *girl please* look. "I'm okay. A little weak right now."

"Go sit down. I'll warm your broth," she offers.

"Thanks so much. I think I'm going to lie down for a minute. Just bring it to the room, and Janelle, thanks."

"Anytime. That's what sisters are for," she says, smiling.

Janelle and I haven't really talked about our personal situations much lately. I didn't talk about mine because I'm just too embarrassed, and I'm sure she doesn't talk about hers because she doesn't want to hear any more of my advice. Little does she know I already vowed on the plane to just be supportive and keep my comments to myself, unless I think she's in danger, in which case she will have to be mad because I will definitely speak my mind.

"Here you go," Janelle says, bringing my food in the bedroom.

"Thanks," I say, trying to sit up without getting dizzy.

"Holly, are you sure you don't need to go to the doctor? You've suffered from sinus infections before, but I don't ever remember them being this bad."

"I'm sure. It's just a really bad case this time. I'll be fine."

"Okay, whatever you say," she says, dropping the subject, but I know it's only temporary.

I try to stand to go wash my hands, but just as I do I fall back on the bed. I'm so dizzy.

"You know what? I don't care what you say, you're going to the doctor. Now, you can come willingly or forcefully—and force means calling your mom for backup."

Janelle knows the last thing I want is to worry my mom over nothing, so to keep down confusion I decide to go willingly.

I make the ride to the doctor's office as miserable for her as possible. I don't like people telling me what to do, and she knows that. I may be easygoing, but I draw the line there. Of course I can never really get mad with her. She's been my rock throughout this soap opera life I'm now living. Each time I look around I'm going through more drama than Victor Newman from the *Young and the Restless*. My life now makes his look like a comedy.

Janelle and I make it to the doctor's office and prepare ourselves for a long wait. I called my doctor and the nurse said they could work me in, which meant "you can come, but expect to be here all day."

It seems the longer I sit, the worse I feel. A sudden wave of nausea comes over me, and I run to the bathroom. Because the bathroom is in the waiting room, I know everyone can hear me, but I'm too sick to care. Now I'm glad Janelle insisted I come, I can't handle this much longer.

"Holly James," the nurse finally calls.

I slowly make my way to the freezing room, while Janelle waits. The nurse takes all my vitals and asks all the necessary questions, then informs me the doctor will be right with me. It's funny how medical time and real time is totally different. It takes him another forty-five minutes to make it to my room. Forty-five minutes is not exactly my idea of "right with you."

"Good afternoon, Mrs. James," Dr. Lee greets me as she walks in the room.

"Good afternoon, Dr. Lee."

"Now, what seems to be the problem today?" she asks.

I tell her all my symptoms and she proceeds to check me out. "Could you be pregnant?" she asks.

I look at her like she's the craziest person in the world. Was she not there when Mark and I were going through all the drama of trying to have a baby? I know she has a lot of patients, but she could've reviewed my chart before she start questioning me.

"No, I have fibroids, remember?"

"Well, that doesn't mean you can't get pregnant, but it does make your chances very slim. However, I would like to do a test just to rule it out before we go any further."

I agree to the test, already knowing the results because I've been down this road too many times before. Dr. Lee's nurse gives me a cup to catch some urine and instructs me to place the cup on the shelf in the bathroom. I do as I'm asked and proceed back to the room to wait yet again.

After what seems like hours, Dr. Lee returns with my results.

"Okay, Mrs. James, your test results came back positive."

Did she say positive? She could not have said positive. There's no way she said positive. *Did they change the terms?* I wonder. Does positive mean you're positively not pregnant?

"Mrs. James, are you okay?" Dr. Lee asks.

"Um, yes I'm–I'm fine," I finally force myself to respond.

"I would think you would be jumping for joy right now. I know how long you and your husband have been trying to get pregnant."

"I am happy. I guess I'm just in shock right now."

"Well, that's certainly understandable. It's not every day you get the one thing you've wanted so badly."

"No, it's not," I respond, still in shock by her words.

"Now, because of the fibroids I'm going to refer you to a specialist who deals with these special cases. He'll take very good care of you and your baby."

She has absolutely no idea how special this case is, and it's not one any specialist can take care of. I never thought I would be one of those women. How is it that the news I've been waiting for years to hear all of a sudden becomes my worst nightmare? How in the world did I allow this to happen? I guess a better question would be who? Who do I call to congratulate, Mark or Dexter?

Chapter 18

"So?" Janelle asks as she drives me home from the doctor's office.

"She said I have a really bad upper respiratory infection." I hate to lie but I have to. How do I tell my best friend who puts me right up there next to Mother Theresa that I'm pregnant and I have no idea who the father is? It sounds crazy just hearing myself say it. I know I won't be able to hold this in forever, but at least for today. I have to come to grips with this myself.

"Poor baby. I can tell you're miserable. Did she give you something to take?"

"Um, yes, she gave me some samples, and I have a prescription if I need more."

"Okay, well we can drop off the prescription and then head to your house."

"No, Janelle, I'm really tired. Just take me home. I'm sure I'll be fine with the samples for now." Okay, I'm really getting good at this. I use to frown upon liars, and look at me. I've become so good I'm starting to believe myself.

"Okay, but it's no problem. If you want, I can drop it off on my way home. That way it'll be ready when you need it."

Why won't she just leave this alone? I know she's trying to be helpful, but I'm getting real annoyed. Deep down I know it had nothing to do with her and everything to do with me and this crazy predicament I've gotten myself into. "It's fine. Dr. Lee gave me a lot of samples, so I'm sure I'll be fine."

"Okay, well I'm sorry but I really need to go after I drop you off. I have to pick Dex up from the airport."

"Who's Dex?" I ask, totally spaced out.

"Dexter, my cousin, crazy," she says, laughing.

"You didn't tell me he was coming to town," I say, trying to sound nonchalant while deep down inside I'm screaming. I really don't want to face Dexter right now. It's going to be hard enough trying to avoid Mark, now Dexter's here too.

“I’m sorry. I didn’t know you would be that interested to know that.”

“What? Oh, I’m not interested. I just thought you would’ve mentioned it before.”

“Yeah. He told us before we left the Bahamas he would come down and visit for a while. His mom isn't doing too well. She has cancer and was in remission for a while, but it's back now and she's in and out of the hospital. I'm sure he'll stay until she's better. However, it's really no telling because Dexter is so unpredictable. ”

“Tell me about it,” I mumble to myself.

“Okay, we’re here. So do you need me to do anything before I leave?”

“No, I’ll be fine. Thank you so much for coming with me. I really appreciate it.”

“Of course. Where else would I be?” she says, smiling.

Janelle and I say our good-byes and she leaves. I want to go inside and bury my head in the pillows and have a good cry, but for some reason the tears won’t come. I guess because I’ve finally heard the news I’ve been dying to hear for so long. My mind is still in shock. I still don’t believe the doctor said I’m pregnant. I thought I’d never hear those words. I’d even convinced myself I was fine, that I didn’t need to carry a baby to be a mother. Mark and I would adopt or we’d hire a surrogate. There were so many options for us to consider. Although I would be happy with either of those choices, my number one choice would always be to be able to carry and deliver my own child. I’ve heard childbirth is the most miraculous thing any couple can experience. I would give anything for this situation to be different. I would love for Mark and me to be here celebrating while he rubs my stomach, and even though it’s still flat as a board, just the thought that there’s a little life in there would be enough for us. The phone rings, and I want to ignore it because I’m enjoying my daydream, but that’s all it is, just a dream.

“Hello,” I say, answering the phone, halfway annoyed because I see its Mark’s cell phone number across the ID screen.

“Hey, I was calling to check on you. Are you okay?”

“I’m fine. Why?”

“I could tell you didn’t feel well when I came by earlier. I wanted to stay around and talk, but I didn’t want to upset you, especially if you don’t feel well.”

“How considerate of you,” I say, this time with much attitude. Now he considers my feelings. Now he wants to play the role of the loving, caring, considerate husband.

“Okay. I can tell this is only going to lead to an argument, so I’ll go now. I just wanted to check on you.”

“Whatever,” I say, hanging up the phone. I have way too much to deal with, and I really didn’t feel like arguing with Mark, not at this particular moment anyway. No matter how much I would like to avoid it, an argument is destined to happen, especially when he hears my big news. I try to put all those thoughts in the back of my head and get some rest. It’s kind of hard to sleep when every time I close my eyes I dream of babies. It’s always the same recurring dream: I’m in the delivery room, and the doctors just keep pulling out babies. They just won’t stop coming. Then I’d look up, and standing to my left is Mark and to my right is Dexter. It’s almost like we’re one huge happy family. I don’t know the meaning of this dream, but I hope it means everything will be fine. I don’t know about all those babies though. I would love to have twins because to me this is a miracle baby. I feel like this is probably my only chance of getting pregnant, which saddens me. I remember the loneliness of being an only child. That’s why I always wanted a big family so my children wouldn’t know the feeling of being an only child. Things don’t always happen in life the way we plan. I feel so unappreciative because I know I should just be thankful for the opportunity to have one child and here I am sad because I may not be able to have more. Hopefully people on the outside can’t tell how messed up I am. I’m very happy with the pregnancy, not so happy with the situation as a whole. I’m just going to concentrate on having a healthy baby and deal with the messed-up part later, whether I like it or not. I decide to let my thoughts rest for tonight and allow my mind to rest. I feel my eyelids getting heavy, which means soon I’ll be off into dreamland. I have to get some rest because I cannot oversleep in the morning. This situation is way too big for me. I’m going to need some divine intervention.

It's funny how when you're in trouble, church seems to be the most logical place to go. I was brought up in the church, so I've always been taught to turn to God when the situation seems too big for me to handle. Mark and I are faithful churchgoers. I'm glad he's out of town seeing to his grandmother or I'd have to see him today. I don't want to have any distractions because today is all about me and God.

The preacher preached a sermon I know is meant just for me. He talks about forgiveness and how we expect God to forgive us when we can't forgive our brothers. Automatically my mind goes to Mark and all the lies he's told over the years. I wonder if God expects me to forgive all of that and if so, how. How do you forgive and move on? Better yet, how do you forget? When it's time for the altar prayer I pray God will forgive me of my sins and show me how to forgive my husband of his. I pray that He, if it be His will, lead us back to each other. I pray for my unborn child and that God allows all of us to look at this as the blessing He means for it to be. Bringing a life into the world is a miracle God blesses us with. It's not a curse, and I need to keep telling myself that.

Sometimes I allow myself to believe this is God's way of punishing me for sleeping with another man. A child that I've wanted so badly can't possibly be anything but a blessing. I'm starting to accept the pregnancy, but I would give anything not to have to deal with the problems that are coming along with it. I wish I didn't have to face Mark or Dexter, but I know that eventually that day will come. *Lord, just give me the courage to handle it.*

"Hello, Sister James. My aren't you just glowing today, and where is that handsome husband of yours? I didn't see him in service this morning," Sister Juanita, the head usher, asks as I try to make my exit.

"Good morning, Sister Juanita. Mark's out of town taking care of his grandmother, but I'll be sure to tell him you asked about him."

"Be sure you do, and tell him next Sunday I'm bringing that blueberry cobbler he's been asking about," she says, smiling.

She's such a sweet lady, which is why I'm sure Mark was instantly drawn to her. She has one son who's strung out on drugs and living on the streets. Each Sunday she stands and requests that the church pray for him and bring him back home safely. I guess she and Mark see something in each other that they're missing. To him she's a mother figure, and to her he's the son she gets to take care of and spoil with rich desserts. "I will definitely let him know. You know he loves your blueberry cobbler."

I make my way to my car and finally start to feel a sense of peace. I feel God is telling me everything will be okay. I just have to keep telling myself that. I've come to the conclusion I have to do what's best for me and the baby. I still don't know what that is, but I'm sure the answer will come. I just hope I'm not too distracted to know it.

Chapter 19

It's killing me to get up this morning. I lay there as I strategize how I'm going to get out of bed. I'm so nauseous, and I know as soon as I pick my head up, it's all over. The best thing for me to do is to lay here until it passes or at least until I know I can make it to the bathroom. I would give anything to be able to lie in this bed all day, but for some reason I think it may look bad if the teacher is out the first day of school. The first day use to be my most favorite day of the school year. Other than the last day, that is. It's just something about the excitement of these days in particular. I love meeting my new students and forming relationships with them and their parents. Although I miss them like heck over the summer, I still enjoy that break.

Once I feel like the nausea has passed, I drag myself out of bed and go immediately to the bathroom. I don't want to take any chances. I'm standing here staring at my toothbrush, talking myself into picking it up. I never knew so many challenges came along with being pregnant. Once upon a time brushing my teeth was a thoughtless task. Now it's the most difficult part of my morning. As soon as the toothbrush enters my mouth I have to immediately run to the toilet. Morning sickness is the worst, especially when you're going through it alone. I don't know what I would expect Mark to do, maybe hold my hair, which I'm obviously not very good at doing myself. I've come to this conclusion as I touch the wet ends of my hair. Washing it is out of the question this morning so I'll have to make due.

My routine changed this morning. I'm not very successful with getting out the house on time, which means I can't stop for my morning coffee. I read that pregnant women shouldn't have caffeine anyway. I really want to do the right thing during this pregnancy, but giving up my coffee is going to be very hard. I really need to ask Dr. Lee about this. If it doesn't harm the baby, then I may have to indulge every now and then. One thing I'm determined to keep the same about my routine is my inspirational music. I allow Yolanda Adams to take me to another level, a more positive level. By the time I arrive at work I'm feeling really good. After greeting my coworkers and signing in I go to my classroom and prepare to meet my new babies, as I so lovingly refer to my students.

The first day goes by really fast. The whole day is gone by the time I talk to the parents who just insist on staying around a little while, introduce myself to the students, go over classroom rules, and collect and organize supplies. The first day is usually a very easy day because most of the students are on their best behavior. I think they use this day to feel me out and see just how far they can go before they push my buttons. I can tell within the first hour who's going to be the problem for the year. There's a very easy way to tell. If I know that student's name, then they're going to be a problem. Of course the only reason I would know their name so well is because I've called it so much, just within that first hour. These students I know I need to give a little extra special attention. I've learned over the years that students act out for several reasons: either they need attention, they're bored because the work isn't challenging enough, or they're bored because the work is too challenging. Being that no real work is given on the first day, naturally I diagnose them as attention getters.

My favorite time of the day—lunchtime—is finally here. The day was so busy that I really didn't have time to talk with my new coworker, Ms. Erica Valentine. Ms. Valentine is a spanking brand-new teacher. She graduated this summer from Louisiana State University, or LSU as it's often referred. Mr. McNair worked out our schedule so we now have the luxury of a duty-free lunch, which means we no longer have to eat with our class. I feel like Christmas has come early this year.

We sit in the lounge and get to know each other in between bites of food. I learn that she's from California. Her parents are from Louisiana and they both graduated from LSU, which is where her desire to be here came from. I almost feel sorry for her because she has no family here anymore. Her grandparents lived here, but they passed away within a year of each other. I feel so sorry for her because I can still hear the pain in her voice as she talks about them. Our lunch is really nice. I'm so glad I made up my mind to get to know her before I automatically decide I don't like her. Once we finish eating it's back to the real world.

With the exception of two talkative kids, the rest of my day is great. I've become really good at masking the fact that my personal life is a complete wreck. Mark's been ringing my cell phone all day today. I'm sure he's just checking to see how my first day's going, but I am not in the mood for small talk. I know I can't avoid him forever, but no one can blame me for trying.

"Hey, I need to go to the school supply store. Do you need anything?" Erica asks as she peeps in my room. Apparently no one gave her the last name memo either because she insists that I call her Erica. It is a lot easier than Valentine. It just flows better to me. When she asked I did get a warm feeling. She reminds me of Smith, who never left without asking if I needed anything. I have a feeling Erica and I are going to develop a beautiful relationship.

"No, not that I can think of, but thank you so much for asking," I say.

The drive home is surprisingly very peaceful, until I hear my phone ring. I pick it up not bothering to look at the screen because I know who it is. "Yes Mark," I answer.

"Are you busy?" he asks.

"No, just driving home," I say, waiting for him to get to the point of this call.

"Oh, you want me to call you later?" he asks. Mark has always had an issue with me driving while talking on the phone. He says it's too distracting. Just because he has trouble concentrating doesn't mean I have that problem.

"No, do you need something?" I ask trying to hurry this call along.

"Okay, well I was just calling to tell you that my grandmother died today," he says, sounding like his whole world has ended.

"Oh, Mark, I'm so sorry to hear that," I say very sincere. In spite of Mark and his cheating ways, I still, and always will, have a special place in my heart for Ms. Emma, his grandmother. "Are you in Varnado now?" I ask.

"No, I'm wrapping up some files now. I plan to leave within the next hour or so."

"Okay, well tell everyone I send my regards and I'll definitely keep you all in my prayers." I know that's not what he wants to hear. He really wants me to say I'm going to come with him because of course that would've been my response if we were still together. If the situation was different and I wasn't dealing with morning sickness I probably would just take off tomorrow and go, but I'm not ready for him to know yet. I could pretend I have the flu or something, but I just don't feel like going through the motions of lying and pretending.

"Okay, well I just wanted you to know," he says, sounding very disappointed. "Do you think you'll be able to make it to the funeral?"

"Yes. Just let me know when you all make the arrangements?"

"What am I suppose to tell them when I get there? You know my sister's going to question why you're not there with me."

"I don't know, Mark. Tell her I'm sick, but I will be there for the funeral," I suggest.

"So you want me to lie to her?" he says, sounding somewhat aggravated.

"Mark, look, I'm not about to go there with you today. I understand you're dealing with a lot right now, but you have to understand my position too. I don't want this to turn into an argument, but you can't get upset with me. I didn't create this situation, you did." I wait for his response, but it never comes. I look at my screen and see the home screen, which tells me our call has ended. I don't know if he hung up or if the call dropped, but in any case I feel we've said all we need to say to each other at this time.

When I enter my house, the unexpected happens. I fall to the floor and I cry uncontrollably. I don't know if it's dealing with this mess with Mark, the craziness of this pregnancy, Ms. Emma's death, or a combination of everything. As I lay on the floor, I want so bad to be held. I want someone to put their arms around me and tell me that everything's going to be alright, but who? I could call my mom or Janelle, but I'm not ready to disclose my dirty little secret yet. I can already see the disappointment in my mom's eyes when she finds out. Just thinking about it makes me cry even harder. How in the world did I get to this place? I'm a professional, well-educated woman. I'm not suppose to get caught up in scenarios like this: I have a cheating husband with a baby on the side, I'm pregnant with no knowledge at all who's the father, and I'm avoiding my best friend and parents for fear they may find out the position my life is in nowadays. Isn't this supposed to be happening to some young ghetto girl? Surely this is not where I'm meant to be in life. Everything was going so good. Sure Mark and I had some issues, but what marriage doesn't. Damn him for taking my life away from me, damn him for ruining my marriage, and damn him for putting me in this position. Had he not been such a male whore, that night with Dexter never would've happened.

I lay on my floor for quite some time before I finally coax myself into getting up. As always when I'm not feeling my best, I go straight to my comfort place, which happens to be my bathtub. I've always wanted a large garden tub because of my love for baths. Every since I was a little girl I've enjoyed taking bubble baths. Whenever I would get in trouble, which wasn't very often, I would always resort to the bathroom. It's just something about indulging in a warm bath surrounded by bubbles and the sweet scent from the bubble bath. It used to be all I needed to make me feel better. My mom always said I would be a great spokesperson for Calgon bubble bath. I wish it could be as simple as the commercial makes it seem. You get in and allow it to take all your troubles away. For some reason I think my problems are going to take a lot more than a bubble bath, but for now it's all I have.

Chapter 20

I hate missing work more than anything, especially the first week of school. I realize that desperate times call for desperate measures. I'm going to do something I feel will assist me with having a wonderful school year. I make up my mind to do something I didn't think I'd ever do. I decide to go see a therapist. When the receptionist says the doctor has an opening Wednesday morning, I immediately take it. The school system pays for one free counseling session, so I decide to take advantage of it. I know it's time to do something when I find myself talking to the telemarketer about my situation. I'm sure I'll never have to worry about her calling again. At the end of the conversation all she could say was, "Ma'am, are you interested in ordering the magazines or not?"

I had to laugh at myself because I truly felt pathetic. I'm still not ready to tell Janelle or anyone else about my situation. I want to avoid it as long as I can. I don't know how they'll react, but I'm not ready to find out. I don't even want to know what my parents will think about me. I'm sure they'll wonder what in the world is going on with Mark and me. What kind of twisted world are we living in? Here he's been having an affair for the last nine years and has a child and I go away, have an affair, come up pregnant and don't know who's the father. Wow! That's a mouthful even for me.

"Hello. I'm Holly James. I have a two o'clock appointment with Dr. Harris," I tell the receptionist when I walk in the doctor's office.

"Good afternoon, Ms…." She pauses, waiting for a possible correction to my title.

"Mrs.," I reluctantly tell her.

"Mrs. James, is this your first visit with Dr. Harris?"

"Yes."

"Okay, I need you to fill out these papers, and I'll need a copy of your insurance card and driver's license.

I give her my cards and sit to fill out the booklet of papers she gives me. *This is going to take forever,* I think. After filling out my paperwork, I sit with my book that I've been trying to finish all summer long and prepare to wait. Just as I'm opening my book, the receptionist tells me I can come to the back. Imagine my relief when I realize I don't have to sit and wait. I walk to the back and she opens it to a very beautiful office. Someone really knows about decorating, I think as I admire the decor.

"You may have a seat on the sofa or chair, whichever you like, and Dr. Harris will be right with you," the receptionist says as she closes the door to the office.

I chose to sit in a chair because I just couldn't see myself lying on the couch spilling my guts about my childhood and what brought me to this point. I guess I've seen way too many TV shows.

"Hello, Mrs. James," Dr. Harris says as she walks inside the room.

"Hello, Dr. Harris."

"Okay, before we get started, I'll tell you a little about myself." She begins telling me about her educational background and her family. She's a married mother of three. She only tells the basics and I'm sure that's just to make me feel more comfortable about my situation. After she finishes, she asks me about myself.

"Well, let's see, I was married for fourteen years—well technically I'm still married, but separated. I'm a third grade teacher." It's sad because telling her about myself makes me realize this is always what I tell people when I'm asked to tell a little about myself. I tell about my husband and my job, and that's usually where it ends. Today, that's about to change because there's way more to my life than my husband and job—way more.

"Okay, so is there anything in particular you'd like to talk about today?"

"Actually, there is," I say, still not sure how I'm going to tell her about my situation. I thought talking to a stranger would make it easier, but I guess not. I don't think it's easy to tell anyone. Even though I don't know this woman from Eve, I still don't want her to think I'm a horrible person. That's how I view myself, so of course others will feel the same way . I guess Dr. Harris can tell I'm very hesitant about opening up.

"Just take your time and begin whenever you're ready. I want you to understand that all sessions are confidential. Anything you say here today is only between us. I also want you to understand it's not my job to judge you or your actions. I'm simply here to listen and offer advice if you want it."

I nod and begin telling her the whole sordid tale that has become my life. "And now I'm pregnant, and I'm not sure who the father is," I finally say. I wait for the disgusted look to come across Dr. Harris' face, but it never does. Actually, her facial expression never changes. I feel better after I tell her my story.

"Would you like to hear what I think?" she finally asks.

"I would love some advice. I'm tired of dealing with this alone, but I don't know what I should do."

"Let me just say that although your situation seems like the end of the world, it's really not. I'm not going to pretend it's going to be easy, but you do have some decisions to make, and putting them off isn't going to make them go away. Obviously, you can't hide your pregnancy forever. At some point you're going to have to come clean with both men. It's up to you if you would like to find out the paternity now or after the baby's born. I would recommend you talk to your physician about that. What scares you the most about telling your family?"

"I just don't want them to look at me differently. My parents have always been very proud of me—well except for marrying Mark at such a young age, but they dealt with that and grew to really love and respect him. I guess I just don't want to let them down."

"That's understandable, but your parents sound like they've been really loving and supportive of you. You said they didn't want you marrying Mark so young, but they stood by your decision. Don't you think they'll continue to stand by you?"

"I know they will." Thinking about my parents opens up the flood gates. Dr. Harris hands me a box of Kleenex as I continue. "Even though I'm grown, I still feel the need to please my parents. I just want them to be proud of me."

"You don't think they'll be proud of you?"

"I don't know."

"Do you have any siblings?"

"No. I'm an only child."

"So this will be your parents' first grandchild?"

"You know, as strange as this is going to sound, I never thought about that, that this will be their grandchild. Oh my God, my mom is going to flip when she finds out." I honestly never allowed my mind to go there. I was so consumed with the situation and how it's affecting me that I didn't allow myself to think of any positives. Now that Dr. Harris has reminded me that my parents are going to be grandparents, I'm actually starting to feel better, when it comes to telling my parents anyway. I'm still not too excited about dealing with Mark and Dexter. I know there's nothing Dr. Harris can say that's going to make that easier for me.

"Now, when it comes to telling the potential fathers, that's different. I'm not going to even sit here and tell you that's going to be easy. In fact it may be the most difficult thing you've ever had to do, but you do have to do it, and soon. Putting it off is only going to make this pregnancy more miserable for you. This should be an enjoyable time for you, and the sooner you tell them and get that burden off your shoulders, then you can spend your time concentrating on taking care of yourself and your baby."

Dr. Harris tells me everything I already know, but it seems different coming from an outside source. After meeting with her I make up my mind I will go ahead and do what I know has to be done.

Chapter 21

The next two days at work are just as good as the first two. I'm really glad I went to see Dr. Harris, the therapist. Just being able to talk about my problem was a big help. I never thought I'd be comfortable telling a stranger such private information, but surprisingly it wasn't nearly as bad as I imagined. I guess it was easy because she doesn't know me; therefore, I didn't have to deal with the shocked expression once I told her what Mark and I did.

My students are in music class at the moment so I use this time to copy a page for a project we'll work on once they come back to class. As I'm entering the office to get to the teacher's lounge, I open the door and coming out is none other than her, the person who's made my life a living hell both personally and professionally. She looks me up and down, then gives me a smile. Not a nice friendly smile, more of a "yeah, I sexed your man, now what?" kind of smile. Through that smile I see nothing but evil. I'm convinced that woman doesn't have a compassionate bone in her body. She finally walks out so I'm able to go through the door.

"I told her I needed an emergency contact number for Tyler," I hear Ms. Craig talking to herself. "Mrs. James, you taught Tyler Davis last year didn't you?" she asks.

"Yes," I reluctantly answer.

"You don't happen to still have his emergency card, do you?"

"No, check with Jones. Remember, he switched to her class before we left for Christmas break," I remind her.

"Oh, that's right."

I walk in the back and thankfully there's no one in the teacher's lounge because I need a moment to get myself together. Seeing her has me so rattled. I should've prepared myself for the possibility of running into her, because I knew it would happen. As a matter of fact, it's going to happen a lot. I'm sure Tyler hasn't changed over the summer, which means his teacher will be calling his mom about his behavior. I really should warn his teacher about his and his mom's behavior, but I really like for teachers to form their own opinions of their students. She's another teacher who's new to the school, so unless someone else told her, she doesn't know about their reputation. Tyler has gone to school here since he was in pre-K, so naturally his name and his mom's name are well known around here. I still can't believe Mark spent nine years with that piece of—okay, I need to calm down. Neither one of them is worth me getting worked up over. I can tell that today's going to be quite a day. First, I run into her and next I have the pleasure of going to meet Mark. I'm driving to Varnado for his grandmother's funeral. The funeral is actually tomorrow, but the viewing at the funeral home is tonight.

I suppress my feelings and will myself to finish the day with my students on a good note. It must've worked because the kids do a really good job on their group project. I am so proud of them I treated them with an extra recess. We had about twenty minutes left before dismissal.

"Okay, boys and girls, if you pack up quickly and quietly we can get out of here and you'll have more play time," I explain to my students. By the time they all pack up and we're out the door, they may have ten minutes of play time left. I watch my students play and remember a time when life was that innocent for me. I remember when my biggest problem was when my best friend decided she wanted to be friends with Angela Banks. My heart was broke because every since kindergarten Nicole and I had been inseparable. Once we entered sixth grade, she for some reason felt we needed to start hanging with more people. I liked things the way they were, which is why I wasn't happy at all when she invited Angela to sit with us at lunch. It's funny, being an only child, one would think I'd like to hang with many people to make up for the loneliness from home, but I didn't. Eventually Nicole, Angela, and I all became very good friends. We remained friends throughout middle and high school. We lost touch after we all left for college. I would love to see them again one day.

"Mrs. James, do you want us to go?" one of my students asks.

"Go where?

"Line up? The bell just rung."

"Oh yes," I say as I motion for the class to come line up for dismissal.

Once I see all of my students off I return to my classroom to straighten up before I leave. For some reason I'm starting to get knots in my stomach thinking about going to be with Mark this weekend. Neither one of us is an actor, so hopefully we can pull this act off this weekend. The last thing we need is his nosy family all in our business. I've come to love Mark's family like my own, so I know nothing I say about them is to be hurtful in any way. I do believe, however, in telling the truth, and the truth is his family is nosy. It's funny because his uncles are just as nosy, if not more, than his aunts. I'm sure they've already grilled Mark about my absence. Mark has gotten really good at lying so I'm sure he was able to put on a good façade.

"Well I'm out of here. You have a good weekend," Erica says as she enters my room.

"Oh, you too, sweetie. Do you have any plans?"

"Not really. I was thinking about going to the mall tonight, but I'll probably just stay in and watch TV."

"You are too young to be in the house. You need to get out and do some things." I can tell someone else this because I realize all the fun I missed when I was her age. I would hate for her to miss out on life too.

"I might get out tomorrow, but I'm just too tired today."

"I understand."

"What about you? Any hot plans?" she asks, smiling.

"Only if you consider going to my husband's grandmother's funeral having hot plans."

"Well, I guess not."

We say our good-byes and she's off. Other than the fact that she's very considerate, there's just something about her that I like. Something familiar, but I don't know what it is. I guess she's just one of those likeable people.

I finish in my room and decide I better get on the road if I want to make it to Varnado in time. I call my parents and Janelle to let them know I'm on my way. They all tell me to call to let them know I've made it safely. Once I end my calls, it's just me and my thoughts for the next two hours. Taking this drive alone in the past would've been a welcomed change, but today it's the last thing I want to do. Everything about this trip is pure misery. I don't want to go bury Mark's grandmother, the person I've grown to love. I don't want to be around him, and I don't want to have to front for his family. So, needless to say this is not my idea of a fun trip. I realize I have no choice because in spite of my feelings for Mark, I cannot deny how much I truly love Ms. Emma.

"I hope you know I'm doing this for you, not your grandson. I know you love him dearly, as you should, but I'm not feeling him at all these days. I know you're not smiling down now, seeing all that's going on with us. I can only hope we can make you proud again. I just don't know if we can do it as a couple. I know it's not what you want to hear, but it's all I can say—for now anyway."

Chapter 22

It's hard to believe it's been three weeks since we buried Ms. Emma. It seems like it was just yesterday. Maybe because being there was a lot harder than I thought it would be. With everything else going on, I really didn't give myself time to grieve properly. I fell in love with Ms. Emma the first time I met her. It was the summer Mark took me to his family reunion. Ms. Emma was there having a great time. You could tell she truly enjoyed being around her family. I think she danced more than the little kids. I remember sitting there looking at her in amazement. She was the same age as my grandmother, but you would never know. She was always so full of energy. My maternal grandmother was always very sickly. I personally believe she just loves the attention, but what do I know? I never met my dad's parents who both died before I was born.

Once I returned to Baton Rouge I make a vow that I will continue seeing Dr. Harris, my therapist. Going to the funeral made me realize how short life really is. Ms. Emma was perfectly healthy one day and the next she was gone. She had a massive heart attack and was gone by the time the paramedics arrived. I do hope I can live a long life as Ms. Emma did, but I never know. I would hate for something to happen to me and I leave without fixing things in my life.

After my third session with Dr. Harris I finally decide to talk with my parents. My session is on Thursday, but I decide to wait until Sunday after church before I actually do the deed, which is what I call breaking the news to my parents. I'm not really sure why I chose to tell them first, but to me it just makes sense to start with them. I guess a big part of me is hoping they'll be the support I need when I do decide to break the news to Mark.

I decide to skip church. I believe a lot has to do with the nervous stomach I have. In an effort to keep from thinking about my upcoming appointment, I've been cleaning the house all day. With everything that's going on, cleaning has been the last thing on my mind. Not that it needs it because Ms. Laura is the best cleaning lady I know. I just need something to do because I invited my parents over for dinner. Tonight's the night I will give them the shock of their lives. My only hope is that they leave here happy. I thought of inviting Janelle, too, but I think it will be best if I tell them alone. Janelle's next on my list.

Just as I'm taking the roast from the oven, the doorbell rings. *Perfect timing,* I think as I head toward the door. I open it, and I'm so happy to see my parents standing there. I haven't seen them in a few weeks, and it's not until I see them standing there that I realize how much I've truly missed them.

"How's my baby girl?" my dad asks as they walk inside. Seeing my dad out the house and doing well makes me feel so good. No one would ever know by looking at him that he's had a heart attack.

"I'm fine, Daddy. How've you been?"

"I guess I'm doing well for an old man," he says, laughing.

My dad always says that when someone asks him how he's feeling.

"That's great, Dad," I say, smiling. "Mom, how've you been?"

"Blessed and highly favored, baby."

My mom also has a traditional response. I don't even know why I keep asking, especially since I already know the answer.

"So, where's my son-in-law?" my dad asks.

"Oh, Mark stayed in Varnado to tie up some loose ends at his grandmother's. He'll be back in a few days."

"Is he okay?" my mom wants to know.

" He's doing okay, considering. "

"Why didn't you stay?" My mom is way too inquisitive sometimes.

"Mark insisted that I come home. He'll be spending most of his time handling business anyway."

"Well that makes sense.," my dad chimes in.

"So, I hope you guys brought your appetite because I have a feast prepared for you."

"I sure hope it tastes like your mama's cooking. You know I usually only eat her food."

"I don't care if it doesn't taste like mine. I'm going to enjoy the fact I didn't have to cook it," Mom says, laughing.

My mom usually cooks every day. Normally when I invite them over she'll cook something to bring. It took at lot to get her to come empty handed tonight.

"Well, I can't say that I'm a prize-winning cook like Mom, but I like to think I come really close," I try to assure my dad. We sit and enjoy our dinner. I conclude by the moans coming from my dad after each bite that he's thoroughly enjoying it.

"Honey, that was absolutely delicious," my dad says as he finishes his last piece of roast. "Your mom taught you well."

"Thanks, Dad. You have room for seconds?"

"No, I'm not going to be a pig tonight."

"Okay, well, what about dessert? I made your favorite, Key lime pie."

"Now that I do have room for," he says, smiling.

"Great. Why don't you two have a seat in the living room and I'll bring out the dessert and coffee?"

"I won't argue with that," my dad says.

"Do you need help, honey?" my mom asks.

"No, Mom, I have it. Just go sit down and relax." It's funny to me how different men and women are. Dad, being a man, has no problem leaving out while I continue to serve them. Mom, on the other hand, is reluctant to leave without at least offering to help. I don't want either of them to stay because I need to take this time to say a little prayer before I deliver my news.

Lord, please guide me and help me to tell my parents my news. I've already asked for forgiveness for my sins, but I'm asking again. I realize this isn't the ideal situation, but for some reason it's my situation. Please help them to accept this news and help them to forgive me as well. In Jesus' name I pray. Amen.

After whispering my prayer I head to the living room with the dessert. I walk back in the kitchen for the coffee and as I turn around I come face-to-face with my mother. "Mom, what's wrong? Do you need anything?"

"That's what I want to know, Holly."

"I don't understand. What do you want to know?"

"Holly, I'm your mother. You think I don't know when something isn't right with you? I've felt for quite some time that something was going on between you and Mark. Coming over here tonight and hearing you say he's still in Varnado without you just confirmed my suspicions. I've never known Mark to go anywhere without you. He hardly went to the corner store alone. Now, I don't know what's going on, but I need you to know that you can talk to your father and me about anything."

When my mom puts her arms around me, I begin to cry. I don't know if she realizes how much I need to hear those words or feel her arms around me at the moment. Mom holds me a little while longer until Dad hollers in and asks about the pie.

"Coming, honey," my mom tells him. "Listen, baby, whatever is going on, you can talk to us. We're your parents, and there's nothing you can do that will make us love you any less."

My mom balances the pie with one hand and holds my hand with the other. I remember she use to do this whenever I had something to confess to my father when I was little. Like the time I used his entire can of shaving cream making pretend pies. My mom had a fit when she saw the mess in my room. Instead of dealing with it herself, she escorted me straight to my dad. Having to confess to him was worse than any punishment he could've given. This time I feel just like I did when I was that little girl so long ago.

I cut the pie and serve my parents, then prepare myself to break the news. "Mom, Dad, I have something I need to talk to you about. Please know this is really hard for me."

"What is it, baby?" my dad asks just as he puts another piece of pie in his mouth.

"Well, a lot's been going on between Mark and me—"

"Like?" my mom interrupts.

"Mom, please, just let me take my time and do this my way," I say, trying not to sound too disrespectful.

"Okay, baby, I'm sorry. Go ahead and tell your story."

"Like I was saying, there's a lot going on between Mark and me. I found out a few months ago that Mark had an affair nine years ago."

"Oh really," my dad says with much attitude. "And how did you find this out?"

"He told me."

"So he just came out and told you? No, there has to be more to this story because it's hard for me to believe he'd decide to come clean about an affair that happened nine years ago," my mom says.

"Okay, I may as well just tell you the whole story."

"Yes, please tell the whole story," my mother instructs.

"About a year ago I started getting harassing phone calls…" I tell them everything from the calls to the flowers, and even to the incident in the grocery store when I realized my troubled student was actually Mark's son. My mom and dad, of course, weren't too happy about this news. I didn't leave out how I added to the drama of our marriage. I told about Dexter and having way too much to drink in the Bahamas. Then, finally, I got to the point of why I really needed to tell them all of that. "Mom, Dad, I'm pregnant, and I'm not sure if Mark's the father," I try to say as fast as I can.

"Come again," my dad says, implying he needs to hear it again to make sure he's heard me right the first time.

"Dad, I know you're disappointed, and believe me I am too," I try to explain.

"Oh Holly," is all my mom is able to say, which is better than my dad who doesn't say anything. That's usually what he does when he's mad or disappointed. He shuts down. It doesn't take him long to come around, but initially he says nothing.

"I know this is a lot to comprehend right now. No one intended on us ending up here, but here we are." I try to think of something else to say because the silence is killing me.

"Does Mark know? Is that why he's staying away?" my dad finally asks.

"No, he doesn't know. I didn't lie to you. He really is handling business at his grandmother's ."

"I don't know what to believe right now. Had I known this is how the night was going to end I would've stayed home."

"Dad, I'm really sorry. I know you're disappointed."

"Yes, I'm disappointed. What Mark did was wrong, no ifs, ands, or buts about it, it was wrong, but for you to turn around and do the exact same thing…now look what happened. Two wrongs do not make a right. It only makes a bigger wrong. What if Mark's not the father? What will the church say when they find out?"

My dad is a deacon at our church, so he always feels he has an image to uphold. I have enough to think about, and honestly the people of the church are the least of my problems.

My dad stands up. “Come on, Mae. We need to get going.” Now I know for sure he’s mad because he only takes a few bites of the pie he was so excited about a few minutes ago.

“Dad, please don’t leave like this. I hate to think of you mad with me.”

“Holly, I’m not mad, but I am very disappointed. You know how serious I feel about marriage. If Mark wants to mess up and break one of the Ten Commandments then that’s him, but I raised you better than that. I’m sorry, but you’re going to have to give me some time to deal with all of this.”

I understand what he means because I felt the same way when Mark broke the news of his affair to me. I have to respect my dad’s feelings and give him the time he needs to digest all this. I walk my parents to the door, and before my mom leaves she hugs me and whispers, “You know he loves you. Just give him a little time, and he’ll come around.”

I know she’s right. It doesn’t make the pain any better though. I think I could handle him being mad better than him being disappointed. Him being disappointed means I’ve let him down, and the last thing I want is to let him down.

I’m cleaning my kitchen when my phone rings.

“Hey, girly, are you still entertaining?” Janelle asks.

“No, they’re gone.”

“So how are moms and pops doing these days?”

“They’re fine.”

“Are you okay?”

“I’m fine, why?”

“You just sound so distant and distracted. Did I interrupt something? Is Mark there?” she says with a smile in her voice.

“No. Mark’s in Varnado, remember?”

“Oh, that’s right. Have you heard from him?”

“He called yesterday. We talked briefly. Nothing new is going on.”

“I see. So how long are you going to put up this charade?”

“Janelle, what are you talking about?”

“Holly, you know good and well that you and Mark are meant to be together. You need to stop acting like you don’t love him anymore.”

“I never said I didn’t love him. All I’m saying is I’m not ready to forgive him yet. I’m sure I will one day, but not today.”

"Okay, I'm going to tell you like you always tell me. Tomorrow's not promised."

I hate when she throw my words back at me. She's not supposed to tell me this. How in the world did I put myself in a situation where Janelle is the one giving the advice?

"So, anyway, I was calling to see if you're up for more company," she says.

"Since when do you care if I'm up for company or not?"

"Whatever. Is that a yes or no?"

"Yes, I'm up for company."

"I think I'm feeling like a daiquiri. What about you?"

Oh you have no idea how much I would love to be able to sip on one right now. "No, I'm fine," I have to say.

"Okay, well I'm going to stop by the daiquiri shop that's near your house then I'll be over there."

"I'll be here," I say before hanging up the phone. When she called I decided to go ahead and tell her tonight also, but I don't know if my nerves will allow me to. I think I've had enough for one night.

Janelle arrives about fifteen minutes later, and she and I sit and enjoy the pie I pulled back out of the refrigerator.

"You must've fed your parents too well. I know how much Pops loves him some Key lime pie."

It used to be strange to me to hear Janelle referring to my dad as Pops, but she's been doing it so long now that it's become natural. I don't think she's ever called him anything else. "Yeah, they were ready to get home."

"I'm surprised he didn't insist on taking some to go."

She knows my dad all too well. If he hadn't left so abruptly, he probably would've taken some to go. I should take him some tomorrow, but I doubt he'll be ready to see me again so soon. I'll give him the space he needs, and when this all blows over I'll have to make him another pie.

"Um, Holly, this pie is off da chain, girl."

Janelle watches too much MTV or BET, whatever it is the young people watch these days. I can tell from her expression that "off da chain" means the pie is good. "Thanks. You want some more?"

"Girl, I shouldn't, I'm still trying to take off the ten pounds I gained in the Bahamas."

"Well, I'll just put this up then," I say, waving a slice of pie in her face.

"Oh, what the hell, give me the pie," she says, taking the slice and laughing.

I knew she was too weak to resist another piece. "You knew you were going to eat more. Why are you sitting up there talking about losing ten pounds? When's the last time you worked out?"

"Girl, you know I hate to sweat. Well, unless…"

"Okay, I get the point," I say, cutting her off.

Janelle and I decide to have a slumber party. We stay up all night laughing and talking about crazy things we've done in the past. We use to have so much fun together. Now we barely get to see each other because life's gotten so hectic, more so for me than Janelle. It amazes me how being with Janelle always seems to take my mind off my problems. She's really good for me and truly is the sister I never had. I just hope our friendship remains the same once I tell her what I did with her cousin. Hopefully she of all people will understand. I guess one reason I'm so hesitant about telling her is because I'm always lecturing her about being careful and telling her she needs to settle down. I often warn her that one day she may find herself in a situation she can't get out of. I was mainly talking about dealing with an irate wife once she found out Janelle was sleeping with her husband.

My situation isn't like that but I still feel like a hypocrite giving her advice I can't even follow. I'm telling her to be careful, and here I'm the one who slipped up. How ironic is that?

Chapter 23

I wake up today feeling very good. Most days I'm dragging out the bed, but today I get right up, brush my teeth, wash up, and get dressed. It's not until I sit to eat breakfast that I realize why I feel so different. I didn't have any morning sickness today. I actually feel normal again. I immediately go from feeling great to feeling very, very nervous. *Oh my God, what if something's wrong with the baby.* I jump up and run for my cell phone, which is where Dr. Lee's number is programmed.

"Dr. Lee's office," I hear what I think is a nurse say.

"May I please speak with Dr. Lee?" I ask very nervously.

"I'm sorry Dr. Lee's office isn't open yet. This is the operator, may I take a message?"

"No, you don't understand I really need to talk with Dr. Lee. I'm pregnant and I'm afraid something is wrong with my baby."

"Ma'am, would you like to leave a number so Dr. Lee can return your call? In emergency cases we are told to advise all patients to report to the nearest emergency room. Do you want to wait for her to call or do you think you should go to the emergency room?"

"I don't know what I should do," I say, beginning to cry.

"Okay, ma'am, calm down. Is someone there with you?"

"No, it's just me," I say, crying even harder.

"Ma'am, do you need to call someone to bring you to the hospital?"

"I don't know," I say then hang up. The operator was absolutely no help. I remember I did tell my mom. She'll know what I should do. I switch to the house phone and call my mother.

"Hello," she answers all chipper. She's always been a morning person.

"Hi, Mom."

"Holly? Baby, what's wrong?" she asks, sensing something isn't right.

"Mom, I think something's wrong with the baby."

"Oh my God. Baby, are you bleeding or cramping?" she asks, sounding just as nervous as I am.

"No, I'm not bleeding or cramping."

"Then what's wrong, baby?"

"I'm usually nauseous every morning, but this morning I'm not, and I'm afraid that something's wrong with the baby." When I say this, my mom does something I'm not expecting. She bursts out laughing. "Mom, what's wrong with you? This is not a laughing matter," I say, beginning to get very angry.

"Holly, I'm laughing because there's nothing wrong with your baby. You had morning sickness, but it doesn't last throughout the whole pregnancy. You should be jumping for joy. I had morning sickness the whole time I was pregnant with you. I envied women like you who didn't have to deal with sickness each and every morning."

"I don't know, Mom. I still think I should go to the doctor."

"Holly, if it'll make you feel better then go ahead, but I'm telling you the baby's fine. If you're not bleeding or cramping, then you should be okay."

"Okay, I'll go ahead and go to work, and if I start feeling bad I'll go see Dr. Lee."

"I think that's a good idea. Call me later."

"I will. Thank you, Mom."

"My pleasure, baby."

I hang up with my mom and continue getting dressed. This whole episode makes me realize I need to talk to Mark. On Friday I'll be twelve weeks. Even though I know I'm not showing, I still feel like people are starting to notice.

My usual morning routine has temporarily changed, at least until after I have the baby. I've read that caffeine isn't good for the baby, so I decided to give it up, for the moment that is. I thought it would be hard, but I'm finding I really don't miss it that much. Unlike most people, I don't need caffeine to get me energized in the morning. I just like the way it tastes.

I arrive at work and I'm pleasantly surprised when I open my classroom door. On my desk sits the most beautiful bouquet of red and pink roses I think I've ever seen. As I approach the flowers, my mind instantly thinks about the last time I received roses. The ones Diane sent in an effort to announce her and Mark's relationship. I feel my heart about to beat through my shirt. I cautiously pick up the card. When I see the handwriting I'm able to breathe again.

Holly,

I saw these beautiful roses and immediately thought of you. I hope you love them as much as the sender loves you.

Much Love,
Mark

I'm happy to know they're not from the psycho, but still not sure how I feel about them being from Mark either. He's making it much harder to break the news to him. I believe my feelings for Mark are the real reason why I'm avoiding him so much. I can't deny I'm still in love with him, and I also can't deny that more than anything I do want our marriage back, but I'm afraid of his reaction when I tell him about the baby and Dexter. I can deal with avoiding him, but I don't know how to deal with him being angry with me.

"Oh, someone must've had a really good weekend," Erica says.

"Morning, Erica," I say, smiling.

"So?" she asks slyly.

"So what?" I ask back.

"Who are they from, or is it a secret?"

"No, they're from my husband."

"Ah, now that's sweet. That's what I want one day. A man who remembers he loves me and shows me often."

"Well, this isn't something he does often, but it is appreciated when he does decide to surprise me."

"So now you have to do something sweet for him."

"I will," I say really wanting to change the subject. "So, are you ready for your kiddos? I'm sure you missed them terribly this weekend," I say, laughing. Most teachers would find that funny because the last thing we try to think about over the weekend is work and students. Erica obviously didn't get it because she didn't crack a smile.

"I did miss them. I love when the weekends are over."

I look at her, waiting for her to burst out laughing, but it never happens so I just have to ask. "Are you being serious?"

"Very. I love teaching."

"Well, so do I, but I also love my weekends. If I had to be with these kids seven days a week, I'd go crazy."

"That's because you have family and friends here. I just have my dog Gigi."

I forgot she's down here alone, but surely she has friends. "What about your friends? Don't you have some down here?"

"No. My two best friends both moved away after graduation."

"What made you stay?" I have to ask.

"I like it here. It's too big to be a small town and too small to be a big city, so it's just right for me. Life here is simple, and I like that."

"I understand. That's why I love it here too. My husband and I considered moving to Houston after I graduated from college, but that obviously never happened."

"Do you wish you would've gone?"

"Some days I do, but overall I'm quite content here in Baton Rouge."

We chat for a minute longer, then she leaves. I spend about five minutes thinking about our conversation. I feel so bad for her. I'm not sure why because she seems like she's happy with her decision to stay. While thinking about her it does cross my mind I should invite her over sometimes, especially when we have family gatherings. I need to remember to include her. I hate the thought of her spending her free time with just her dog. She needs some human interaction as well.

My day is going really well. I don't think I could ask for a better class. This year instead of dealing with fighting and disrespect, I'm now dealing with two talkative girls. Normally this would drive me crazy, but compared to last year, I'm in heaven.

My students are just finishing a science project on lights and shadows and they are lining up for lunch. I still cannot believe I get to enjoy lunch with adults this year. Each day I look forward to lunchtime. Last year it was the most dreaded time of the day. Hollering and screaming in the cafeteria is not my idea of a good time. As I'm walking my class to the lunchroom, I feel my cell phone vibrating. Mr. McNair instructed us not to talk on the phone around the students, so I hurry and get them situated, then rush back to my room to see who called. I feel better when I see it's Janelle. However, it has to be an emergency for her to call knowing I'm at work. I nervously dial her number, and the chipper voice on the other end is not what I expect to hear.

"Hey. You called?"

"Yeah. I was calling to see if you're busy after work today."

"No. Why?"

"Because I want you to meet me at Zea's for dinner."

"Is that the new restaurant on Corporate Boulevard?"

"Yes. It's in Town Center, the new Outlet Mall."

"I don't know, Janelle, I really need to get home. I have papers to grade that I meant to do last night until someone kept me up."

"Girl, whatever. Okay well I tell you what, you meet us for dinner and I'll help you with your papers."

"Wait, who's us? You said meet you, not us."

"Oh, Dexter. He asked about you, and I said maybe we can all go out tonight."

I'd just truly made up my mind to tell Janelle about the baby. I never got around to it last night. We got so caught up in reminiscing, and I didn't want to spoil the mood, so I didn't bring it up. When she mentioned dinner I thought this would be the perfect time, but hell no. There's no way I'm telling Dexter before I talk with Mark.

"So do we have a deal?" Janelle asks.

"Fine, Janelle. I know if I say no you're just going to keep calling until I change my mind. And please don't think I'm coming because I actually believe you're going to help me with grades. I fell for that once before, remember?"

"Oh, yeah, well next time remind me. I just forgot," she says, laughing.

"Whatever. What time are we meeting?"

"How about 7:30?"

"Sounds good."

We say our good-byes and I hurry to warm my food before it's time to get my students. When I see Erica in the lounge, I immediately get the best idea.

"Erica, are you free tonight?"

"I have no plans that I can think of. Why? Do you need something?"

"I do actually. My best friend just called and invited me to dinner with her and her cousin and I was hoping you could join us."

"Oh, I don't know. I really don't like to do too much during the week."

From what I can tell you don't like to do too much on the weekend either, but I leave that comment in my head. "Come on. We're meeting at 7:30. You'll be home by 9:00 at the latest."

"Where are you guys eating?"

"We're trying a new restaurant in Town Center called Zea's."

"Oh, I've heard of that place. From what I hear it's really good."

"Well, come tonight and find out for yourself."

"Okay, but I can't stay too long."

"Me either. We'll eat, talk for a minute, then leave. I promise."

"Well in that case, I'll see you tonight. Thanks for inviting me."

"We'll be happy to have you."

As I'm eating my food, I do feel a slight sense of guilt. I know the only reason I invited Erica is so the dinner won't be so awkward for me. I feel that having someone else will help to calm my nerves some. I haven't seen or talked to Dexter since the Bahamas trip. Just as I was working up my nerves to deal with Mark, Dexter shows up. Maybe tonight won't be so bad with Erica as my sidekick.

The end of my work day comes way too fast. I'm just not mentally ready to deal with Dexter. I have absolutely no plans of telling him anything about the baby, but just being in his presence is not something I'm looking forward to. I almost decide to call Janelle and cancel, but that's more trouble than it's worth. All she's going to do is beg and beg until I finally give in. Janelle's the most persistent person I know. She doesn't take rejection easy.

Before I know it I'm pulling into my driveway. I decide not to park in the garage since I'll be leaving in a couple hours. Just as I walk through the door the phone rings. I rush to answer it, and just as I pick up the receiver my eyes land on the table by the door. Sitting there, where my keys would normally lay, I see a very huge bouquet of roses just like the ones I received at school. I press the off button on the phone, never bothering to say hello, and make my way over to the roses. Unlike the roses I received today, these do not come with a card. It doesn't take a rocket scientist to know they're from Mark. Who else has access to my house? I pick up the phone to call Mark and there's no dial tone.

"Hello," I say just to see if I forgot to pay the bill or if in fact someone was on the line.

"Hello, Mrs. James," I hear Erica say.

"Erica?"

"Yes."

"Hey, what's going on? Is everything okay?"

"Everything's fine, but I don't think I'll be able to make it tonight."

"Why not? Come on, Erica, it'll be fun."

"All I want to do is curl up on my sofa and get into a good movie. I'm not really the going-out type."

"Erica, for God's sake, we're going to dinner, not to the club. I tell you what, if you get there and you feel uncomfortable then fake sick and excuse yourself. My feelings will not be hurt, I promise, but at least give us a chance. We really are good people," I say, smiling.

"Okay, fine. I'll come."

"Oh, and before I forget, if you call me Mrs. James one more time I will not answer you," I say, only halfway joking.

"I'm sorry. I keep forgetting," she says, laughing. "Okay, Holly, I'll see you tonight."

"It'll be fun," I say as I hang up the phone.

The next few hours seem to fly by. I look at the clock and can't believe it's already six-thirty. I put on my favorite black sandals, which Janelle affectionately refers to as my "come and get me" shoes. I decide to go casual, yet sexy. My bootcut jeans and black halter is just the look I'm going for tonight. I would say I'm putting so much thought into my attire simply because I want to look good, but who am I kidding? I love the attention Dexter gives me, and I'm sure the compliments will be soaring my way tonight. I give myself a once-over in the floor-length mirror I insisted on having in my bathroom. After deciding I look great, I head out the door.

As I approach my car I notice something on my windshield. It looks like a small piece of paper. I cautiously move toward the car to retrieve the paper. Once again I'm able to breathe when I notice Mark's handwriting. The note simply reads:

Still loving you with all my heart.
Mark

I suddenly start to feel sick to my stomach. I don't think this feeling has anything to do with the baby or morning sickness, which I heard I can have at any time. This is a feeling of pure guilt. I know in my mind I'm not doing anything wrong, but my heart tells me otherwise. I'm putting a lot of time and effort into looking good for some other man tonight when I should be putting all this attention into putting my marriage back together. I don't realize how long I'm sitting in my car until my cell phone vibrates. When I see Janelle's number I decide to crank up my car and ignore the call. I'll be a little late, but better late than never. Or is it?

I arrive at Zea's to find Erica waiting outside for me.

"I'm so sorry, I was held up," I try to explain.

"It's fine. I just made it a minute ago myself."

"Ready?"

"After you."

As soon as we walk through the door I spot Janelle. She's sitting alone. When I see her a strange feeling comes over me. Almost like I'm, dare I say, disappointed. Surely it's not because of Dexter. What's going on with me? Whatever it is I need to shake it off and fast.

"Hey, girl," I say as I approach Janelle.

"Hey. I thought you were trying to renege on me."

"Who me?" I ask, pretending to be quite hurt.

"Girl, please. Save it, okay?"

"Anyway. Janelle, this is my coworker and new friend Erica."

"Nice to meet you," Erica says as she extends her hand to Janelle.

"Same here."

We sit for a minute until I can't hold it in anymore. "So is it just us tonight?"

"No. Apparently he's running late as well."

"You haven't talked to him?" I ask.

"I called him right before I left home, and he was just getting out of the shower. You have to know Dexter. He reminds me of a woman because it takes him so long to get dressed."

My mind is still stuck on he's getting out of the shower. I have an image in my head that is so bad, but it looks oh so good. *Damn it, Holly, stop it! Don't you think you're in enough trouble?* I try to lecture myself because I feel like I'm starting to lose control here. My life is a web of lies and deceit and on top of that I'm drooling over a man that has already done quite enough for me.

I'm so deep in thought that I totally miss Dexter walking up to the table.

"I must be in heaven because there's no way on earth I'm having dinner with three of the most beautiful women in the world," he says as he sits next to Janelle and directly across from Erica. I introduce him to Erica, and we make very small talk before we order drinks. I order red wine because my mom assured me I would not harm the baby with one glass.

"So, Erica, is it? You're a teacher too I assume," Dexter says.

"I am. Are you in education as well?" she asks him.

"Oh no. I couldn't be a teacher. I have much respect for you guys and your profession, but I would probably hurt someone's child," he says, laughing.

"Oh come on. They're not that bad. We need more men in the classrooms. You should really consider it," she says, obviously joking around with him.

Do I sense some flirting going on here? That's a good thing, right? Now I can concentrate on my husband and our issues. Tomorrow I'll tell Mark everything, next I'll tell Dexter. We'll get a paternity test and let the chips fall where they may. I'm hoping with everything in me this is Mark's baby, but something tells me that's simply not the case. I've been wrong before, and I pray I'm wrong now.

Dinner isn't as bad as I thought it would be. We all thoroughly enjoy our meal, and the company isn't half bad either. I could've done without the nauseating flirting between Dexter and Erica, but hey they're both single adults and are allowed to do whatever they want, right?

I couldn't wait to get home to my bed. I said my good-byes to everyone and we all leave. I have no idea what they plan to do after this because the idea of going to the casino was thrown out there. Erica and Dexter seem to be the only ones interested in going. Janelle and I both expressed how tired we are. I'm shocked Janelle doesn't want to go and that Erica does. For someone who didn't even want to come out, she sure loosened up once she met Dexter, but anyway, what do I care?

I go home, take off my clothes, get in bed, and mentally prepare myself for my day with Mark. I'm going to need all the rest I can get because I already know the next day's going to be emotionally draining. I wish I can say I'm able to immediately put my thoughts aside and allow sleep to take over, but it's obvious sleep is not my friend tonight.

Chapter 24

I'm a bundle of nerves today. I talked to Mark and agreed to sit down and finally talk things out with him. I know I prayed for our marriage, but honestly I just don't see how we'll ever be able to get through this. Not only do I have to work to get over the fact that Mark cheated, but now he has to get over the fact that I did the same. I don't know why, but I think it'll be a lot harder for him to accept the fact that I was with another man. It's no walk in the park for me either so I know it'll be ten times worse for him.

I guess adding the baby to the equation isn't exactly going to make things easier. I would love to be able to tell him I'm carrying his baby, but I can't guarantee that. It's strange because with each passing day I'm beginning to believe more and more that it's not Mark's baby. The only reason I'm having doubts now is because of the many years we've tried with no success. I keep reminding myself of the advice we received over the years. Everyone kept saying, "It'll happen once you stop stressing about getting pregnant."

Lord, how I hope that's the case now. Even though I'm unsure about the direction our marriage will take, at least I know Mark, and he is my husband. I don't know Dexter well enough to say I'm having his baby. I definitely didn't know him well enough to sleep with him, but what's done is done. Oh, what I wouldn't give for this baby to be Mark's. Life will be less complicated.

I arrive at the park a little earlier just to give me some time to sit and relax my mind. Mark and I decided to meet at the park because it's the one place we both love. We use to come out here and sit for hours watching the children play and the ducks swimming in the pond. Everyone around seemed so carefree and happy. I guess that's why we enjoy being here so much. It takes your mind off your worries. It's hard to be sad when there's so much laughter around you. I hope that's the case today. I'm praying Mark and I will come to some type of agreement that will make both of us happy.

I'm still looking at the ducks when Mark comes and sits beside me. I made up my mind I won't give him a hard time today. We will talk things out like sensible adults.

"Good afternoon, Holly," Mark says, sounding like he is greeting one of his medical clients.

"My, aren't we formal today?"

"I didn't know how the mood would be so I felt I would be safe with good afternoon," he says, smiling.

"Whatever." We make more small talk. It's obvious we are both feeling awkward and very hesitant about bringing up the situation at hand. Mark thinks we're only here to discuss his wrongdoings. Little does he know we have to discuss mine too.

"So, Holly," he says, finally breaking the silence, "tell me what you're thinking."

"Well, I'm thinking I wish we weren't here."

"I thought you wanted to meet here."

"Not here at the park, but here at this place in our lives. Unfortunately, this isn't a movie where you can rewind and go back to your favorite part."

"If it was, what part would you go back to?"

"The day we met. Sometimes I still find it hard to believe you were actually interested in me."

"I still remember the look on your face when I asked if I could speak with you alone. I remember you looked around at all your friends."

"I was trying to figure out who you were talking to."

"I was talking to the most beautiful girl standing in that circle."

"Really? More beautiful than Miranda?"

"Miranda? Who's Miranda?"

"Oh, don't even sit there acting like you don't remember Big Booty Miranda," I say, laughing because I haven't thought about her in years. She had a major crush on Mark and up until now she was the only girl who couldn't stand me.

"Oh, that Miranda." He says trying to sound nonchalant.

"Yes, that Miranda."

"Please. All she had was a big booty. She wasn't much to look at. She definitely doesn't have anything on you."

"Well, can I ask you something?"

"Anything."

"If I'm so beautiful to you, what made you cheat on me for all those years?"

"I know this is going to be hard for you to understand, but what I did had nothing to do with my love for you."

"Well, what did it have to do with? I'm asking because I'm trying hard to understand. Maybe if I understand it then I'll be able to get over it."

"Holly, I wish we didn't have to discuss this."

"Mark, I wish we didn't either, but this is the only way we'll get to the root of our problem. We need to fix it to assure it never happens again."

"I can assure you it'll never happen again."

"How can you say that if you don't know why it happened in the first place?"

"I know why it happened."

"Well, tell me why. Don't you think I should know?"

"Not really, but I'll tell you anyway."

I sit there giving Mark my undivided attention because finally I'm about to find out what happened in our marriage to get us to this point. I've thought of everything that could have caused it, but none of my answers make sense to me. Now I'm about to find out the truth, and I hope I'm ready to hear this.

"Well," he starts, "after many months of trying to have a baby, it seems our lovemaking became more of a job than something we did to please each other. There were no feelings involved anymore. We only did it when you were ovulating, and afterward we played the waiting game until the next time. I was always so disappointed when you weren't getting pregnant. I felt it was my fault and that I'd let you down. I'm your husband and can't give you the only thing you want the most. Do you know how that made me feel? How much pressure I was under each time we had sex? Each time before we started I would pray and ask God to please let this be the time you got pregnant."

"But I don't understand how you could feel it was your fault when the doctor said I have fibroids."

"But it was too late by then. I'd already started seeing Diane."

"Well why didn't you stop once you'd found out about the fibroids?"

"I did stop, but so did you. Each time I tried to have sex with you you'd push me away. You acted as if it was pointless, like there was no need anymore. I still wanted to be with you more than you know. I told Diane it was over between us. After so many rejections I found myself back with her again."

"So basically all of this is my fault?"

"I'm not saying it's your fault. I'm simply letting you know what drove me to that point. I know it's my fault. I'm a grown man, and I should have more self-control than I did. I know that what I did was wrong. I should've stayed with you and been there to support you instead of doing what I did."

I don't know what I'm supposed to say at this point. Should I apologize for pushing him away? I had no idea he felt this way. I guess the old folks are right when they say if you don't take care of your man, someone else will. I never thought that would apply to Mark and me. All this time I thought he just accepted I wasn't ready to have sex again. He has no idea how hard it is for a woman to know she may never have her husband's child. He has no idea how torn up I was inside.

"See, knowing doesn't make the situation any better, does it?"

"It does for me because it opens my eyes to how you were feeling. I can tell you one area we need to improve on is communication. While you were feeling like you let me down, that's exactly how I was feeling too. Once we knew for sure I was the reason we couldn't have a baby I really started to feel guilty. I felt like less of a woman, and I thought eventually you would start to feel the same way about me. Having sex was a constant reminder I would never be able to give you the child we so desperately wanted. I thought you would eventually start to despise me. That's why I needed time to deal with my feelings. We both should've talked to each other versus trying to deal with it alone."

"I see what you mean now. I didn't even realize that. It never crossed my mind that something deeper was going on. It's funny how two people can be together for so long. Stay up late at night and have long talks, but when it comes down to it, the root of all our problems is communication. We fell in love with each other because we enjoyed talking to each other. We've had some really deep conversations and communication is our problem." He keeps saying it as if he just can't believe we would have communication problems. I guess this revelation is a lot for him to take in.

"Is that thunder?" I ask, looking up at the now dark sky.

"I think it is. We'd better go before it starts to pour. Did you drive?"

"Yes. My car's right over there," I say, pointing toward the parking lot.

"Do you mind if I follow you back to the house so we can finish our conversation?"

"No, I don't mind."

Our house is about five minutes away from the park so the drive is very short. Mark calls me on my cell phone to see if I want him to pick up some food. I didn't realize I haven't eaten much today because my nerves won't allow it. We agree on Chinese so I wait until he arrives with the food. Just as I'm about to go to the bathroom the phone rings. I know it may sound nasty, but I really have to go so whoever is on the phone will have to accompany me to the ladies' room.

"Hello," I say as I'm unzipping my pants.

"Holly?" a very familiar voice says.

"Yes, this is Holly. Who's this?" I have to be sure my ears aren't misleading me.

"It's Dexter. Can you talk?"

"Um, I'm a little busy right now. Is something wrong?"

"No. I was just hoping I could see you again before I leave."

"When are you leaving?"

"I'm scheduled to fly out tomorrow night."

"I don't think that's such a good idea, Dexter," I say, exiting the bathroom. I decide to save the flushing for later—no need to be that obvious.

"I just thought we could get together for dinner tonight. I promise to be on my best behavior. I won't even follow you home to make sure you get in safely," he says jokingly.

"Please don't," I say, laughing.

"So, what do you think?"

"About?"

"Dinner tonight?"

"Can I call you later with my answer? I'm really busy right now."

"That'll be fine. Do you have my number?"

I repeat the number that showed up on my ID.

"That's it. I'll be expecting your call," he says, hanging up.

Just as I hang up the phone with Dexter, Mark rings the doorbell.

"Hope you're hungry because I bought a little of everything," he says, bringing the bags in the kitchen.

"I see. Are we expecting company?"

"No, just us."

"We can't eat all of this."

"Speak for yourself."

I never understood how Mark could eat so much and still maintain his high school physique. I, on the other hand, could eat a small crumb and blow up. That's why I try to work out so much. If I don't I will be obese. Talk about slow metabolism, I don't think I have any metabolism whatsoever.

"So," Mark says, sitting down at the table, "where were we?"

"I don't even remember."

"Well, let me ask you something."

"Okay."

"Are you ready to give up on our marriage?"

"It's funny because if you'd asked me this a few weeks ago I would've said yes with no hesitation. Now, I can't say that I am."

Mark sits there with a big smile on his face, like he's just won the lottery or something. I didn't say we were getting back together. Once I tell him my news he may say it for me. I know Mark, and it's not going to be easy for him to accept my infidelity. I feel like we've made progress today, but I have a feeling we're about to be back at square one, again.

"Why are you smiling so hard?" I ask, smiling myself.

"Because for the first time in a long time I feel like there's hope for us."

"You do?"

"Yeah. Don't you?"

"I don't know, Mark. There's still so much to work out."

"I know it's going to take a while for you to forgive me and this whole situation, but I'm willing to do whatever it takes to help you trust me again."

"What about Tyler?" I ask, suddenly remembering there are two children involved here.

"What about him?"

"Are you involved in his life now?"

"I try to be, but his mom doesn't make it very easy."

"What do you mean? What does she do?"

"Anything she can to prevent me from seeing him."

"Why? Isn't that what she wanted, for you to be an involved father?"

"She wants me to be involved, but not with Tyler."

"Oh, so I guess she and Tyler are a package deal."

"In her mind they are. I've already threatened to take her to court, and it seems I'm going to have to go that route in order to get through to her."

"So she won't let you see him at all?"

"She will, but only if I stay at her house with him."

"What's so bad about that? At least you get to spend time with him."

"Yeah, and with her too. The whole time I'm there she's constantly giving him something to do in order to distract him from her advances. I feel like I'm constantly fighting off a wild tiger."

"I guess she doesn't take rejection very well."

"You already know that. Remember, that's why she started harassing you in the first place. She couldn't handle that I didn't want to continue our affair, and she decided hurting you was just the revenge she needed."

"Oh, I remember all too well. It's a shame though because Tyler needs a good male figure in his life. Maybe that'll help with his behavior."

"How would you feel about Tyler staying with us?" Mark asks out of the blue.

"What?" I can't believe he's asking me this now. I didn't even say he could move back in and here he's trying to bring his kid.

"I'm saying, if we work things out and get back together, would you be totally against him coming to stay sometimes?" he asks, obviously reading my expression very well.

"Mark, if we decide to move forward and make this marriage work, then no, I would not be against him coming to stay sometimes. I know that he's your son, and naturally you would want to have a relationship with him."

"Holly, that's what I love about you. You are so caring and understanding."

I wonder if he'll still have those feelings once I tell him my big surprise.

"Mark, I agreed to talk with you today not only for us to talk out what you'd done, but also for me to tell you what I did."

The big smile he wore a minute ago is long gone. I guess he can tell by the tone of my voice this is serious.

"I'm listening," he says, obviously very anxious to hear what I have to say.

"Mark, you aren't the only one who has some confessing to do."

"I'm not?"

"No. I have something to confess to you too."

"Okay, well let's hear it."

"Don't rush me. This isn't easy."

Mark just sits there staring at me. He puts his fork down and focuses only on me.

"Mark, I cheated on you," I say very fast before I lose my nerve. Once it's out there's no turning back. I have to go ahead and tell him everything.

"You did what?" he asks in disbelief.

"I cheated. I know two wrongs don't make a right, but for some reason I allowed myself to go there. I don't remember it happening, but I'm sure it happened."

"What do you mean you don't remember it happening?"

"When I went away with Janelle this summer I met someone. I guess I had a little too much to drink at the reception, and the next thing I know I was waking up in bed with him."

"So you slept with some island man you'd just met?" he asks, sounding totally disgusted.

"I didn't mean to sleep with him. Like I said I had too much to drink and…"

"Oh, Holly, please, that kind of stuff only happens on television."

"Well, consider this *Primetime* because I'm telling you it happened. I have no reason to lie to you."

Mark just continues to stare until he's obviously seen enough. Without saying anything he gets up, retrieve his keys, and heads out the door. The next thing I know he's cranking up his car and pulling out the driveway. "Wow," is all I can say. I expected him to be upset, but I definitely didn't expect him to just leave. So much for talking out our problems.

Chapter 25

"I'm so glad you accepted my dinner invitation, Holly."

"Well it's not like my social calendar is booked these days."

"So that's the only reason you agreed to dinner with me, because you didn't have anything better to do?" He says smiling.

"That's not what I meant."

"I know. I'm just playing with you."

"Okay, Mr. Comedian, how's your trip home been so far?"

"Could be better. My mom's been in and out of the hospital so that part's been pretty stressful."

"I know it's very stressful when your parent gets sick. My dad had a mild heart attack a while back and that nearly drove me crazy with worry."

"How's your dad now?" He asks sounding very concerned.

"Oh he's much better. I would say pretty much back to his old self again"

"That's great. I'm praying the same outcome for my mom. She battling cancer and so far the cancer seems to be winning. "

"I don't think I've ever met your mom, but if she's anything like you and Janelle, I would bet that she's a real fighter. She knows the battle isn't over. "

"She is, she really is a fighter." He says as his voice starts to sound very distant. It's obvious he's very concerned about his mom.

"So, I didn't know this was home for you until Janelle mentioned it one day. Were you born here in Baton Rouge?" I ask trying to lighten the mood up a little.

"Oh yeah. I grew up here. I didn't move to Atlanta until I graduated from college."

"What college did you attend?" I ask.

"Southern University—SU, baby." He responds proudly.

"Oh, so you're a Jaguar, I see."

"You know it. What about you?"

"SU, baby," I say, mocking him.

"Really? What year?"

"I graduated fall '99. How about you?"

"Spring '93."

"You were long gone before I came."

"I come back every year for homecoming and of course the biggest rival game of the year."

"Let me guess, that would be the Bayou Classic."

"Southern University battling it out with Grambling State and it all taking place in New Orleans, I mean really does it get any better than that?"

"I guess not."

"What do you mean you guess not? Don't tell me you have all this excitement right under your nose and you don't bother to partake in it."

"I don't. I'm just not into football like that. I use to go with Mark, but not because I wanted to."

"Not into football? What's wrong with you?"

"It's just not my thing, but I try to watch it sometimes."

"I bet you're one of those people who asks a million questions during the game," he says, laughing.

"I am. That's probably why Mark would always go with his friends instead of me, and guess what? My feelings were not hurt. I tried to be annoying so he would stop asking me to go," I say, joining him in a good laugh.

"Okay, so now I have some blackmail information so you better stay on my good side."

"You wouldn't…"

"Oh yes, I would."

Dexter and I have a great time laughing and talking about absolutely nothing of importance. Life's been so hectic these days, I'd forgotten how good a great laugh can feel. One of those laughs that makes your eyes water and stomach hurt. Dexter kept me in stitches. He really is quite the comedian.

"You missed your calling," I tell him as he walks me out to my car.

"I did, and what would that be?"

"You should've been a comedian. I would pay to see you do stand-up."

"Oh no. I'm way too shy for that."

"You…shy? Whatever."

"No, I really am. There's just something about you that makes me feel comfortable and allows me to be carefree and goofy. I really like that. I've never met anyone like you before. The total package brains, humor, and most of all beauty," he says as he leans in to kiss me.

"Dexter, I–I can't," I say as I move away from him.

"Holly, I'm sorry. I don't know what comes over me when I'm with you. I don't mean to cross the boundaries. I just can't help myself."

"Well please try, I can't afford another slip-up."

"Holly, about that."

"Dexter, please not tonight. I'd really rather not discuss it anymore. It happened and I can't change that, but I can't keep reliving it with you."

"Fine, but can I at least say I'm sorry? I never got the chance to apologize."

"Apologize for what? It wasn't your fault."

"Well you were obviously very upset that morning when you realized what happened. The last thing I wanted to do is to upset you." he says sounding very sincere.

"Dexter we were both to blame for that night. I accept just as much responsibility as you do, if not more because you were right about one thing. I should've told you I was married."

"Well it's water under the bridge now, I'm just happy to know that we're okay. Well can I at least have a hug before we part."

"Sure," I say as he draws me into his embrace. I want to tell him about the baby. I know I should tell him before he leaves, but I can only handle so much in one night. Dealing with Mark is enough.

Dexter and I say our good-byes. I'm sure he feels in his mind that it's probably forever, but I know differently. Dexter and I have some unfinished business we'll definitely have to deal with, and soon.

Chapter 26

As soon as I pull up to my house I see Mark's car sitting in the driveway. I have mixed emotions about him being here. I'm happy he's back, and I really want to make sure he's okay, but another part of me really doesn't want to deal with this anymore tonight.

I walk up to the car and see Mark still sitting inside. He still has his key to the house, but I guess he wants to respect my boundaries. "Mark, are you okay?" I ask as I lean down to the window.

"We need to talk," is all he says.

"Okay, well come inside and we'll talk."

"No, not inside. Come take a ride with me."

"Mark, I'm really tired. I just want to go inside."

"Holly, please just come ride with me so we can talk."

"Fine, Mark." I give in because the sooner we get going the sooner we'll get back. I certainly don't plan to stay outside all night arguing about where we should talk. I get in the car and we're off. I have no idea where we're going, but I have no reason not to trust Mark.

"Listen, Mark," I begin.

"No, Holly, please let me talk."

"Okay, then talk."

"I've been doing a lot of thinking, and I'm trying very hard to wrap my mind around this whole mess. I keep replaying your words over and over in my head. I keep hoping I heard you wrong that you didn't actually say you'd slept with another man."

I notice the more Mark talks, the faster he drives. "Mark, slow down." Mark is either ignoring me or so into what he's saying he doesn't respond to me at all.

"I just keep thinking not Holly, not my special innocent little Holly," he continues.

"Mark, I really need you to slow down. You're driving way too fast!" This time I holler because his speed is getting increasingly faster. I look over at him and see he's crying. "Mark, please just stop the car and we can talk."

"Not the woman I married. Holly would never give her body to another man, I kept telling myself. Surely I'd heard her wrong," he continues talking, again, like I've said nothing. "But each time I replayed it I always heard the same thing. I always heard that you'd slept with another man. Please tell me I heard you wrong, Holly. Please tell me you didn't say that because I don't know if I can live with the fact you've given your body to someone else."

"Mark, please, please just stop the car," I say, crying uncontrollably because I just know my life will end tonight. Mark seems to have in his mind that he will kill both of us to end his misery. I can't die like this. I can't. I have too much to live for now. I have a child on the way. I can't leave this earth, not like this. I guess something comes over Mark because he begins to slow the car down. Next thing I know we're parking on side of the road. I still don't know what to expect. Did he pull over to kill me in the middle of nowhere?

"Oh God, Holly, I'm so sorry," he says as he stops the car.

I jump out of the car shaking all over. "What in the hell is wrong with you?" I holler. By this time Mark is out too.

"Holly, I'm sorry. I'm just so overcome with grief. I feel like a big part of me died when you told me that. Please believe the last thing I want to do is hurt you in any way."

"Really, Mark? Because I think you're trying to kill me."

"I'm not trying to kill you, Holly. I would take my own life before I hurt you any more than I already have. I don't know if this is your way of getting back at me, but just know that it worked."

"Mark, I was not trying to get back at you. I don't even remember that night or anything that happened."

"Okay, so you say you don't remember. If you don't remember, how can you be sure something happened?" He looks somewhat hopeful that I may be wrong.

"Because I woke up in his bed the next morning and we were both naked." Mark puts his head down and I can tell he doesn't want to hear any more. "Look, Mark, you know me better than that, and you know I would never sleep with someone else in an effort to punish you. You know that's not me."

"I thought I did know you, but the Holly I know would not have drunk so much that she was too inebriated to remember sleeping with another man."

"Well, in my defense, I did have a lot on my mind at the time. Maybe I was doing things that were out of character for me, but that's because I was at my lowest during that time. I'd lost all the self-esteem I'd once had and someone was giving me some attention—attention my husband had stopped giving me a long time ago."

"I know I can't be mad with you. I have no room to point a finger at you, but it doesn't lessen the pain. I keep having these visions of you and him, and it's killing me inside."

"I know it's torture. Don't you think I experienced the same thing when I found out about you and Ms.... you and Diane? The pain is unexplainable and you feel like your world has just been crushed. I know exactly how you feel."

"How in the hell did we allow our marriage to get to this point?" he asks, not really expecting an answer.

"I don't know. What we need to decide is if it's worth saving or should we cut our losses now and move on." I want to tell him about the baby, but if finding out I slept with someone caused him to act like this then I can only imagine how he'll act once he finds out I may be carrying the other man's baby. My mama didn't raise no fool. I'm not about to tell him this out here on this lonely dark road.

"You know how much I love you, and you know I don't want to lose you. I have to be honest with you, Holly. I'm sure I'll be able to forgive you, but it's going to be really hard to forget."

"I feel the same way."

"What kind of marriage will we have if we're both holding on to these bad memories? What's going to happen the next time I'm late coming home from a meeting or you're late for whatever reason? You know we're going to automatically assume the other person is out with someone else. I think we have a lot of work to do, but I'm definitely willing to give it a try."

"I am too," I respond. "I know this isn't going to be easy, but we have to do it for the ba..." I stop when I realize what I was about to say.

"For the what?" he asks.

"Nothing. Just forget it."

"No, what were you about to say? Holly, we're working on proving ourselves trustworthy, remember?"

"Yeah, I remember."

"Okay, then just tell me. It's obvious you're keeping something from me."

"I was about to say we had to at least try for the baby."

"Holly, don't tell me you're ready to put yourself through that again. You know the doctor said the likelihood of you getting pregnant is very slim."

He totally misunderstood my statement. "No, you don't understand. I'm not saying we have to try to have a baby. I'm saying we have to try to save our marriage for the baby."

"Okay, now I'm totally lost. What are you talking about?"

"Do I have to spell it out for you? I'm pregnant."

He stands there for a minute in shock. He looks like he's waiting on me to say I'm playing, and when that doesn't happen he does something that's a total shock to me. He picks me up and swings me around. It's obvious he's very excited about the news. I definitely didn't expect this reaction.

"Are you serious? We're going to have a baby? Why didn't you tell me this sooner? Why did you wait to…"

He looks at me again, and this time I don't see enthusiasm in his face. I see sadness and concern.

"Is it my baby?" he asks sadly.

"I honestly don't know. I wish I could tell you without a shadow of a doubt that yes this baby is yours, but I can't."

"Did you tell him?"

"No. Besides my parents, you're the first person I told."

"You mean besides your parents and Janelle."

"No, I mean besides my parents. I haven't told Janelle yet."

"That's surprising. You tell Janelle everything. What made this so different?"

"I just don't want her to know yet."

"Did you tell her about the guy in the Bahamas?"

"No. I didn't tell her anything."

"I thought she was your best friend. What happened?"

"Nothing. She's still my best friend. I just didn't want her to know until I told you."

"You know all of that is so irreverent. The situation at hand is that my wife is pregnant and it could be mine or it could be for the island guy. This is a lot, Holly. This is a lot for me to deal with right now. I think you and I need more time apart. I can forgive the cheating, but I don't know if I'm ready to raise some other man's baby."

"Isn't that what you expected Mr. Davis to do for Tyler? He not only cared for your child, but he gave him his last name. How could you ask something of someone you can't do yourself?"

"Diane already had Tyler before she even met Trent. He didn't have to deal with the fact that his wife cheated on him and got pregnant. Tyler was already a part of the equation when he decided to make that commitment. It's not exactly the same, Holly."

"You know what, Mark? Whatever. If you need time, then by all means take all the time you need."

"You can't be mad at me for wanting to sort things out before I come back. I thought you would be happy because now you know if I come back it's because I've had time to truly think it over and I've decided I can live with this. Wouldn't you rather that than for me to tell you yes, just to realize later down the road it's too much for me to deal with?"

"You're right. I would rather you think it over before you make a decision. The last thing I want is for you to be in and out of this child's life. I may not be able to give him or her much, but I can offer stability and love, and I plan to do just that."

"Listen, it's getting late. Let's get out of here."

"Only if you allow me to drive back," I state firmly. I guess Mark has had enough arguing for the night because he doesn't say a word. He just walks over to the passenger side to get in.

Mark's interested to know how I found out about the pregnancy, so the ride home consists of me telling him about my doctor's visit and how shocked I'd been to hear the diagnosis. Our ride home is actually a very pleasant one. Mark just listens as I talk. He does say something that gives me a glimmer of hope. He says, "Once we get passed this we should have a rock-solid marriage that can withstand anything." It feels good to know he hasn't given up on us because I know I haven't. I can deny a lot of things, but one thing I can't deny is I'm still very much in love with my husband. I just hope after he has time to think things over he comes to the same conclusion and we can work on building this family together.

Chapter 27

The next few days pass by without any excitement. I've officially hit the four-month mark in my pregnancy and things are progressing along nicely.

Mark and I have talked every day since our car ride nightmare. It's taking him a lot longer than I thought to accept the idea that I'm pregnant. Actually it's accepting that I slept with another man. If it were just the baby news he would've moved back home that night. It is a lot for him to deal with though. Talk about weaving tangled webs. We started off as your typical married couple, and now we're everything but typical. Mark has a child, whom I can't stand, and ironically it has nothing to do with the fact that Mark's his dad. My feelings for him were ruined the first time I met his mother. Not only does Mark have a child outside of the marriage, but I very well may be doing the same thing. Christmas should be quite interesting around our house in the years to come. If Mark decides to give us a chance, that is.

Who would've thought I would find myself praying for normalcy. I never thought I would crave the boring life I once led. This experience has made me realize I wasn't bored at all. I've always heard the saying to be careful what you ask for. I'm learning that the hard way. It's funny because although this isn't my ideal situation, especially the not knowing who the father is part. I was raised in the church my whole life, so I know I've broken a commandment, but don't we all sin? Some more than others, but in my eyes a sin is a sin. Maybe this is just what I tell myself in an effort to keep my sanity in check.

I decide I will spend today relaxing. I already made my appointment at the spa and have reservations at a very upscale restaurant. I never thought I would find joy in doing these things alone, but I feel I really need to be alone right now. This will give me time to think things over and prepare myself for whatever my future brings.

I have a few minutes to spare before I leave, so I decide to sit out on the porch for a little while. I still really love my house. I love the neighborhood, and especially the view from the back porch. Being outside looking at all the flowers and trees is so serene to me. Mark and I both have green thumbs, so even though we haven't given them much attention lately, our flower gardens still look as beautiful as ever. Just as I'm settling into my lounge chair, I hear the house phone ringing. I notice St. Mary's hospital on the screen. Immediately I think my dad has had another heart attack or something.

"Hello," I answer nervously.

"Hello. Is this Mrs. James?"

"Yes, it is."

"Mrs. James, are you the wife of Mr. Mark James?"

"Yes, I am. May I ask what this is in reference to?"

"Yes, ma'am, I'm a nurse at St. Mary's Medical Center. I'm calling because your husband was just brought into the emergency room. He's been in a very serious accident. I got your home number from his cell phone."

I stand there shaking like a leaf. My palms are sweaty, and suddenly my whole body feels numb. My mouth is open but no words are coming out.

"Mrs. James, are you still there?"

"I'm here. How is he? Is he okay?"

"I'm sorry, Mrs. James, but I can't give any information over the phone."

"Can't you just tell me if he's okay!" I'm able to scream between sobs.

"Ma'am, I'm really not suppose to, but I will tell you he is still alive and that's the only information I can give you."

"Okay thanks," I say, hanging up the phone. I feel I should call someone, but right now my first concern is to get to the hospital and check on Mark.

I don't even remember driving to the hospital. My mind is racing a mile a minute. Every thought imaginable is in my head. When I find myself thinking negative thoughts, I start praying. I can't allow myself to go there. I have to think positive for Mark's sake.

I hurry and park and race to the emergency room. I ask the first person I see in uniform about my husband. Each person I stop directs me to the front desk. Why can't these people answer questions around here? Exactly what did they know? And these are the people who are responsible for saving lives? That's scary. I rush to the front desk where I'm told to have a seat in the family room and a doctor will be right with me. Just as I'm opening the door I hear someone calling my name. I turn around to see the doctor coming toward me. He isn't moving fast enough, so I rush to him.

"Doctor, I'm Mrs. James. Is my husband okay?"

"Mrs. James, do you mind stepping in the family room so we can sit down and talk?"

I know this can't be good. Anytime someone asks you to sit down, it's usually because there's bad news to follow. I do as I'm asked and I sit patiently waiting on him to give me Mark's prognosis.

"Mrs. James, I'm not going to sugarcoat the situation. I have to tell you it doesn't look good. Your husband has sustained some very life-threatening injuries. He arrived unconscious and he's still unconscious. He has several broken ribs, a broken arm and leg. We're about to take him up for a CAT scan now to see what, if any, head injuries he may have."

"But these are all injuries he can recover from, right?"

"The broken bones, yes, but the head injury…well, it's too soon to tell. I'm concerned he's still unconscious. There could be a number of things going on, but I won't know until I do the scan."

"Can I see him?"

"Once we bring him back down then you'll be able to see him. I really should get going. I just wanted to give you an update before I took him up."

"Doctor," I say as he's getting ready to leave, "please save my husband."

"I'm going to do all I can, Mrs. James. I promise you that. Right now we're really going to need some divine intervention. I don't know if you're a praying woman or not, but if you are, now would be a good time to start praying."

The doctor leaves, and I sit there for the longest crying and praying. I can accept Mark and me not being together, but I cannot accept him dying on me. I've been with him so long, I can't even begin to imagine life without him. *Lord, I know Mark and I have made a complete mess of things. I've gone astray and I've allowed myself to get into situations I'm not proud of, but right now I'm begging that you please spare Mark's life. I know I don't deserve any favors, so if you don't do it for me, then do it for his family. Do it for his son, who needs his father in his life. Please, God, let him pull through this. Please.*

While I wait, I call my parents and Janelle. I really need the support right now. Janelle arrives first, and boy, is she a sight for sore eyes. I run into her arms and cry like a baby. "He can't leave me, Janelle. He can't leave me. I didn't tell him that I love him. He can't go like this," I say as I hug her even tighter.

"Holly, Mark's going to be fine, and don't worry, you'll have plenty of time to tell him you love him, even though he already knows it."

"But so much has been going on. We've been constantly at each other's throat lately. I don't know if he knows that through it all I never stopped loving him. I just need him to know that."

"Holly, he knows, sweetie. He knows," she reassures me as she rubs my back. I'm so glad she's here. I don't know what I'd do without her. Just as we sit down, my parents arrive. Once again the dam breaks and the tears start flowing. My mom sits with me and rocks me like she use to do when I was little. Being surrounded by them somehow makes me feel hopeful, like everything is going to be okay. I tell them what the doctor said and how he suggested I start praying because Mark's condition doesn't look too good. My dad immediately stands up and beckons us all to the prayer circle. He gives a powerful prayer on Mark's behalf. I know God hears it, and I'm sure He's going to answer.

We're all sitting around making small talk when the doctor walks in again. I don't like the look on his face. I have a feeling something is terribly wrong.

"Mrs. James, I'm afraid my suspicions were right. Your husband has TBI or traumatic brain injury. He has what's called edema, which basically is swelling of the brain. I'm afraid the only way to try to save him is to operate to try and relieve some of the pressure. Again, I can't sugarcoat this and tell you it's not serious because it is. This operation is very complex, but I can assure you we have the best brain surgeon in the state of Louisiana here to take care of your husband. The operation is about three hours long. There's a phone in the room we will move you to. Someone will call you at the halfway point to let you know how things are going."

The doctor leaves to prep for surgery and it's time for us to play the waiting game. I realize three hours is a long time to ask everyone to wait with me, so I tell them they can leave and I'll call them once I hear something. Everyone insists on staying, and I'm so glad they do. I told them they could leave to be polite. God knows I didn't really mean it.

I must look at the clock on the wall every ten minutes. Time is creeping along so slowly. My dad offers to treat us all to dinner downstairs in the cafeteria, but I decline. I do insist they go to eat. This time I really mean it. My dad and Janelle decide to go ahead, but my mom refuses to leave my side. She and I sit there, and she allows me to talk and cry. It's amazing she always knows exactly what I need and when I need it. She knows I just need someone to listen. She doesn't say a word, she just listens.

We're still sitting in the room looking at the television when the phone rings. Mom and I exchange glances.

"Answer it," she says.

"Hello," I answer nervously.

"Mrs. James?" the nurse asks.

"Yes. This is Mrs. James."

"I'm calling from the operating room. I just want to let you know we're at the halfway mark. and so far everything is going along well."

"Okay. Thank you," I say as I hang up the phone.

"Well?" my mom asks.

"She said that everything is going well," I tell her.

"Oh praise God," my mom responds.

The next hour and a half is the longest ever. My mom has to touch my knee several times because I'm shaking my leg so much. I don't even realize it's shaking until she touches me. I try to find ways to occupy my time. I make small talk with Janelle, and I watch as much CNN as I can stand. By the time it feels as though I'm about to jump out of my skin the doctor walks through the door. We all stand up when he comes in.

"Please, everyone have a seat," he says. We all do as we're told.

"Well, the surgery was a success. We were able to relieve the pressure from the brain. He's still in critical condition. Once we get him back to his room and settled, we'll let you go in to visit with him. I must warn you that he's very swollen. He has a lot of tubes hooked up to him, so don't be alarmed. There's going to be a nurse sitting at his door to monitor him for the first few hours. If he makes it through, then his recovery process is going to be very long. He's going to need a lot of support, which I'm sure you'll be there to offer. Before I leave, do you have any questions for me?" he finally asks.

"I do," I say. "I just want to know what are his chances of survival."

"Mr. James's condition isn't uncommon. We see trauma cases like his all the time. He has a very good chance of survival, but tonight is going to be the most critical. If he makes it through the night then his chances of a full recovery increases. I have to tell you I do feel better about his outcome now than I did when he first arrived. I didn't even expect him to make it through the surgery, but he pulled through it like a champ. I hope that answers your question," he says, looking at me.

"Yes, it does. Thank you, doctor, for everything you've done."

"You're very welcome. The nurse will be in shortly to bring you to his room."

"Okay, thanks," I say as he's getting ready to leave the room. The doctor's words are somewhat encouraging, but I know Mark's in for the fight of his life tonight. I hope he knows he doesn't have to fight alone. I plan to stay with him and help him fight as long as it takes.

I keep telling myself I'll be able to hold it together. I will walk in Mark's room and be the strong woman he needs by his side. I keep saying it, until I actually walk in his room that is. I take one look at my dear husband and break down. Mark's unrecognizable. I have to ask the nurse to be sure we're in the right room. His face is at least three times its normal size. He looks like he has tubes coming from every opening of his body. I cannot believe this is the same person I was with just last night. He looks completely different. My dad is the first to approach him. He stands over him and immediately begins to pray. I guess I'm not the only one who feels this situation is really bad.

Janelle and my parents stay only a few minutes before they decide to go home. I hug them good-bye and express again how much I appreciate them being there for me and Mark. The nurse tries to get me to leave. I just can't bring myself to do it. I just know the minute I leave someone will call to tell me bad news. I just can't take that chance.

"Mrs. James, there's really nothing you can do here. You may as well go home and get some rest. You'll need your energy for when he gets out of here," she tries to tell me again.

"I can't leave him here like this," I explain to her.

"There's really nowhere for you to get a good night's sleep. The only thing in his room is a chair."

"I'll sit in the chair if that's okay. I won't get a good night's sleep no matter where I am."

"Okay. Do you need a blanket or pillow or something?"

"No, thank you. I'm fine."

"Just let me know if you change your mind."

"I will," I say, talking to her but never taking my eyes off Mark. It's funny how just yesterday my biggest problem was telling Mark he may or may not be the father of my baby. That was really hard to do, but compared to standing here looking at him fighting for his life, yesterday was a walk in the park. I'm sure I hurt his feelings, I may have even crushed his male ego, but at least he was still breathing on his own and healthy. I believe I'm able to deal with a lot of things, but seeing him lying up here with all the tubes and a breathing machine is just too much for one person to handle. It's times like these my faith is really tested. I believe with all my heart he will get better. I have to believe that not only for him, but also for me.

Chapter 28

"Hold up, stop the damn press. So you mean to tell me all of this has been going on and you conveniently forgot to tell your best friend?" Janelle says as we sit in Copeland's for dinner.

The restaurant is right across the street from the hospital, so I felt safe leaving Mark for a little while. I've been spending my days at work and my nights here with Mark. This past week has been such a roller-coaster ride that I almost forgotten I hadn't broken the news to Janelle yet. I can tell I'm getting bigger because of my clothes, but I'm still not big enough for anyone else to notice. I decide to tell her today so this will be behind me and I can focus the rest of my attention on getting Mark home and nursing him back to good health.

"Janelle, you have to understand…"

"Understand what, Holly? That you're going through one of the most difficult times in your life and you didn't even trust me to help you?"

"I do trust you. You know that."

"I thought I knew that, but after this I don't know what to think. There's never been anything I didn't feel I could tell you."

Okay, now I don't know what to do. I expected Janelle to be shocked, but the last thing I expected was for her to feel hurt. It's true in the past we have told each other everything. I probably shared more with her than I do with Mark. I guess I can understand how her feelings could be hurt. I did change the rotation. Usually when I have big news I tell Janelle, Mark, and then my parents. It just dawned on me that I did that. I can never remember anything she didn't know first. When I found out about Smith's murder I called her from my cell phone on the way home. We didn't talk because her voice mail picked up. I guess Mark got the news first by default.

"Holly, what are you thinking about?"

"I'm sorry. My mind just wandered off."

"Well could you bring it back because I'm still trying to deal with this news? I can't believe you're pregnant."

"Well join the club. I found out three months ago, and I'm still having a hard time believing it."

"So you're three months?"

"No actually I'm four months. I was a little over four weeks when I found out."

"Wait a minute? Did you find out when I took you to the doctor?"

"Yes. I wanted to tell you then, I really did, but I was still trying to sort things out in my head."

"Talking about a upper respiratory infection, yeah you got the infection alright. It's called a baby bug," she said, laughing.

"Ha-ha," I say, smiling.

"What I don't understand is how you kept this a secret for three whole months? You can't hold anything."

"It wasn't easy, believe me. I wanted to tell Mark first, and the next day he had the accident so that distracted me. I didn't feel right discussing the pregnancy with him being in such critical condition. I wanted the focus to be on him, not on me and the pregnancy."

"So how did he take the news? I'm sure he wanted to jump out of his skin with excitement."

"Well, that actually takes me to the next part of my big news."

"Next part? You mean, there's more?"

"Oh, there's so much more."

"Well, spit it out already."

"Okay, well you see, we're not actually sure if Mark's the father of this baby." The next thing I know I'm being sprayed by soda that she spit out. I guess this was just too much to take. Mental note: Never tell someone such big news when their mouth is full of anything.

"Oh, Holly, I'm so sorry, but I really think—no I know—I heard you wrong. I had to have heard you wrong because what I think I heard you say is you don't know if Mark's the father of your baby. That's what I *think* I heard. Please tell me I didn't hear that correctly."

"I wish I could but…"

"May I get you ladies something else?" the waiter asks as he approaches our table.

"Yes, do you all serve Patron?" Janelle asks.

"No, we're fine," I say to the young man who looks very confused.

"Okay, well let me know when you're ready for your check."

"We will. Thanks."

"Why did you do that? I really need that drink," Janelle insists.

"You do not need a drink. You just need to sit and listen."

"Okay. I'm listening because I know I'm missing a very big part to this story—like who you've been creeping with behind my back."

"I wasn't creeping. It just happened."

"I'm listening."

"Well, you know how difficult your sister's wedding was for me. I mean it was a very lovely wedding, but I was still dealing with possibly losing my husband and the life I'd known for so many years."

"Okay, can you please skip the soap opera and get to the part where you end up naked with some other man?"

"Could you please not say it like that?"

"Well, it's the truth, isn't it? Unless you found a way to do it with your clothes on."

"Anyway," I continue, totally ignoring her uncalled-for comments. "That night after the wedding apparently I'd had a little too much to drink, and I ended up sleeping with Dexter."

"Dexter who?"

"Your cousin Dexter."

"Oh my God!" she screams as everyone in the restaurant turns to look at us.

"Shhhh! Can you control yourself, please?"

"No more than you could, I suppose," she says, being very sarcastic.

"Are you going to listen or what?"

"Fine. I'm listening."

"Anyway, the next morning I woke up with him next to me. I don't remember having sex with him, but apparently we did."

"So what I don't understand is where the confusion comes in. If you slept with Dexter and a month later found out you were pregnant then obviously the baby's for Dexter."

"I wish it was that simple, but it's not because I slept with Mark too."

"Oh my, and the plot thickens. When did you sleep with Mark?"

"The night after I slept with Dexter. The night we arrived back from the trip."

"Oh, you little slut. I've taught you so well," she says, laughing.

“This isn’t funny. I’m not proud of that. I should’ve never allowed myself to get that drunk.”

“Holly, you get drunk off one wine cooler, so why did you think you could handle so much champagne?”

“That’s just it; I think in my mind I knew I couldn’t handle it. I didn’t want to feel normal anymore because normal didn’t feel good. I drank one glass and felt myself starting to loosen up, I thought the more I drank the more relaxed I’d get.”

“Oh, you were relaxed alright.”

“Part of this is your fault, you know?”

“How in the hell is part of this my fault? I didn’t put you two in bed together.”

“No, but if you would’ve been in the room and not out being loose with some island guy, then I would’ve never ended up with Dexter.”

“Oh, I see. So since I wasn’t in the room then you felt compelled to go and sleep with him?”

“No. I told you I don’t remember sleeping with him.”

“So what did he say?”

“About what?”

“About possibly being a father?”

“Nothing because he doesn't know.”

“Why? You think he'll be upset? He can’t be upset with you. He was an active participant too.”

“I know, but you know how some guys can be. Besides Mark wants to keep it between us for now, so don't go running your big mouth.”

“Well when you do decide to tell him, I can reassure you that Dexter’s not your typical man. He’s living the bachelor’s life because he can. Right now he doesn’t have a wife or kids, but I know Dex, and he won’t run away from his responsibility. If he’s the father then believe me he’ll definitely do all he can to be there for his child and you if you need him to.”

“I believe you, it's just that this whole situation is very complicated right now..”

“Well I guess so. Don't worry it'll all work out somehow." she tries to reassure me.

“That's my prayer.”

“Oooh, I just thought of something,” she says, smiling.

“What?”

"You could possibly be carrying my little cousin. My best friend could be having my cousin."

"Well, please don't take this the wrong way, but I'm praying I'm not carrying your cousin. I hope with everything in me this is Mark's child."

"I know you do. Everything's going to work out one way or another."

"I believe it will. I just feel so guilty because I should be enjoying this pregnancy. You, more than anyone, know how much I cried about not being able to have a child. Now that I'm having one, it's still stressful. My ideal family would be Mark, the baby, and me. " I say sounding just as sad as I feel.

"I know a place that'll make you feel better." Janelle says obviously sensing that her friend needs some uplifting and bad.

"Where?"

"You'll see. Check please," she says as she motions to our waiter.

After paying for our food we head out. I call the hospital to check on Mark and his nurse tells me he's still resting. I guess it's okay for me to venture off a little farther than the restaurant. I follow Janelle to this mystery place. We drive for a few minutes before we finally pull into Babies R Us. I knew telling her would make me feel better because as soon as we walk in and I see all the tiny clothes I feel an instant sense of joy. I hope this feeling lasts for many more days to come.

I arrive back at the hospital and find things exactly as they were when I left. Mark is sleeping soundly with the monitors beeping each second. I check on him, then go out to the nurse's desk and talk with the nurses. They've become like a part of the family. I'm grateful for them because they've made my stay here as pleasant as one can be in a hospital. I actually look forward to grading papers these days because at least it gives me something to do while I'm here. There's only so much TV and crossword puzzles I can do. My laptop has also been a big life saver,. At least I'm able to send and retrieve emails. I've also become a big MySpace and a Facebook fanatic since I've been here. I always felt these sites were for younger people, but I am surprised to see so many of my old high school classmates on them. I've had quite a few Internet reunions. I can't wait to tell Mark. Some of these people we haven't seen since we left Varnado. He'll be so shocked to know I've found them, especially some of his old football buddies. None of them can compare to Mark. They've really let themselves go. I put some pictures of Mark and me on my site so everyone can see how great life is for us. At least they were when the pictures were taken. Everyone expected Mark and me to live the fairytale life. Who am I to disappoint them? Mark and I know fairytales only exist in the storybooks, but no need to share that little secret with everyone else.

Chapter 29

It's been three weeks and Mark is still in a medical-induced coma. Being at work is the only time I'm able to have a somewhat normal life. Being around the kids helps to take my mind off everything that's going on in my personal life. I remember when I was in elementary school. I couldn't imagine any of my teachers having a personal life. I thought they were teachers twenty-four seven. I remember one time I saw my third grade teacher in the grocery store. It was a Saturday and she looked nothing like she looked at school. Her hair was up in a ponytail and she had on sweatpants and a t-shirt with tennis shoes. I can vividly remember following her around the store because I could not believe this lady was my teacher. *She looks normal,* I can remember thinking. I'm sure that's the way my students feel about me. Huh, if they only knew. Thank God they don't. I can only imagine what they would think of me if they knew the life I'm now living. I don't know what to think of me most days.

During lunch, Erica and I sit and catch up. We haven't been able to talk much during our breaks. Every day I'm either on the phone with the hospital checking on Mark or on the phone with his sister, filling her in on his progress. Today's different because she drove down to spend some time with him, and to give me a little break. Thankfully, she was able to take some time off work.

"So, how's your husband?"

"He's about the same, but I feel good about his prognosis. Mark's a very strong man. He won't give up without a fight."

"That's good. You know I've always heard that one's attitude plays a big role in how they recover. It sounds like your husband will be just fine."

"He will. So how are things going for you? Have you been out again since our dinner date?"

With a very sly smile she says, "Yes, actually I have."

"Oh, what's that look about? You holding back on me?"

“No. Actually I’ve been dying to tell you, but you’ve been so preoccupied, and it just seems insensitive to share my good news when you’re going through something so traumatic.”

“Well, I’m fine now so please share the good news.”

“Okay. Well, I sorta met someone.”

“Shut up, you did not,” I say, smiling.

“I did.” she says blushing.

“Well, who is it? Tell me about him.”

“His name is Sean,” she whispers with the biggest smile I have ever seen her wear.

“Sean, oh he sounds like he's a cutie.” I say smiling.

“He is, he actually reminds me a lot of my ex, just not as obnoxious. I've only known Sean for a couple weeks but we have the most fun together. Right now I'm just enjoying things you know? I'm not trying to rush into a relationship or anything.”

“Erica you have no idea how happy I am for you. Even though we've only known each other a short time, I can just tell there's something very special about you. I really hope this works out for you because you deserve to feel the way you're feeling now.” I say as I feel my voice starting to crack. I'm trying hard not to cry, but it's hard when all I can do is remember when I once felt that way and had that type of fun relationship with Mark. Lately things have gone from bad to worse and it's quite depressing.

“Holly, are you okay?”

“I’m fine. Just reminiscing that's all.” I say trying to conjure up a smile.

“You look a little pale. Are you sure you’re okay?”

“I’m sure. I’ve just been really tired here lately.”

“I certainly understand. It must be hard to have to divide your time between working full-time and going to the hospital to take care of your husband.”

“It really is, but it’s my duty. He’s my husband, and I wouldn’t want to be any other place than by his side.”

“You’re such a good wife, Holly. I hope I can have that one day.”

“You will, just be patient and like you said take things slow.”

“Oh trust me I've learned my lesson about moving too fast. I'm the type of person that seems to fall in love very quickly so I'm working on myself and learning to just live in the moment.”

“Well, I have a feeling you'll be just fine. Just trust your instincts.”

"Thanks for listening and for your advice. I will be careful. I promise."

"That's all I ask."

"Well, I think that's our time. We need to go pick up our kids from the cafeteria."

"Would you mind getting mine with yours? I really need to go make a phone call."

"Sure, go ahead, take your time, and we'll be outside for recess."

"Thank you so much."

Erica can't get out the lounge fast enough. The tears immediately start streaming down my face. I know with the pregnancy I'm a lot more emotional, but I believe these emotions would exist with or without the pregnancy.

I compose myself and join Erica and the kids on the playground and try to make it through the rest of the day without having another breakdown.

On my way to the hospital, Shelia, Mark's sister calls to tell me she has an errand to run.

"I'm on my way. I should be there in five minutes," I tell her.

"I asked Nurse Jackie if she could sit with him and to call one of us if there are any changes before we return." she tells me. She knows I hate for Mark to be there alone.

It only takes me about three more minutes before I make it to the hospital. I arrive at Mark's floor only to find the nurse sitting behind the desk."I thought you were sitting with Mark," I say, somewhat annoyed.

"Oh, I was, but he has company. I believe she said she's his cousin. I hope that's okay."

"Yes, that's fine," I respond,.

"Hey, when did you…" I begin but am totally shocked when I see who the nurse thinks is his cousin.

"You look like you've seen a ghost," Diane Davis says smugly.

"I feel like I have," I respond with a lot of attitude. I normally stay away from confrontation, but in my mind right now anything goes.

"Well that's just too bad," she responds with just as much attitude as I've given her.

"What do you want?" I finally ask.

"What do you mean, what do I want. I want to see my child's father, that's what I want."

"Well you see him, so good-bye."

"Lady, please don't play with me. I'll leave when I'm good and damn ready, and I'm not ready."

"Look, this is neither the time nor place for this. If you're here to cause trouble then be careful because you just may get it today. My husband—and hear me well when I say *my husband*—is in this bed fighting for his life, and right now I feel like I'm at the end of my rope, and believe me, I can use a good stress reliever. If taking you out in the parking lot and using you for a punching bag is the answer then I'm good and ready."

I cannot believe these words are actually coming from my mouth. I'm the least violent person you'll ever know. I've never had a fight a day in my life, but I'm tired of her trying to intimidate me. She has to know I'm not afraid of her.

"Look, if that's what I wanted, then trust me I would've whipped yo' ass a long time ago. If I were you, I would not make the mistake of threatening me, or you and your husband will be fighting for your lives, which doesn't sound half bad to me," she says with that evil smile of hers.

"You know what? I don't have the time or energy to spend on you so either you can leave on your own or I'll call security to escort you out."

"Fine, I'll leave, but just know as soon as Mark is well I'll let him know how you wouldn't allow his son to see him."

"His son isn't even here."

"Well, he doesn't know that, now does he?" she says as she exits the room. I don't know why I allow her to get me worked up the way she does. I know in my mind we're going to have to find a way to at least be civil to each other, but in my heart I'm just not ready. I guess I could be a little more tolerant if she wasn't still so persistent when it comes to Mark. I just don't know what it's going to take to open her eyes to the fact that we're still together and that's not going to change. She's going to be in for the fight of her life if she thinks I'm going to lie down and hand Mark to her on a silver platter. He is and always will be my husband. So if it's a fight she's looking for then I'd say she's met her match because a fight she will definitely get.

Chapter 30

"That's it. Easy, easy be careful," I tell Mark as I help him inside the house. He stayed in the hospital a month and a half. Each time we got over one hurdle, another one would arise. He's dealt with everything from excruciating pain to high blood pressure, from high blood pressure to possibly having more bleeding around the brain. We're blessed the CAT scan showed no bleeding. His doctor explained why they thought that to be the case, but honestly I don't remember. I had so much going on, and so much medical lingo was thrown at me I'm just happy I still remember my name at this point.

"Holly, I'm not helpless, you know?" He is annoyed because he's still not able to get around the way he would like.

"I realize that, Mark, but you have a broken leg, a broken arm, and four fractured ribs. I can't say I know how that feels, but I do know you can use a little assistance, so you sit here and I'll go get you some pillows."

"Holly, I don't need any pillows. Please, just sit down. I need to tell you something."

"Mark, you know I don't like sit-downs. That only means bad news is coming."

"Will you sit down, please?"

"Fine."

"Listen, the nurse told me you were there every hour on the hour. She said you refused to leave my side. I just wanted to say thank you. I really appreciate you being there for me when I needed you the most."

"Mark, you don't have to thank me. You're my husband. Where else would I be?" After saying that Mark gives me the strangest look. "What?"

"I was just wondering."

"About?"

"The baby." Because the accident happened right after I told him, we never really had a chance to talk about the baby.

"What about the baby?"

"Did you tell the other guy yet?"

"No, I haven't told him yet."

"Have you thought of not telling him?"

"What? No ."

"Why not?"

"Because it wouldn't be right. Would you want someone to do that to you?"

"I just think it would be best if we kept this to ourselves, at least for now."

"I don't know Mark. This is very serious. It's not like we're keeping a minor secret. This is a child we're talking about. I just wouldn't feel right not letting him know something."

"I agree that he needs to know and he will if we find out the child is his. If not then there's really no reason for you to ever have any contact with him again."

"Is that what this is about, me contacting him? If that's the case, then we can discontinue this conversation right now. I know it's going to take some time, but we both have to learn to trust again. Believe me when I tell you that being with him again is the furthest thing from my mind. There's a child involved, and that's my main concern."

"That's my main concern too. I guess I was hoping we could raise this child as ours."

"Mark, no matter what...."

The phone rings. *Saved by the bell,* I think.

"I'd better get that," I say in an effort to put a halt to this conversation.

"No, let it ring. We really need to talk about this."

"And we will, but let me answer this first," I insist.

"Fine," he says, but I can tell he isn't happy at all.

"Hello."

"Hello. Mrs. James?"

"Yes. This is Mrs. James."

"Hey. It's Shirley Jones."

It takes me a minute to realize who Shirley Jones is. I guess because work isn't on my mind at the time.

"Oh, hello Ms. Jones," I finally respond once I realize she's my former coworker. Jones decided to retire at the end of last year. It was a decision she struggled with all year, and after everything with Smith and her murder, Jones decided to go ahead and hang up her teaching hat. Her husband retired a year earlier and was really pushing her to join him in retirement heaven, so he called it. They plan to spend the rest of their days together traveling and just enjoying life. I'm happy for both of them because that's how life should be.

"I'm calling to check on your husband and to see if you'd heard the latest on Smith's case."

"Mark's doing much better. Thanks for asking."

"Oh, I'm so glad. Please let him know I'm still praying for you two."

"Thank you so much. We need all the prayer we can get. I haven't heard anything new about Smith's case. Have you?"

"I'm surprised you don't know. It's been all over the news."

"I can't tell you the last time I watched the news. I've been so distracted with working and taking care of Mark."

"Oh, I understand. Well let me fill you in. You know the police suspected it was a home invasion, right?"

"Right. That's the last I heard."

"Well, they got a tip it may have been someone she knew."

"What!"

"Yes, now that was about a month ago."

"Okay, so did they find out who did it?"

"Are you ready for this?"

"Probably not, but tell me anyway."

"Have you ever heard of her talk about this guy Steve?"

"The one she met on the Internet?"

"That's the one."

"He killed her?"

"Initially, he was a person of interest; however, he was ruled out because apparently he was out of town. They still think he may have been involved though."

"How?" I ask totally engrossed.

"According to the police, Steve was heavily into drugs."

"He used drugs?"

"No, he sold drugs. The police believe Steve may have gotten involved with the wrong people, like a drug deal gone bad or something. Right now the police are trying to figure out if she was the intended target or if it that bullet was meant for Steve. Either that or she could've just walked in on a burglary in progress. They're speculating that Steve could've had something they wanted."

"Like what?"

"I don't know, either drugs or money I guess."

"But that doesn't make sense. Smith would never allow drugs or drug money in her house. That just wasn't her. This whole thing doesn't make sense to me. Was all of this on the news?"

"No, just the part about Steve being ruled out as a person of interest. The rest I got from my nephew who's a policeman."

"Is he working on this case?"

"No, but he keeps me posted about information from her case. He knows she was my coworker and that I'm very interested in hearing anything about the case."

"All this just doesn't make sense to me."

"It didn't make sense to me either until I remembered some things she'd said about him."

"We didn't talk about him much. She knew how I felt about the whole Internet dating thing. What did she tell you?"

"She would just tell about all the things he bought her and all the trips he'd take. She was so fascinated with his lifestyle, but she never knew what he did for a living. I would always ask her about his job because, according to him, it allowed him to travel."

"That sounds reasonable. They're many jobs that require their employees to take business trips."

"Business trips to the Bahamas, Hawaii, and Las Vegas? Not to mention all the expensive things he bought for her and the money he would give her just because. I don't know any hardworking man who gives his money away the way he did. It just didn't add up to me."

"You're right. That doesn't sound right. She should've known something wasn't right with him."

"Maybe she did and chose to ignore it. You know how she felt about being alone. It's sad, but some women will settle even though they know it's wrong."

"Now I wish she would've talked to me about him. Maybe I could've said something to get through to her."

"She knew how you felt about her seeing him. I'm sure that's the only reason she talked to me. You know it was very unusual for us to talk about anything other than work."

"I told her the first time she mentioned him that Internet dating is very dangerous, and now you see why I feel that way. She didn't know a damn thing about this man and look what happened," I say, beginning to cry. "I told her time and time again she's way too trusting of these men. She was a sweet, loving woman, and I believe God had her mate, but she wanted to take matters in her own hands." I feel like I'm going from hurt to angry. I'm hurt Smith is gone, and I'm angry at her for not being more cautious.

"I really don't think there was anything you, me, or anyone could have said to change her mind about him. She truly felt he was the one for her. She would often say he treated her better than any other man, her dad included. She enjoyed the attention from him."

"I know. I just wish things could've been different."

"We all do. Lately, I've been trying to think of things we could do to hopefully prevent this from happening to anyone else."

"You know I would love to help. Please keep me posted on whatever you come up with, and if I think of anything I'll let you know."

"That sounds good. Well, I'll let you go. I just wanted to check on you and your husband and to make sure you were updated on this case."

"Thank you so much for keeping me informed. I'm sure we'll be talking again soon."

"Yes, definitely. Okay, well take care."

"You too. Bye."

"Bye."

"What happened?" Mark asks once I hang up the phone.

"That was Mrs. Jones giving me an update on Smith's case."

"Any new developments?"

"More than you can imagine."

Chapter 31

It's been four months since Mark's been home and things have been going great for him. He's progressing very well. He just stopped going to physical therapy a few weeks ago. His doctor wasn't happy with that decision, but Mark's so bullheaded, once he makes up his mind to do something, that's it and there's nothing anyone can say to change his mind.

I can't believe my shower's today. This pregnancy has been really good. Everything was smooth sailing after the morning sickness ended. My glucose level and blood pressure is normal. My doctor was a little concerned about my weight, but the baby's a good weight, so she's not as concerned as she was in the beginning. It's funny because I've always heard that women gain all this weight when they're pregnant, and that's what I thought I had to look forward to, but thankfully not. So far I've only gain about ten pounds, most of that is baby so I'm very proud of that.

I've been looking forward to this day every since Janelle started planning it, which was actually the same day I told her I was pregnant. She insists I have to have the biggest baby shower ever. I haven't felt pretty in months because I've been so tired, and just not in the mood to put much thought into my looks. I already know the next few weeks are going to fly by. Mark and I still have so much to do to get the house baby proofed and get the nursery ready. My body's ready, but my mind sure isn't, and my house certainly isn't. I'm so nervous about having a baby. I don't know the first thing about taking care of a baby. My mom promised she will come stay with me, at least for the first couple of weeks. I don't know what I'd do without her. Mark keeps insisting we can handle it on our own, but he's just as lost as I am. The hospital offers parenting classes, I jumped at the opportunity. Mark was disappointed because he really wanted to share that experience with me, but he still has to take it real easy. I don't want anything to cause him to mess up the progress he's made. The classes are very good and very informative, but it's a little too overwhelming. I feel more confused now than I did when I went. I'm just so afraid I'm going to do something wrong, and the last thing I want is to hurt my baby.

"You need help in there?" Janelle asks through the bedroom door.

"No. I think I can manage," I respond.

"Okay. Well, don't take too long. Your guests will be arriving soon."

"I'm suppose to take long. I'm the guest of honor. I have to make a grand entrance," I joke with her.

"That only applies when you actually go somewhere, not when the event's at your house."

"Oh, okay," I say, laughing.

My mom, of course, was the first to arrive. Janelle pins her "I'm the Grandma" button on her, and she can't stop smiling. She is so excited about being a grandma. Lately she's been thinking about what the baby will call her. She's gone through so many different names. I think she's finally settled on Nana. Even though I told her that's what children call their godmothers, she doesn't seem to care. She likes the name and she's sticking with it—this week anyway.

"Oh, everything looks so nice, Janelle. I wish you would've let me help you out," my mom says.

"No, Mom, it was no trouble at all. I enjoyed every minute of it. I don't know who's more excited, Holly or me," Janelle says, smiling. Just as she calls my dad "Pops," she also refers to my mom as "Mom". My mom loves it; she always wanted more children, so she has taken Janelle in as her own.

"Well, I know I'm excited. I can't wait to spoil my little precious baby," Mom responds.

"There will be no spoiling of the baby," I say as I enter the kitchen where they're gathered.

"Oh, baby, you look so pretty. I love that dress on you."

"Thanks, Mom. Can you believe Mark actually picked this out? I ordered it from Motherhood online. I'm glad it fits. You know I hate buying clothes that I can't try on first."

"Well, tell Mark he has excellent taste."

"I'll be sure to let him know."

"Okay, well it seems almost everyone is here. How about we get this party started?" Janelle says as we all start to gather in the living room.

"Welcome, everyone, to Holly's first annual baby shower. We plan to do this at least once a year or maybe every other year," she says, being silly.

"Oh yeah, right. The next baby shower will be Janelle's," I say mainly to her.

"I have no objections to that. Right after the wedding," my mom interjects.

"Well, I guess that idea's out the window," Janelle says. She always says she's not meant to be a wife. She's not the submissive type and she can't see herself changing for any man. I keep telling her that's not what marriage is all about. It's not about the husband being in control and the wife bowing down to him as if he's her master. If that were the case then I wouldn't be married either.

"Okay, ladies, let's get to the fun part," Janelle says as she begins giving directions to the games. I begged her not to play any god-awful baby games, but she insists. That's the one thing I hate about baby and bridal showers. I can deal with everything else except the games. I think they're pointless and a pure waste of time. Why can't we just socialize, eat, and open presents? That's my ideal shower. Janelle said everyone loves to play games. Apparently this shower has nothing to do with me and everything to do with Janelle. She's right in her element, which is entertaining. I'm happy because that's less work I have to do.

Finally, it's time for my favorite part, the gifts. I open tons of gifts and listen to all the *oooh*s and *ahhh*s. I feel like I'm ready to burst out of my skin with excitement. Actually having all of these cute little baby things in my house is just making me more anxious to have my baby here. Just as I'm finishing up with the gifts my cell phone rings. Janelle tries to hand it to me, but I motion for her to go ahead and answer it.. She does and before I realize it she's nowhere to be found.

After opening all the gifts, I thank all my guests for coming and invite everyone to help themselves to the spread of food. Meanwhile, I go down the hall to find the hostess sitting in the guest bedroom sitting with her back to the door holding the phone to her ear. I start to say something when she begins talking again.

"I don't know what you hope to accomplish, but trust me you're fighting a losing battle" she says.

Okay, now my interest is piqued so I decide to remain quiet and listen in before I make my presence known.

"What has gotten into you? I've never known you to be this way."

In my head I'm trying to process who she could be having this conversation with? Obviously it's someone we both know. Maybe it's

Mark, but no he would've called the house phone. Come on Janelle say something so I can figure this out.

"You're asking for trouble. I'm telling you to let this go."

She sits there listening to the person on the other end talk, then she hangs up. No goodbye or anything. I'm still standing there when she turns around to see me standing in the doorway.

"What's going on?" I ask, more curious than ever now.

"I didn't know you were there. Come in, close the door we need to talk."

"Oh no, not the closed door talk. That means big trouble."

"Just close the door." she instructs again.

"Okay" I do as I'm directed. "Hurry up you know my mom will be back here looking for us soon. "

"Okay well I'll give you the condensed version. Basically, Dexter has decided that he's in love with you."

"Wait, what?" I ask because I was not expecting to hear that.

"I'm serious. He was calling to tell you. He's in love with you."

"We've known each other for a week, how can he say he's in love with me?"

"According to him he knows how he's feeling and what he feels for you is very real."

"Janelle, this is not good. I'm trying to put my marriage back together I can't go through this with Dexter."

"I told him to let it go, but I don't think you're going to get rid of him that easy."

"What am I going to do? Mark thinks the guy I slept with lives in the Bahamas. If he found out that he's right here in Baton Rouge he will have a fit."

"Okay listen. Just play it cool for now and after everyone leaves we'll sit down and think of something."

I try to take Janelle's advice, but it's very hard. Had this conversation come up a year ago I would've just laughed it off as nonsense, but because things are the way they are now I have to take all situations seriously. One slip up can put Mark and me right back at square one.

"You go ahead. I'll be out in a minute," I say as I go toward the bathroom. I just need a little more time to compose myself. The thought of

Mark finding out is very scary. The last thing I want to do is jeopardize what we've been working so hard to build back up.

I stay in the bathroom a few more minutes before I decide to leave my safe place. I have to go back out there and rejoin the party. I'm glad I do because I really did have a good time with my family and friends. Everyone cleared out by 6:00 P.M. Of course Janelle stays around to clean up. She insists that my mom go home and get off the road before it gets too dark. My mom still gets around very well, but she hates driving at night because her sight isn't as good as it used to be. Janelle worked in silence for a while before I decide someone has to say something.

"So, what am I going to do?" I ask hoping she can help me handle this the right way. Mark is my first concern, of course, but I also don't want to hurt Dexter's feelings.

"I would say talk to Dexter. Just let him down easy. He's still under the impression that you and Mark are separated. I told him you were working on your marriage, but I think the walls understood better than he did. You need to tell him yourself. Besides isn't there something you need to discuss with him anyway?" She says eyeing my stomach.

"Mark wants to wait until we find out the paternity."

"So you're not going to say anything? Holly you know that's not right."

"Janelle, what am I suppose to do? I'm trying to make everyone happy, but it seems the harder I try the more I mess things up." I say as I began to cry, again.

"Holly, I'm sorry I didn't mean to upset you. I just want you to do whatever makes you happy." She says as she comes over and rub my back.

"You know I'm starting to wonder if I can be happy. It's been so long, I think I forgot what happiness feels like."

"I know you've been through a lot, but trust me you will be happy again. Just wait until this little baby comes and you and Mark are parents, something you've been waiting a long time to experience together."

"I know you're right. I'm just so afraid to get my hopes up just to be disappointed again."

"Hold up," she says putting her hand in the air. "I know this isn't the same person who's always preaching to me about being positive and having faith. Now why does that apply to me, but not to you?"

"It does apply to me. I guess I just needed to hear it again. Sometimes it's very hard to encourage yourself you know?"

“Girl please, you're preaching to the choir. Why you think I ring your phone so much? If it weren't for you I don't know what condition I'd be in. Which isn't saying much I guess because I'm still a mess.” She says laughing.

“You're not a mess, just a little confused that's all.” I say as we both fall out laughing.

Chapter 32

I find it very hard to focus this week. My mind is so preoccupied with making sure everything is just right for the baby's arrival. Everything in me is saying this baby is coming really soon. I don't think I'll make it to my due date.

"Hey, did you hear the announcement?" Erica asks walking in my room.

"I heard him say something, but couldn't really make out the words. I was outside with my class looking at our shadows. What did he say?"

"He said we have a brief meeting after school." she informs me.

"Oh come on, you've got to be kidding me. I have plans after school. I don't have time for a meeting."

"Well, he said brief, let's hope he means it."

"I hope so."

After dismissing my students I call Mark to inform him I'll be a little late. Normally I wouldn't call, but lately he's been so worried about me and the baby. He's actually a little upset that I'm still working. He's ready for me to stay home and take it easy until the baby comes. He mentioned it a couple times, but dropped the issue because he knows I'm going to work until I can't work anymore.

I make a detour to the bathroom before going to this dreadful meeting. I walk in the lounge still obviously upset, when I see a big sign that says: WELCOME BABY JAMES. It doesn't take me long to realize the sudden meeting is actually a surprise baby shower for me.

"Oh my God," I say as I begin to cry. I was totally not expecting this. "You guys, how could you do this to me?"

"Because you deserve it," Erica says as she comes up to hug me.

"I can't believe you kept this from me. How long have you known about this?"

"Known about it, she planned it," Mr. McNair chimed in.

"Oh, you really shouldn't have," I say again, but this time to Erica.

"I couldn't think of a nicer person to do this for. I'm so happy for you and your husband. This baby is so lucky to have such caring, loving people for parents."

I'm listening to Erica and sitting here thinking how wonderful my coworkers are to me. I also wonder how they would feel about me if they knew the truth. If they knew I'm not the person they think I am.

"Earth to Holly," I hear Erica say.

"I'm sorry. I'm just so overwhelmed with all this. I cannot believe you were actually able to pull this off. Do you know how many times people have tried to surprise me, and I've managed to find out about each and every one of them? I must say, you're good."

"I think so," she says, laughing.

The work party is so much fun. The faculty gave me a three-hundred-dollar gift card to Babies R Us. I'm so excited because now I can go get the bedroom set I really want. I'm bubbling over with excitement. Mr. McNair and a few of the teachers assist me with loading my car with other gifts I received. I thank them all again, then I'm off to surprise my husband with a carload of baby goodies. Mark is your true macho man, he lift weights, he runs, he plays basketball with the fellas from time to time. It's funny seeing him, the manly man, go crazy over baby items. He's more mushy than I am. That's why I love him so much. Even though he's all man, he's never afraid to show me his sensitive side. I have an overwhelming feeling of calmness and for the first time I really believe everything will work out just fine.

Chapter 33

I cannot believe the big day is finally here. I knew it was only a matter of time. After putting all our baby things away, Mark and I sipped on hot tea and decided to watch a movie. Well, I watched the movie because I believe Mark was asleep before the first scene began. Just as I'm really getting into my movie, I feel a pain unlike no other. There's no mistaking I'm indeed in labor. “Mark! Mark! Get up, ” I say, shaking him like crazy.

“ What Holly, ” he says upset that his sleep is being disturbed.

It takes me a minute to tell him what's going on because I can't talk through the pain. “Mark I'm in labor.” I say after the pain is a little less intense.

“What!” he yells as he jumps off the couch. “Why are you sitting there, come on we have to get to the hospital.” he says obviously starting to panic.

“I'm sorry, I'm just experiencing some excruciating labor pains, please forgive me for not getting up and getting everything together while you enjoyed your rest.” I say trying really hard not to get up and slap him.

“Okay, calm down. Is this all you need?” he ask as he pulls my suitcase out of the hall closet.

“Yes, can we go now?” I say trying to get to the door before another pain hit.

Mark is once again driving like a madman, this time I don't try to stop him. As long as he gets us there safe. He swings in the hospital emergency room parking and runs in to grab a wheelchair. I'm admitted immediately because I had the good sense to preregister. My doctor isn't on call tonight so I have to settle for her partner, which is her husband Dr. Lee. I've met him a few times and he seems really nice, but my only concern at this moment is him getting down there and getting this baby out of me.

I'm made to suffer a while longer before my Godsend comes in to save me. I believe his name is Dr. Washington and he's my anesthesiologist. He comes in and gives me the best stuff in the world. Mark asked me if I was sure I wanted and epidural. The look I gave him said it all. He didn't bother to ask again. My parents and Janelle arrives just as the medicine is kicking in. Lucky for them, they get to see the calm and collected Holly. Unlike the monster Mark had to deal with. We sit and talk for a minute before Dr. Lee comes in and asks everyone to step out while he checks me. I was so happy when he said "Mrs. James, it's time."

"Push, Holly, push," Mark says while I'm trying to concentrate on getting this child out of me. "Come on, baby. We're almost there. I can see the head. Oh, honey it's such a beautiful head."

"Come on, Mrs. James. Just one more push and the baby will be out," the doctor finally says.

I give one more big push and the next thing I know I'm staring in the face of the most beautiful baby girl I've ever seen. Even though she's covered in what looks like slime, I can still tell she's beautiful.

"We're going to get her cleaned up and we'll bring her right back to you," one of the nurses says.

"Do you have a name picked out?" another nurse asks.

"Yes. It's Kirsten Noel James," I respond.

"Kirsten Noel. That's beautiful," the nurse says.

"Thanks," I say proudly.

After the baby is cleaned up they allow Mark and me to spend some time with her. I don't need a paternity test to tell me this is indeed Mark's child. She is the spitting image of her daddy. The baby is soon rolled to the nursery where she'll take her first sponge bath. We explain everything to Dr. Lee and he's going to do the paternity test before we leave. Even though it's obvious to me, I still don't want there to be any doubts.

Our hospital room is full of our family and friends. Everyone's so excited to welcome Kirsten to the world. My parents and Janelle were here the whole time, of course. My mom insisted Mark and I should be in the delivery room alone. I asked her to come, but she thought it should be a moment for Mark and me to share together. I mean how many times do you get to welcome your first child into the world?

Later that night, I can't sleep a wink. I can't keep my eyes off her. She's the most perfect baby I've ever seen. I know I'm a little bias and I'm sure every parent feels that way, but for me this moment is unlike any other. I do feel better knowing I'm not the only paranoid one in the room. Each time I look over I see Mark staring at the baby. He looks like he's afraid to take his eyes off her too. If I didn't know it before, I definitely know it now. This family was meant to be. It's a part of God's perfect plan for us.

"I feel in my heart that she's mine," Mark says.

"I do too," I say, totally agreeing with him.

"I guess we'll have our proof soon enough."

"Dr. Lee said he'll put a rush order in. So we should know something before we leave the hospital."

"That'll be great," he says as he continues looking at his little miracle baby. I decide to give in to the medicine and let Mark stay up with the baby. I simply can't go any longer.

After two days in the hospital, I'm finally being discharged. Mark loads up all the flowers and fruit baskets we received from friends, family, and a few of my coworkers. My students made a giant card they all signed. I already miss them.

Just as the baby and I are being wheeled to the elevator, I hear Dr. Lee calling my name. I turn around and see her running toward me with a big brown envelope in her hand. I know it's the paternity test, and all of a sudden I start to feel sick. All the certainty I had a couple days ago has gone out the window. I now feel this could go either way. I still feel Kirsten resembles Mark, but not as much as she did when she was first born. I'm wondering if I just willed her to look like him. Maybe I wanted it so badly that in my mind she really looked like him. I've learned that the mind is a very powerful tool.

"I was told to make sure you get these," she says handing the envelope to me.

Once Mark figures out how to work the car seat, he gets in the car. I'm sitting there holding the envelope in very sweaty, shaky hands.

"Is that what I think it is?"

"Yes. Do you want to do this now or wait until we get home?"

"No time like the present, right?"

"You're right. Let's open it." I say the words, but don't attempt to open the envelope. I don't think my nerves will allow me to open it. Before I know it, Mark is reaching over to take the envelope from me. I watch nervously as he does something totally unexpected. He rips the envelope and the results to pieces.

"Mark! What are you doing?" I ask in shock.

"Holly, I don't need no paper to tell me this is my child. I know she's mind. Look at her? She's definitely a James." he says very convincingly.

The ride home was pure misery for me. I wanted the speculation and everything to be over with. No matter what I was prepared to deal with it and move on the best way possible. Now I'll have to wait a while longer because I can't live not knowing the truth, the real truth.

After only being home for a few hours I can already say I have to admit I do agree with Mark. Things would've been better with just the three of us. I love my mom to death, but she's definitely the take-charge type. I can barely touch the baby without her coming to, in her words, relieve me. Many times I have to tell her I actually want to hold my child. I know she just wants to spend time with her, but so do I. I hate I feel like I'm competing with my own mother. It's literally like a race most of the time. The unspoken rule has become whoever gets to her first gets to hold her. So naturally I make it my business to always try to get to her first.

It's funny because for the past week my mom has worked my nerves, but now that she's leaving I want to cry. I didn't realize how much I really did depend on her. Now everything's going to be on Mark and me. The feedings, the diaper changes, and everything in between will depend on us. I know Kirsten's our child and that's what we're supposed to do, but my mom spoiled us. We had a nice little schedule worked out where we would take turns with the nightly feedings. Now since it's only two of us, my turn will come around a lot quicker than before.

"Mom, I can't thank you enough for staying this long and helping us out. I know it was a great sacrifice for you and Dad," I say, hugging her as she heads for the door.

"Yeah, Mom, we really do appreciate all your help. Holly and I never would've made it without you," Mark adds.

"Oh, stop it, you two. You know you don't have to thank me. There's no place on earth I would be but here helping to care for my grandbaby who, by the way, is going to call me Grandma." She decided she likes that name after all.

After all the hugs and kisses, Mom is on her way. Mark and I look at each other like we don't know what to do next. It's funny how such a little being can change the whole dynamics of a house. We've never been uncomfortable in our own house. Now we're too afraid to make too much noise because the last thing we want is to wake the baby.

"So?" Mark finally says.

"So, what?" I ask.

"What do we do now?" I know exactly what he means, but I can't let him know I'm just as lost as he is.

"What do you mean? Now we do what we have to do." That's the best I can come up with. I know eventually we'll get it together.

"Why don't you go and get some rest? I'll listen out for the baby," Mark insists. I can't pass up that offer because I'm exhausted. Just as I lay my head on the pillow, I hear the baby starting to cry. I want to let Mark handle it, but I can't. I walk to her room to find him rocking her in the glider. Mark is such a great dad. He's so attentive and never complains. I know we're all still in the honeymoon phase, but I believe with everything in me we're going to be just fine. I believe the bad days are behind us and we've been given the opportunity to start over.

I changed my cell phone number and asked Janelle to handle Dexter. She swears she can get through to him when no one else can. I have absolutely no idea what she said or how he reacted, I told her I didn't want to know. I'm trying very hard to put that part of my life behind me. I really have no desire to talk to him ever again. It was a mistake that I can't take back, but I can surely learn from it. I know what's really important in my life. Now my focus is on my family. Maybe Mark's right. We should just leave well enough alone. We have the child we've always wanted, the life we've been working so hard to put back together. There's really no need to go digging for trouble. Mark believes she's his and so do I, so I would say that's enough proof. I can't wait to see what the future has in store for us—all of us.

Chapter 34

"Holly, I need to talk to you about something," Mark says as he walks into the nursery where I'm feeding the baby. She's made two months today. How can I be so happy and yet so sad at the same time? I go back to work in a few weeks and I need to start thinking about going to get my room ready. I'm sure the substitute did a wonderful job, but she's not me and there's a certain way I like things organized. It has to be that way or my whole day will be thrown off. I want to go, but I'm having so much fun taking care of my baby, and I really hate to leave her, but I have to. Mark has decided that since he works from home the baby will stay with him. On the days when he has meetings or something, my mom has agreed to step in and help out. It seems everything's working out, so why am I so sad? I know there are some mothers out there who would love to be in this situation. There are many mothers who have to send their baby to day care, and I'm so blessed I don't have to go that route.

"Sure, come in and join us," I respond. Things have been going really good for us. After my mom left, both Mark and I thought we would lose our minds, but these last few weeks haven't been bad at all. We are naturals at being parents. This further confirms that Kirsten was definitely meant to be.

"You know, I've been thinking," he begins as he sits down in the chair across from us, "I really love our family, and I love spending time with my two favorite girls. I realize now that I have Kirsten how much I missed out on with Tyler."

An instant chill goes down my spine. I'm sure I know where he's going with this, and I have a feeling I'm not going to like it. I like our family just the way it is, and excuse me if I'm being selfish, but I'm not too excited about the idea of anyone else coming into it, especially Tyler, and especially if he comes with his good-for-nothing mother.

"I know I can't go back and change things, but I don't think it's too late. If it's okay with you, I would love to invite him into our family."

"And by that you mean?"

"I mean I want him to start coming to stay sometimes and just spending time with us. He needs to know his little sister and get to know more about his dad and stepmom."

There goes that chill again. Little sister? Stepmom? I think we're pushing things a little too fast. I don't want to hurt Mark's feelings because I can tell he's genuine. What am I suppose to do, ask him not to be a father to his child? I do admit I would definitely prefer for him to spend time with him here versus being around Diane Davis. I really wish we didn't have to visit this right now. Why can't we just enjoy Kirsten? Maybe when she's, I don't know, say five or so then we'll introduce the two of them.

"So what do you think, Holly?"

"How about we take some time and really think about it before we decide anything? I'm sure this is going to open up a whole new can of worms, and we have to think of how we're going to handle it."

"What's there to handle?"

"Your baby mama," I say before I know it. I immediately wish I can take those words back. His whole facial expression changes. The wide-eyed excited look he just wore is now gone. I know it's my fault, and for that I feel really bad. "Look, Mark, I'm sorry. I shouldn't have said that. I do know how she is though, and I'm not ready to spoil what we have. You know as well as I do she's not going to willingly allow Tyler to come and spend time with us. We're going to be in for the fight of our lives, and we have to be sure this is what we want. Besides, Tyler may not even want to spend time with us. His mom and her family is all he really knows. Do you think it'll be fair to just come in and interrupt his world? Don't you think that's a little selfish of us?"

"Holly, Tyler is a child. He doesn't know what's best for him, and at this point he has no wants. I'm his father, and we're his family as well. I didn't realize how much I could love another human being until we had Kirsten. You know I love you with everything in me, but what I feel for her is different, and I know it's because she's a part of me. I need to make things right between Tyler and me. I know you don't like it, but he's a part of me too. I'm willing to fight with everything in me to be a part of his life."

I can tell he's determined to make this happen. I realize there's nothing I can say to change his mind. When Mark decides he wants something, he doesn't stop until that happens, no matter how difficult the road may seem.

"Well, I can see you've been giving this a lot of thought. If this is what you want, then I say let's do it." Now the look on his face is priceless. He looks like a man who just won the lottery, and I guess to him he has.

After my talk with Mark, I decide today will be a good day to spend some time with Grandma and Grandpa. Mark has a lot of work to catch up on so I know he can use some time alone. This is Kirsten's first road trip. I don't know if five miles can exactly be considered a road trip, but to us it is. I feel like it takes me forever to leave the house now. I know I tend to over pack for the baby, but my mom always taught me that it's better to be safe than sorry. Kirsten and I say our good-byes to Mark and we're on our way. I try to put on my brave face, but inside I'm terrified. I've never been in the car with her alone. What if she starts crying? What if someone hits me? What if… Okay I'm going to stop thinking like this and just trust that everything will be okay. I had Mark to put her mirror up so I can see her from the rearview mirror. The thought of not being able to see her is just totally unacceptable to me.

"I can't believe my girls are leaving me all alone," Mark jokes as he walks us out to the car.

"Oh right. You know you can't wait to get rid of us," I joke back.

"I have a lot of work to do. If I didn't, you know I would go with you."

"I know, honey. It'll be good for all of us. You can work in peace, and Kirsten and I get to spend some time with Mom and Dad, and when I return, Mommy and Daddy will spend some much needed time together."

"Now that sounds like my type of plan," Mark says, grinning.

The ride to my parents' house isn't nearly as bad as I thought it would be. I make sure to feed and change the baby before I leave home so she sleeps the whole way there, not that we had so far to go. When we arrive, my parents are outside waiting on us. They look like they're expecting the President or something. I never remember being greeted at the front door. Usually Mark and I have to knock at least three times before someone comes to the door. "Boy, Kirsten you must be one very special little girl," I say as I take her carrier out.

"Oh, hurry up so I can see my precious little baby," my mom says as we walk up to the front porch.

"Well hello to you, too, Mom," I say, smiling at her.

"Hello, baby girl," my dad says as he hugs me. For a while my relationship with my dad was strained. He just couldn't seem to get past the fact that I cheated. It didn't seem to matter too much that Mark cheated first, but anyway. He's over it now and couldn't be happier for Mark and me. As far as they know we're one hundred percent sure Mark's her father.

My mom totally ignores my smart remark. She's too concerned about taking the baby from me.

"Come on in," she finally says.

"Does that include me too?" I joke.

"Oh, I'm sorry, baby. Of course that includes you too," she says, smiling.

Once inside, we all make ourselves comfortable in the living room. I love coming to my parents' house because it reminds me of my childhood. I don't care how much I beg and plead, my mom will not depart with her living room décor. Everything looks exactly the same as when I was living here. I can't tell you how many times Mark and I made out on this couch. My parents would die if they knew. We never went all the way, but there was a lot of kissing going on.

"So, Holly, are you ready to go back to work?" my mom asks.

"Not at all. The only thing I want to do is stay home with my baby."

"Holly, you can't smother this poor child. Going back to work will be good for you. You can't spend every minute with her, you know?"

"I realize that, Mom, and I think things would be different if the circumstances were different. Kirsten is most likely the only child I'll ever have. God blessed me with her, and I want to enjoy it. I'll never have this moment again."

"I understand, honey, believe me I do. I just don't want you to get too consumed with her. You had a life before her, and you should still have one now that she's here."

"I plan to have a life. I don't think I'm consumed by her."

"Oh really? Well when's the last time you spent some time without her?"

"That's not fair. She's still a baby, so of course I haven't spent much time away from her. Besides, I'm still breastfeeding."

"I hope you understand I'm just looking out for you. I made the mistake of doing that with you, and believe me it's not fun. I thought I would lose my mind when you left home. I just want to spare you from experiencing that pain."

"I know you're looking out for me, Mom, but please just let me enjoy her right now. I don't want to think about any of that."

"Well I'll leave it alone then," she says, gazing down at the baby.

She always says that, but she never does. We may not discuss it anymore today or tomorrow, but believe me, we will discuss it again. Just as I was making myself comfortable sitting watching reruns of *Sanford and Son* with my dad while my mom sat holding the baby, my phone rings. "Hello," I answer, puzzled by the long-distance number on my phone.

"Hey. How's it going?" the voice on the other end asks.

"Okay," I answer, somewhat surprised by the call.

"How're you doing?" Dexter asks.

I excuse myself from the living room and go to my old room to finish the call. "Dexter, why are you calling me?"

"What, I can't call and check on you?"

"Check on me for what? Did you talk to Janelle?"

"Yes, and I must say I'm very disappointed in you Holly. Why couldn't you be woman enough to come to me yourself?"

"It had nothing to do with being woman enough, but everything to do with respect. I was not going to disrespect my husband any more than I already had. Contacting you would've been very disrespectful to him.

"So we're over? Just like that?" he asks.

"Over? What do you mean over? We'd have to start something for it to be over."

"So you want me to believe that you felt absolutely nothing when we were together in the Bahamas. We had fun together and you know it."

"Yes, we had a lot of fun, but that's all it was, a fun time. Definitely nothing serious. Look, Dexter I'm sorry if I made you believe it was more than that, but trust me that's not how I felt then, and it's certainly not how I feel now. I'm not sure how you got my number, but I'm asking you to please not call me again." I say as I hang up the phone.

I decide to put the phone call in the back of my mind for now and go into the living room to finish my visit with my parents. After a few hours I pack up the baby and get ready to make our trip back home.

"I'm so glad you came to spend the day with us," my mom says as she hugs me.

"Yeah, baby girl, you definitely have to come back soon. I really enjoyed your company," my dad adds.

"We will be back soon, I promise," I say, hugging them before I get into the car to leave. The ride home is normally very short, but I can't get my phone call with Dexter out of my mind. I take the scenic route home so I can call Janelle and tell her about my phone call. I'm so glad I have her to talk to because I cannot keep this to myself. I need someone to help me understand what's going on with me.

"Hey, girlfriend," she answers the phone.

"Hey."

"Girl, what's wrong with you? You sound like you just lost your best friend."

"I've lost something, but it's not my best friend."

"What you lost?"

"Apparently, my damn mind for spending so much time with your cousin."

"What happened?"

"Girl, he called me and…"

"Oh my god, did Mark find out?"

"Are you making arrangements to come to my funeral? You know good and well Mark would kill me if he found out Dexter called me."

"Girl, don't do that to me. My heart is about to pound through my chest."

"Well, calm down and listen. He called me while I was at my parents' house visiting."

"And your crazy behind answered the phone?"

"I didn't recognize the number. I was prepared to tell the caller they had the wrong number until I heard his voice."

"What did he say? I talked with him a few weeks ago and he seemed fine."

"Well apparently he isn't. For some reason he just can't let the Bahamas go. What happened there was a mistake and nothing I ever plan to do again."

"Did you tell him that?"

"In so many words, I did."

“No. Don't tell him in so many words. You have to be straight up with him. Forget about hurting his feelings because he's obviously not getting it. I told him that you and Mark are back together. I told him that you had a baby and you’re happier than you’ve ever been.”

“You didn’t tell him that we thought he could've been the father, did you?”

“No, but he kept asking questions and started putting dates together. He asked me was the baby his and I said no. He thought I was lying for you, but I told him about the paternity test.”

“What was his reaction to that?” I ask curiously.

“He really didn't have much to say after that. He told me he needed to go and he'll talk with me later. That's the last time I talked to him.”

“I just need to tell Mark what's going on.” I say thinking out loud.

“Don't do that. That'll just cause more trouble. Let me try to handle Dexter.”

“I just love my husband and my child so much. The last thing I want is to mess things up again.”

“You won't trust me, I won't allow it. ” she says smiling.

The rest of the ride home is spent with me reminiscing about how simple life use to be. A time when my biggest concern was getting dinner started on time. I use to look at the soap operas and imagine living that kind of life, full of hurt and turmoil. These days I have not need to watch them; my life is a real-life soap opera.

Chapter 35

I spend all day Saturday in my classroom trying to get it ready for next week. My six weeks flew by, and leaving Kirsten really was bitter sweet. I'm ready to feel some sense of normalcy again, but I don't won't to leave my baby all day. I am blessed that Mark is a stay at home dad though. The thought of having to put her in a daycare really was depressing to me. I just like the idea that she's with her dad all day. Now I don't have to wonder if she's being neglected or mistreated. I know there are a lot of really good child care centers out there, I'm just not ready to send my baby to one of them yet.

I haven't seen Erica since she came to the hospital to drop off a fruit basket. I can't wait to catch up with her and hear how everything's going with her and her friend Sean. I make a mental note to give her a call later, then I try to hurry and work so I can get home to my baby girl. I've only been gone an hour, and already I feel like I'm about to lose my mind. I work for a few more minutes when I hear my cell phone ringing.

"What's wrong?" I ask when I see my home number on the screen.

"Nothing's wrong. Will you calm down? I am capable of taking care of a baby, you know."

"I'm sorry, Mark, I'm just so nervous when I'm away from her," I apologize.

"Holly, the baby's fine. I was calling because I need you to meet me somewhere."

"Where?"

"That's for me to know. You'll find out soon enough."

"Okay. When?"

"How much longer will you be there?"

"Actually I was wrapping things up. I should be leaving in about thirty minutes."

"Can you make it an hour?"

"I suppose, but Mark, what's this about?"

"Holly, listen to my voice. Do I sound nervous?"

"No."

"Then you shouldn't be either. Just trust me, okay?"

Easier said than done. "Okay Mark, fine. I'll stay another hour and then what?"

"Then meet me at the gas station on the corner by your school."

"Okay," I say, still very unsure about all this.

I continue working in my room until my hour is up. It wasn't as hard as I thought being that I still have so much to do. This is the one part about teaching I don't like. I hate putting up bulletin boards and all the other decorations around the room. I love the way it looks, but I don't like being the one to put it up.

I grab my purse and walk to my car. I'm very curious to see what Mark has up. He's been full of surprises lately. I don't know if this is his way of saying he's happy we're back together or if he's buttering me up for something. I hate I still have these negative thoughts each time he tries to do something nice for me, but I'm hoping that will change in time.

I pull up to the gas station and spot Mark's car by the gas pump. I pull up behind him and get out the car to try and get a little more information from him. As soon as I close the door, I look to my right and who do I see?

Oh my god, not today, not now. I pretend as if I don't even notice him as I continue walking to Mark. Getting back in the car now will look a little too obvious.

"Hey, babe," Mark greets me.

"Hey, where's the baby?" I say as I look in the empty backseat.

"She's with your mom. She's too funny."

"Who? Kirsten?"

"No, your mother. Didn't she just see Kirsten a couple days ago?"

"Yeah, when we went to spend the day. Why?"

"Because she was so excited to see her. You would think it's been months since she's last seen her."

"That's mom alright. Remember this is the woman who almost had a heart attack when Wal-Mart became Super Wal-Mart. She could hardly contain herself when we went to the store with her, remember?"

"I do. That was hilarious," he says as he puts the gas nozzle back on the pump.

"So, where are we..."

"Hello Mrs. James." Hearing his voice behind me sends my blood pressure right through the roof. I don't want to acknowledge him, but not acknowledging him will be a little too obvious.

"Hello, Mr. Foster."

"This is your husband, I assume?" he says as he holds his hand in an effort to shake Mark's hand.

"Yes, Mark James. And you are?" Mark says as he shakes Dexter's hand.

"Honey, this is Mr. Foster. I taught his daughter last year." Oh God I cannot believe this is happening right now. I know for sure this whole thing is about to blow up in my face.

"So I hear congratulations are in order." he says never taking his eyes off me.

"I assume you mean the baby." Marks says smiling like the proud father that he is.

"That's exactly what I mean... the baby." again he never stops looking at me. His glare feels like it's piercing right through me.

"Well, Mr. Foster, it was really nice seeing you, but we really must get going," I say as I turn to walk to my car. I'm surprised I'm able to make it because my legs feel like they're about to shake completely off my body. I'm relieved when I'm finally able to sit in my car. Mark better pull off fast or I'm leaving him right here. As if he's read my mind, he pulls out of the parking lot. I jump when I hear my cell phone ringing.

"Hello."

"Hey. Just follow me, okay?"

"Okay."

I'm following Mark, just as he asked me to do and I have a funny feeling I know where we're going. I could be wrong though because I'm not thinking straight at all at the moment. I pick up my phone to call Janelle, but her voice mail picks up. I start to leave a message, but decide against it. What I need to say does not need to be left on a voicemail.

When Mark exits the interstate, I know for sure where he's going. We drive for a few minutes longer before we pull into the parking lot of Ninfa's Mexican Restaurant. This is where Mark brought me the night he proposed. In the past whenever we would argue and he wanted to make up, he would bring me here. We haven't been arguing so all I can assume is he just wants some alone time with me.

"Surprised?" Mark asks as he opens my car door.

"I must admit that I am. To what do I owe this little surprise?"

"We hadn't been on a date in a while. I saw how sad you were today when you left out, so I thought this would maybe put a smile on your face. I know how much you love your Mexican food."

"I didn't realize I looked so sad. I must admit I wasn't happy about leaving my baby, but I didn't know it showed."

"Good afternoon," the hostess greets us as we enter. "Table for two?" she asks.

"Yes," Mark and I both respond.

"Right this way. Your waiter will be right with you," she informs us after we're both seated.

"Thanks," Mark and I both say.

We are only seated for a few minutes when two drinks arrive at our table. "Oh no, these aren't ours," I tell the waiter who ignores me and walks away.

"Well looks like we have some free drinks," Mark says as he proceeds to drink.

"Mark, don't drink that, that's not for you. Someone is probably looking for their order."

"They'll be okay."

Just as he says that, two plates arrive. "I'm sorry, sir, but we haven't ordered yet." Again he totally ignores me. "Okay, this is ridiculous. I need to find a manager."

"Holly, please just calm down. I'm sure they'll figure out their mistake and fix it."

I look at the food and something looks very familiar about these dishes. As I continue to gaze at them, I hear music. I look around and find a saxophonist entering the room. I know he's not playing what I think he's playing. He's not playing "Always and Forever." Just when I think I can't get any more confused, Mark stands up and begins to serenade me. He has a voice that can put anyone to shame, but he doesn't use it.

I cannot believe he's doing this. This is the song he sang to me on our wedding day. I have tears in my eyes then just like I do now. I have so many emotions going through me. As I sit here listening to him it finally dawns on me that the food and drinks are exactly what we ordered on that night, the night he asked if I would change his life forever and become his wife. I was so happy back then. Life for me was just beginning. The man of my dreams wanted me to be his wife. I felt like I was the envy of all women because I was marrying Mark James.

Mark continues singing. When he finishes everyone in the restaurant, including me, stands up in a rousing applause.

"Talk about being surprised," I say when he returns to our table.

"I just want you to remember how happy we were that night. I know a lot has happened since then, but I do still love you just as much, if not more, today as I did back then."

This time the tears really begin to fall. Not because I'm so happy, but because I'm so sad. Sad because of all the lies and deceit we've allowed to come into our marriage. Sad because as much as he wants to believe it, things will never be the same again. The things we've done cannot be erased, no matter how bad we wish they could. I'm sad because Mark planned this great surprise for me and I can't enjoy it because I'm too afraid Dexter will walk in at any minute and tell everything.

"What are you thinking about?"

"How nice this is and how much I appreciate you for doing it for me."

"I've neglected you for too long, Holly, and you didn't deserve that. You're the most honest, respectable woman I know. It still tears me apart that I was so stupid."

"Mark, please. We've both made our mistakes."

"You were drunk, I was just stupid."

"Well, we can spend our time comparing who messed up worse or we can enjoy the rest of our time together. Which would you prefer?"

"You're right. Let's toast to new beginnings and a bright future for us and our family."

"I'll certainly drink to that," I say as I take a sip of my drink. "Um, Mark, you do realize I'm legal now?" I tease him about my drink because he ordered a virgin daiquiri. I was still eighteen when he proposed, which meant I couldn't drink alcohol back then, but hell I'm grown now and I need a grown woman's drink. Bad.

"I know, honey? Would you like me to order you something a little stronger?"

"How about a lot stronger," I say, laughing.

Chapter 36

I wake up this morning with Kirsten snuggled under me and Mark spooned right behind me. Last night was truly magical. After dinner, I went to get Kirsten and Mark went home. The first couple hours we continued our stroll down memory lane. We spent the next hour playing with the baby. We fall asleep with him holding me and me holding her. While our night wasn't filled with sex, it was still very magical. I've wanted this my whole life. More than anything I wanted to have a family with the man I love. So why can't I fully enjoy it? I know I've made a mess of my life, but don't I deserve another chance? Don't I deserve to have this happy family that I've always dreamed of? Am I that terrible? Is this God's way of punishing me for committing adultery? Mark did the same thing, why is he able to just move on?

"You up?" Mark asks as he kisses my neck."

"Yeah, I'm up."

"Good. Want you put Kirsten in the stroller and join me for a morning run."

"No thanks I'm not *that* woke," I say, turning over to get comfortable.

"You sure?" he asks as he gets out the bed.

"Very," I moan.

"Okay suit yourself, but just so you know running gives me energy. So if you're there when I return I'll assume it's to help me burn some of it off."

"Hey, watch your mouth around my child." I instruct as I pretend to cover her ear.

"For some reason I don't think she has a clue what I'm referring to." he jokes.

I give him a smile as he disappears into the bathroom. *Why can't life be simple?* As soon as that thought leave my head I hear my phone vibrating on the end table next to the bed. It's probably Janelle. We didn't' talk at all yesterday so she's doing her check to make sure I'm still alive. She says that whenever we miss a day of talking. I feel like I can just die whenever I see Dexter's number. I pick up Kirsten who's sleeping soundly and walk out of the room. I may be frazzled, but not enough to leave my baby alone in my bed. I press talk on the phone as I'm walking downstairs.

"Can you talk?" He says when I answer the phone.

"Why are you calling me?"

"Damn, so it's like that?"

"Dexter, look. I can't keep playing this little game with you. I know I've made it clear that you are not to call me ever again."

"Holly, we're talking on the phone, now having sex. Who are we hurting by conversing?"

"You don't get it do you? What happened between us was a mistake. Trust me when I say it will never happen again. And, stay away from me and my husband."

"The look on your face was priceless." He says laughing. "Did you really think I would tell him?" Isn't it obvious that I really care for you? I wouldn't do anything to hurt you. Do you think I take this abuse from just anyone?"

"This is not a game, this is my life and I take it very seriously."

"Really? You could've fooled me Holly."

"What the hell does that mean?"

"It means…"

"Alright, babe I'll be back." Mark announces as he comes downstairs. "I think I'll go to the YMCA down the street since it looks like it's about to pour down outside."

"Okay, have fun."

"You should come with me, instead of sitting on the phone gossiping with Janelle all morning."

"No thank you."

"If he only knew." Dexter says breaking the silence.

"Look, I know that I messed up, okay. I take responsibility for that…"

"Really? You're taking responsibility for that. And just how are you doing that?"

"Dexter what do you want from me?"

"I want you. Can't you understand that? I want you. I didn't mean to fall in love with you, but I did and I'm sorry I just can't let you go that easy. I'm not asking you to leave your husband. I understand that will never happen, but can I at least have a piece of you?"

“You talk about me as if I’m a slice of pie or something. Can you just have a piece of me, what does that mean?”

“That means all I want is what we had. Nothing more, nothing less.”

“Dexter you need to move on. What we had really wasn't that serious. What's wrong with you?”

“Holly, It’s not like I’m saying you have to choose me or your family. You get to have your cake and eat it too. What’s wrong with that?”

“I’m hanging up now, and I’m begging you to please stop calling me. If you don’t I will change the number.” I say as I hang up the phone. I want to scream. I want to go somewhere and just scream. What in the hell have I done. Everything in me tells me that this is going to get bad. Dexter just won’t let go. Why didn’t someone warn me that he’s a complete psycho.

By the time I hang up with Dexter, Kirsten pops her head up from the play pen. She sleeps hard just like her daddy. I just knew she would wake up when I picked her up from our bed, but she didn’t. I go to the kitchen to warm her morning bottle and try hard not to let my conversation with Dexter consume my every thought today.

After feeding and bathing Kirsten. I put her in her swing and start my Saturday cleaning. I’m so worked up today that I clean the house from top to bottom. I clean things that don’t even need cleaning. I just need some way to work off all of this negative energy I’m feeling. Maybe Mark’s right. Maybe I should’ve joined him for a workout. That’s a great stress reliever.

I’m upstairs hanging up some of Kirsten’s clothes when I hear Mark coming in. I hear him talking and initially think he must be on the phone that is until I hear another voice. I walk downstairs and when I see Dexter standing there I pray and ask God to just take me now because dying will be a lot better than living hell on earth.

“Oh hey honey.” Marks says when he sees me standing on the stairs.

I can’t open my mouth. My eyes are locked on Dexter. My whole body feels like it’s frozen in place.

“Holly, you okay babe?” It’s not until he touches my hand that I’m able to respond. I didn’t even notice him walking my way.

“I’m fine honey, but what…”

“Oh, I’m sorry. I ran into Mr. Robinson…”

“Please, call me Dexter.” Dexter interrupts.

"Well, I ran into Dexter at the Y. He remembered me from the gas station yesterday."

"Oh. Really? So, Mr. Robinson, to what do we owe this surprise visit?" I ask glaring at him so hard and willing him to blow up right in front of our faces.

"Well," Mark began "as we were working out we discovered that we have something in common."

"Yes," Dexter says "we have something in common." he smirks as he eyes me up and down.

I again direct my attention back towards Mark because I'm starting to get sicker by the minute. "Mark, may I speak to you in the other room?"

"Sure honey. Hey, make yourself at home." he says to Dexter.

"If you say so," he says with quite a smug expression on his face and with a lot of sarcasm in his voice.

Once in the other room I try hard to keep my composure. "Mark, what is he doing here?"

"I told you honey, we…"

"Yes, you have something in common, I know, but what is it?"

"We both love antique cars. After talking to him during our workout I mentioned that I'd just bought a fixer upper and he was interested in seeing it. Holly, are you upset that he's here?"

"What? No, of course not. It's just that, well you know how I feel about parents or students knowing too much about my personal life, and the fact that you just showed up with him. Could you have called and given me a heads-up that we're having company. What if I was walking around here naked, then what?"

"Holly, you never walk around naked."

"That's beside the point. Just give me some kind of warning before you bring company home please?"

"I promise. Now come on before he thinks we're talking about him."

We leave the room and I'm thinking hard of how I can get this lunatic out of my damn house. He has really crossed the line this time. I don't know how, but some way I have to get him out of my life. I look outside as Mark and Dexter admire his 58 Porsche convertible. I remember when Mark bought it at the auction a couple years ago. He came home like he'd just won a million dollars. He was so happy to have that car. Who ever owned it before really took good care of it because it still looks good, but of course Mark, being a man, has a lot of things he wants to do to it. I'll never understand.

Mark looks so happy to have someone to share his love of cars with. My whole body feels like it's on fire, I'm so angry. Messing with me is one thing, but now he comes here and pretends to befriend my husband, now that's totally different. Why do I feel like I've opened Pandora's Box, and all the evil it contains is being unleashed on me?

Chapter 37

My favorite part of the day is bathing Kirsten and getting her dressed for bed. In spite of everything's that 's going wrong in my life, my baby is still my bright spot. Having Kirsten reminds me of my childhood and playing with my baby dolls. Since I'm an only child, my dolls were my only source of company. I still remember all of their names. I have to ask Mom whatever happened to them. For the longest she kept them packed away. My mom believes in keeping things, especially my things. My back-to-the-past moment is interrupted when the phone rings. I wait for Mark to answer it, but as usual he's doesn't.

"Mark, can you get the phone, please?" I holler into the living room where he's working on the computer.

"Got it," he hollers back.

I can never understand how he can sit right by the phone and let it ring. That drives me nuts. He always says he know it's not for him so he doesn't bother answering it. I always look at him like that's the dumbest thing I've ever heard. I hear him talking and wait on him to bring me the phone, but he never does. I guess this time he's wrong, the call is for him.

I finish dressing the baby and I'm preparing to feed her when he walks in the kitchen.

"Hey, who was on the phone?" I ask curiously.

"Diane," he says, looking and sounding confused.

"Diane who?" is all I am able to say.

"Do we know any other Dianes?" he asks.

"No. We already know one too many if you ask me."

"Well, that would be the one."

"What does she want now?"

"Honey, I have no idea. She said she wants to come over and talk to us about something."

"Did she really say us, or did she say you?"

"No she said us, honestly."

"If she wants to talk to both of us then this cannot be good."

"I know. I'm not getting a good feeling about this either."

"Well, let's not jump to conclusions. Maybe she's finally come to her senses and wants Tyler to spend more time with us."

"Holly, I wish I could think like that, but I know Diane, and nothing is ever that simple with her."

"Well, I guess we'll find out soon enough. What time is she coming?"

"She's waiting on me to call her back."

"For what?"

"I wasn't going to tell her to come to our house without discussing it with you first."

I smile because he's trying so hard to walk a straight line. I can tell he doesn't want to do anything he feels may upset me. "Mark, it's okay. She can come because I want to know what this is about."

"I'll call and let her know."

Mark goes into the living room to call her back, and I'm sitting here wondering all over the place. What in the world could she be up to now? I never put anything past her. With her, there's always a motive, and usually it's to get Mark all to herself.

Mark and I are sitting in the living room watching TV—or at least pretending to be watching when the doorbell rings.

"I'll get it," he says, getting up to go to the door.

"Diane," I hear him greet her.

"Hello, Mark," she says.

"Come on in," he says, showing her to an empty spot on the sofa.

"Hello, Diane," I say, not to appear too rude.

"Hello, Mrs. James."

Mrs. James seems so formal considering all we've been through, but I can't bring myself to allow her to call me Holly. That just seems way too friendly, and we're nowhere near that point.

"I know you're wondering why I requested this visit," she says, interrupting my thoughts.

"The thought has crossed our minds," Mark says, being sarcastic.

"Just so you know, this isn't easy for me at all. The last thing in the world I want to do is sit here and have this conversation with the two of you."

Obviously she doesn't know me very well because if she did she would know I'm really good at reading between the lines. I know exactly what she means by that. She would much rather have this conversation with Mark, but not me. Unfortunately for her, Mark and I are a package deal, and I'm assuming she's come to realize that because she asked to meet with both of us.

"Diane, what's this about?" Mark asks, getting really frustrated really fast.

"I want to talk to you about Tyler."

"So I guess you've come to the realization you do need help with him," he says.

"I do, but not for the reasons you may be thinking."

"Then what? What's going on?" I finally chime in.

"Well like I said, this is really hard for me. I know you may not believe this but besides from Tyler you're the closest thing I have to family," she says, looking at Mark.

"I'm not your family, Diane," he responds, looking from her to me.

"I know that, but considering the fact that I don't have anyone else in my life, I guess I've come to see you as that."

"Okay, so what is it you need?" I ask, getting really frustrated with this conversation.

"I'm sick," she says.

"Sick how, Diane? Would you please just come on and get this out so we can go on with our lives," Mark says, now more irritated than before.

"I'm very sick, which is why I needed to talk to you. I got a call from my doctor last Wednesday and she asked me to come in to discuss some tests. I met with her the next day, and she informed me that I have brain cancer. I tried to call you several times to tell you. I'm sure you saw the missed call, but obviously you decided not to return my calls. I'd just received the most devastating news of my life, and I really needed someone, and forgive me, but it's not like I have many people to lean on," she says to Mark.

I know I shouldn't care about her feelings, but for some reason I'm starting to feel a lump in my throat. I don't even know if this fool is being honest now, while I'm getting all emotional. "Diane, why should we believe you now? Mark has already said you've pulled tricks in the past in an effort to get him to stay. How do we know this isn't just another one of your little games?"

"I understand why you would be hesitant to believe me. I haven't given you any reason to trust me at all, but the fact that I felt compelled to come here and talk to you should tell you something," she says, trying to convince me of her honesty.

I look over at Mark who's sitting there like he has no emotions at all. I don't even know if he heard what she just said. He looks like he's a million miles away."Okay, so you're sick. What does that have to do with us?" Mark finally asks in the coldest, most non-caring voice I've ever heard from him. I don't know much about their relationship other than they've messed around for nine years, had Tyler, and according to him, she's very manipulative, but it's obvious from his expression and his voice that he has no care at all for this woman. I don't know if this is a front for me or if this is really how he is with her now. I really don't know what emotion I'm supposed to display. Should I have a cold heart and tell her to just deal with it or am I supposed to let the bull go and try to be there for her? She is obviously in need. Why else would she come to us?

"It has everything to do with you." she says to Mark. "I'm taking care of your child, or have you forgotten that?"

"No, have you?" he responds.

"Okay, look, this back-and-forth isn't going to get us anywhere," I tell the two of them. "Diane, I'm very sorry that you're sick, and I know it must be a lot to deal with, but you still haven't told us what you want from us."

"Holly, I can't believe you're sitting here entertaining her. She's made our life a living hell. Can't you see this is her way of trying to gain my sympathy? Well, I have news for you, Diane. It's not working," he says.

"Mark, can I speak with you alone for a minute?" I say, silently daring him to tell me no.

"Sure, honey," he says.

"Excuse us a minute, Diane," I say as Mark and I exit the room.

"Holly, I don't care what you say, I'm not going to allow this woman to destroy us again. I'm not even giving her the opportunity," he begins when we make it to the kitchen.

"Mark, look, I hope you don't take this the wrong way, but she wasn't the only one involved in ruining our marriage. The last time I checked you were a willing participant. The point is, I forgave you, and now it's time for us to forgive her. I truly believe she's sick, and from what I know about brain cancer, it's very serious. If she's reaching out to us for help, then it's our Christian duty to help her. I know we've strayed away from our Christian life, but we were both raised in the church, and when it comes down to it, we know right from wrong. We may not always make the right decisions, but we can at least try, especially in a case as serious as this. Anyway, if she's lying then we'll find out, but for now we have to trust she wouldn't lie about this."

"Holly, she lied about so much in the past. Why wouldn't she lie about this?"

"Maybe she wasn't in a good place then, Mark. Who knows why people lie, but we can't let her past lies be the determining factor to if we're going to help her or not. We have to do this, Mark."

"Look, this is your call. If you want to trust her then fine, but just know I don't believe a word out of her mouth."

"Let's just go back in there and see what else she has to say," I insist.

"Fine," is all he says before he walks out of the kitchen.

Once we sit down Diane begins explaining her real reason for coming to talk to us.

"I know this is very difficult for you all to believe, and I understand that, but just know I'm not here for personal reasons. I'm here because of Tyler. My doctor is trying to sound optimistic about my prognosis, and she's encouraging me to do the same, but I know the possibility of me dying is very real and very likely. Right now I'm the only one Tyler feels he can depend on and trust, and I know that's my fault, Mark. I know you tried to have a better relationship with him, but my selfishness got in the way. I felt like you'd already taken away my hope of having a real family, and next, you would try to take Tyler away too."

"It was never my intention to take Tyler away from you, Diane."

"I know that. Like I said, I was being selfish. I wasn't thinking about what was best for Tyler, which is to know his dad and the rest of his family," she says, looking from Mark to me.

I'm shocked. She must really be sick if she considers me to be Tyler's family. I know in her healthy mind she would have never muttered those words.

"Obviously, when I die Tyler will have to come and live with you guys. Like I said I'm estranged from my family, and I don't have any real friends that I would trust to raise my son. I would like to make his transition as smooth as possible. If the offer still stands I would like for him to start coming to spend more time with you here. The more he's here, the easier it'll be for him once, well…you know," she says, beginning to cry.

"Diane, we would love for Tyler to start coming to spend more time with us. You know I'd never do anything to hurt him," I say, trying to reassure her he'll be well taken care of.

"Okay, well I'd better get going. Tyler will be getting off the bus soon, and he'll have a fit if I'm not there to meet him."

"Well take care, and I'm sure we'll be in touch," I say, trying to be the cordial one since Mark isn't moving from his spot.

I walk her out and walk back inside with my mind full. I'm thinking about everything Diane just laid on us. Even with everything Mark, Diane, and I have gone through, my heart still hurts for her. Being a mother, I know how I feel just thinking about leaving my child. My prayer is always to live long enough to see her grown and able to take care of herself. I know Mark loves Kirsten and will do anything in his power for her, but the bottom line is he's not her momma. I walk past Mark and go straight to Kirsten's room where she's still sound asleep. I can't help myself. I go over and pick her up and rock her in the glider. I know the importance of cherishing each and every moment.

I stay in Kirsten's room a lot longer than normal. I still have so many thoughts running through my head. My life is truly turning into a roller-coaster ride, but unlike the theme park ride, my roller coaster is ongoing. I can't choose to get on and off. This is my life and I would say it needed a little tweaking, but this is more than I bargained for.

After putting Kirsten back in her bed, I go to my bedroom to call Janelle. I have to tell her about this. It's funny how the table has turned. I use to be the one receiving the "girl, you're not going to believe this" phone calls, and now I'm calling her with them almost every day.

I tell her the whole story, and she's beside herself with disbelief.

"Okay, so is this the part where you kicked her lying behind out the house?" Janelle asks after I tell her about the whole ordeal with Diane.

"No, Janelle, I didn't kick her out," I explain.

"What? Well why the hell not?" she asks.

"Did you hear what I said? The woman is dying. I'm not heartless."

"Well I'm not heartless either, but I'm also not gullible. Did you see her doctor's report? I wouldn't believe anything she says without concrete proof to back it up. He's told you that she's lied before, I mean she can do it again. Why wouldn't she do it again? What exactly does she have to lose?"

"Okay, and on the flip side of that, what exactly does she have to gain?" I ask her.

"Oh Holly, please. Your skin may be damn near white, but you are not blonde. Don't tell me you don't see her strategy. She gains sympathy from the one person in this world she wants more than anything else—the person who happens to be your husband. Why would you take that chance?"

"I don't know, Janelle. I just truly believe she's telling the truth. I mean think about it, she's willing to allow Tyler to spend time with me. Don't you think that says a lot?"

"Yes. I think it says now she's playing her trump card. Tyler is the one true connection she has with Mark. Why wouldn't she use him to bring his daddy home?"

"Maybe I'm too trusting, I really don't know, but a huge part of me trusts that is not her angle. I don't believe she would stoop so low."

"Girl, please, I know conniving women like her. Hell, I am like her. When we set our sights on someone we do whatever we have to do to get them. Believe that."

"Janelle, I'm not making excuses for her, but she's a woman scorned. She did what she did to me and Mark because she was hurting. Why else would she make those calls and slash my tires? Does that sound like a happy person to you?"

"Hell no she's not happy because you have what she wants, and scorn my ass. That bitch is crazy, and I'm sorry I didn't realize that made it right."

"I didn't say it made it right, but I do understand."

"All I have to say is you're a much better woman than I am. If it were me I would not let that woman within ten feet of my husband."

"I forgave Mark, which means I have to trust him. Diane can try anything she wants, but it's up to him to consent. I guess I need to remind you just like I had to remind him. Diane was not the only one who did wrong. Mark played a big part, actually a bigger part because he's the one I'm married to, not her."

"Holly, I hear what you're saying, but I don't know. Please just be careful. You have no idea what this woman may be capable of doing. We've both heard of women who went off the deep end because they couldn't have the man they wanted."

"Okay, you really watch way too much television."

"Say whatever you want, but it does happen in real life too. I just don't want you to get yourself into something that could end up hurting you."

"I hear what you're saying, and I do understand you're coming from a good place, but please trust that I would never do anything that I feel will put me or my family in any danger. I simply cannot turn my back on another human being who's reaching out to me for help. It just so happens this person is my husband's ex-mistress."

"Okay fine, but just know I think this is a very, very bad idea. Oh, and did I mention this is a bad idea?" she just had to throw that in there, yet again.

"Yes, I think you've mentioned it a few times," I respond.

"Okay, well change of subject. Have you started planning my godchild's Baby Blessing? What are your plans after church?"

"You are so behind. I started planning that the day I found out I was pregnant."

"Why doesn't that surprise me?"

"Anyway, yes, I have started, and Mark thinks I'm going way overboard, but what does he know?"

"Does he not understand the significance of this day? What's wrong with him?"

"He's a man. They don't understand. You know I'm finding that out a lot since I've had the baby. Mark doesn't let much bother him, whereas I get nervous about everything. If Kirsten coughs wrong, I'm ready to head to the emergency room."

"You had to have a baby to find that out? I could've told you that a long time ago."

Janelle and I spend the next few hours talking about the difference between men and women and everything else under the sun. It's funny how we’ve known each other for years and can still find so much to talk about.

After hanging up with Janelle I retreated to my bathroom—my thinking place, my in-house getaway. Tonight is definitely a bubble bath night. I want to relax and let all my troubles wash away. I wish it were that simple. I wish I could just pull the plug and all my problems would just go down the drain. I would wave good-bye to Dexter, Diane, and God forgive me, but even Tyler.

Just as I arrange my bath pillow and get in my most comfortable position, my cell phone rings. I look at the screen and see that it’s Dexter. I immediately push the ignore button and decide it's time to change my number once again. I don't know what excuse I'll give Mark, but I have to do this. I cannot let this continue. If this isn't the answer then I'll have to take more drastic measures. I've never been put in this position before, where I'm scheming to get rid of someone. This is more Janelle's thing. I can say when it comes to my family, all bets are off. Just because I've never done it doesn't mean I can't do it. If Dexter insists on playing this game, then I say bring it on.

Chapter 38

It's been two weeks since I had my number changed. Obviously it worked because I haven't heard a word from or seen Dexter since that night. I'm praying he's decided it's just not worth it and moved on with someone else. Janelle did mention that his mom's prognosis wasn't very good. I'm assuming he's devoting all his time to taking care of her these days. Whatever the case, I'm just thankful for the two weeks of peace and hopefully there are many more to follow.

Today is a happy day, and there's nothing anyone can do to ruin it for me. The baby blessing was simply beautiful and now Janelle is officially Kirsten's Godmother and Larry is her Godfather. Our pastor was so nice to agree to do the ceremony on a Saturday. Larry has to go out of town and won't be here tomorrow. Janelle swears we're trying to set them up, but I wouldn't dare do that to poor Larry. He thinks he's a player, but he has nothing on Janelle. I feel like today is not only a celebration for Kirsten, but for our family as well. We've managed to get through a lot and now it's time we truly put our focus into our family. I guess I'm the one who needs to refocus on family. Mark's been great as a husband and a father. I feel like I've been absent for so long. My body's been here with them, but my mind has been everywhere else. I'm just hoping I can finally get on track and start to live the boring life I've come to miss here lately.

Kirsten's celebration dinner will start in a couple hours and I'm running around the house like a madwoman. One would think this party is for me. I guess in a sense it is because it's not like Kirsten is going to remember any of this. Mark still thinks I've lost my mind. He simply cannot understand why I'm spending so much money on a party for a baby who will most likely fall asleep in the middle of the festivities. I can't make him understand how special this day is for me. I've dreamed of this day for a very long time. I just want to share it with all of our family and friends.

"Holly, did my sister call?" Mark says as he comes in the family room.

"Yes. She should be here around two."

"Great. Did she say if she's staying here?"

"She insisted on staying in a hotel, but you know I didn't let her get away with that. In the end we decided she'll stay here." I say smiling.

"She knows you always get your way. I don't even know why she tries with you," he says as he comes up behind me and wraps his arms around my waist.

"Please, that only works with you. Your sister is a tough cookie, you know that," I say, laughing.

"So exactly how many people are we expecting today?" he says as he looks around at all the decorations and food.

"Well, it's not like I know that many people. I did invite a few coworkers and a few people from the church, but other than that, just my parents, Janelle, Larry, and your sister."

"You did all of this for them?" he says, pointing at the banner and balloons. I went way out for this day. I went with a princess theme because Mark and I always refer to Kirsten as our little princess. I must've bought every princess decoration there was at Party City. The balloons practically cover the ceiling. There's a big CONGRATULATIONS, KIRSTEN banner hanging near the kitchen, which overlooks the family room. I have streamers everywhere. Mark says I've turned our family room into the Pepto Bismol room with all the pink. He can say what he wants, but I love it.

"No. I did all of this for my baby."

"For your baby? Oh, okay," he says, being very sarcastic.

"I know she won't remember it, but we'll have plenty of pictures and not to mention the video her dad's doing."

"Oh he is, is he?"

"Yes he is, so get ready."

Just as I'm putting the finishing touches on the decorations, the doorbell rings. I'm so excited our first guest has arrived.

"Oh hey, Janelle," I respond, somewhat disappointed.

"You don't have to sound so excited," she says.

"I'm sorry, girl. I'm just so anxious to start the celebration."

"Okay. You're going to have to chill. If you're doing all this now, I can't wait to see what the first birthday is going to be like. You probably have a scrapbook of ideas already," she says laughing. When she notice I'm not laughing with her, she immediately cuts it off.

"Holly, you don't?"

"Well, how am I suppose to remember my ideas if I don't keep them all together?" I say trying to convince her I'm not crazy, not that crazy anyway.

"You are truly a special case." she says laughing again.

I had to laugh at that one. I tell Janelle that all the time, so now she has the chance to get me back. In the midst of the laughter I'm reminded how thankful I am to have such a special friend like Janelle she really helps me out a lot. If it weren't for her I probably would've completely lost my mind dealing with all the mess in my life.

"Girl, anyway enough about that. Back to my goddaughter's party: Do you need me to do anything?"

"No. I actually just finished when you rang the doorbell."

"Oh, I have such perfect timing."

"You always do," I say, smiling along with her.

"I'm about to change the little honoree, and we'll meet you in the family room," I tell her then head to the bedroom.

I hear the doorbell ring and Mark answers it. I can't tell who it is, but I do hear little people, which means it's one of Kirsten's guests. I'm so excited. I can't wait to see her interacting with the other kids. She's always with Mark and me, and she hardly ever gets the opportunity to play with kids her age.

It's now a little after two, and the party is going well. The kids are running around playing and having fun. It's so good seeing Kirsten interacting with the other babies. I guess at her age there's only so much playing you can do. The main thing is that she's having fun and I'm enjoying seeing her have fun. We allow them to eat and play a little longer. Afterward, I decide to bring out the beautiful Bible shaped cake. Her cake is absolutely gorgeous. Just as we're about to cut the cake I hear the phone ring. Mark excuses himself to answer it.

"You guys go ahead," he says as he hands the camcorder to Janelle.

"Oh wait," I say. "I forgot the plates. I'll be right back."

I run to get the pack of plates off the kitchen table and I hear Mark on the phone.

"What?...Wait. You have to slow down. I can't understand you."

I'm looking at him because it's obvious by his tone the call is serious.

"She did what?" he says. "Okay. Where is she now?"

I'm still trying to figure out what's going on because he's not paying any attention to me to tell me anything.

"Look, just calm down and I'm on my way," he says then hangs up the phone.

"What's wrong? Who was that?"

"I don't know what's wrong. That was Tyler saying something about his mom being on the floor and he can't wake her up. I have to get over there. I'll call you later," he says as he runs out the door.

"But…" I try to say but it's too late because he's already gone. I put on my "everything is okay" face and go back outside to continue my baby's celebration. We decided that things were getting a little too crowded in the house, so we moved outside so the kids could run around and play.

"Okay, everyone, cake is being served." I say trying to pretend like I'm not sick with worry.

We eat and enjoy the rest of Kirsten's day. I'm really glad I invited the other children because initially it was just going to be a small family gathering. I'm talking to the other moms, and it's really insightful to hear them talking about their children. I think mothers are the only people who find great joy in sitting and talking about children all day. The festivities are almost over when Erica shows up. I invited her to be nice, but I really didn't expect her to come. Not that I didn't want her here, but I just didn't think she'd be comfortable around a bunch of people she really don't know. I guess she decided coming here was better than being home alone all day.

"Hey, Holly, I'm so sorry I'm late," she says as she comes up to me.

"Oh, no don't apologize. I'm just happy you came."

"I didn't know what to buy, so I got a gift card. I hope that's okay."

"You didn't have to bring anything, but thank you so much for the gift card," I say, as she hands it over to me.

"So where is the beautiful princess anyway?" she says looking around for Kirsten.

"She's over there sitting on her grandpa's lap," I say, pointing toward my dad.

"Oh my God, oh my God, Holly, I have to go," she says as she turns to leave.

"Wait. Where are you going? Why are you leaving? You just got here?"

"I really have to go," she says, obviously disturbed by something.

"Wait. Come here," I say as I escort her inside so we can talk alone.

"Now, what's going on? You look like you've seen a ghost."

"Holly, we're leaving now, thanks for inviting us." Monica a young lady from church says as she walks up to Erica and me.

"Okay, thank you all so much for coming." I say as I walk them to the door. I turn to motion for Erica to stay right there. I really need to get to the bottom of her strange behavior.

Once I walk Monica out, I quickly return to Erica.

"Okay, what's up with you?" I ask.

"I feel like I've seen a ghost," she says with this far-away look in her eyes. I have no idea what's going on, but something has her shaken up. I take her to the guest bedroom so we can talk in private.

"Erica, talk to me. What's wrong?"

"I just saw my dad." she says quietly, almost whispering.

"Your dad? I don't understand. Aren't your parents in California?"

"Yes, my mom and my stepdad are, but my dad is in your backyard."

"Okay, Erica, you are confusing me and scaring me all at the same time. What do you mean your dad is in my backyard?"

"Holly, I know this is going to sound crazy because it sounds crazy to me too, but the man that's holding your baby is my dad."

"Oh no, honey, that's my dad. Does he favor your father or something?"

"No, Holly. I'm positive that's my father."

"Erica, I really don't know what you're trying to do, but I'm telling you that he is not your father. He couldn't possibly be your father because he's my father."

"Okay, well let me prove it to you."

"How are you going to do that? You have a home DNA test in your purse?" I say, getting very agitated by her accusations. There's no way that's her dad. I wait while she goes in her purse and pulls out her wallet. I wait for what feels like an eternity for her to find her proof.

"Look, Erica, I really don't have time for this. I need to get back and see my other guests out." Just as I get those words out she shows me a picture. I feel like my legs are too weak to hold me up. There right in front of my face is a picture of a younger version of my dad. "Where did you get this?" I question.

"From my mom. She's never lied to me about who my real father is. I've always known the man that raised me and loves me as his own was not my biological father. My mom gave me this picture when I was in high school and was really going through the unwanted child syndrome."

"The unwanted child syndrome? What's that?" I ask, still staring in disbelief at the picture.

"When I was in high school I went through a depressed period. I'd convinced myself I did something wrong to make my dad not want me. I was almost sixteen, and I didn't even know what his voice sounded like. He never visited. He never called or wrote to me. He didn't know if I was dead or alive, and he obviously didn't care. Do you know what that does to a child to think your own parent doesn't want you? Let me tell you it's not good," she says.

It took everything in me to stay in this room with her. I wanted so badly to run outside and confront my father about this. How in the hell did this happen? Does my mother know she's married to a cheat? This girl is at least eleven or twelve years younger than I am, so that means he stepped out of his marriage. The nerve of him. He practically blew up when I told him about Mark and me, and he did the same thing. Well now, isn't that the pot calling the kettle black? Talking about marriage and how serious it is. I guess that only applies to other people's marriages because his wasn't very important to him. I guess I'm so wrapped up in my thoughts that I don't even notice that Erica left.

Once I go back outside, most of the guests have already left. Janelle and my mom are cleaning up and my cheating dad is still sitting with Kirsten. I know I have some nerve getting upset with him after everything I've done, but I'm not the one going around preaching about the importance of marriage and the vows. Giving all this advice he couldn't even follow. I guess he assumed it was water under the bridge and no one would ever find out about his little secret. He's old, he should know by now that secrets always have a way of rearing their ugly little heads. I want so badly to discuss this with him, but I decide tonight's not the night. I need time to process this myself. If I talk with him tonight, I already know it's not going to be pretty, and I have to remember he's still my father and I have to remain respectful, even if I don't feel he deserves it.

Apparently my sister-in-law is tired because it doesn't take her long to fall asleep. I'm glad because now I don't have to hide my emotions anymore. I haven't heard from Mark since he left earlier today. I tried to call him several times but only got his voice mail. I'm pissed off with my father, and I don't think I can hold it in any longer. I'm still wondering how I was able to hold it together considering I had every emotion possible running through my body.

I decide to take my bath and get ready for bed and hopefully by that time at least one of my worries will be over—Mark will be home and I'll finally find out what happened. I go to the medicine cabinet for Tylenol because my head feels like it's about to split open. I want so bad to take the Tylenol P.M, but I need to stay coherent, at least until Mark gets here. I swallow my pill and can't wait for it to work its magic. Just as I begin to run my bath water I hear the bell from the house alarm, which lets me know Mark is home. I can't get out the room fast enough. I put on my robe and run to the front room to meet him. I can't get to him fast enough before I throw my arms around him and start to cry hysterically.

"Babe, what's wrong? Did something happen? Is the baby okay?" Mark asks, becoming worried by my behavior.

I shake my head because I can't open my mouth to respond right now. He holds me for a while longer, then he leads me over to the sofa.

"What's wrong? Why are you so upset?"

"Today was just very stressful, and there's a lot I need to tell you, but first tell me about Diane. What happened to her?"

"Well apparently she had a seizure. I'm sorry. I know I ran out of here without really telling you anything, but I didn't know what was going on. Tyler called and he was hysterical. He kept saying his mom was on the floor and he couldn't wake her up. I just knew I had to get to him and fast."

"Mark, you don't have to apologize to me. I knew something terrible was going on. I just wish you would've called me to let me know what was happening. I sat around here all day worried about you."

"I was going to call you, but I couldn't find my phone. I assumed it was in the car. On the way here I thought about calling again and couldn't find it. I see now that I left it here on the table."

I called him all day and never realized his phone was here all along.

"Anyway, how's Tyler? Where is he?"

"He's so scared. I couldn't get him to leave his mother's side. He'll be fine. The nurses promised to look out for him and to call if there are any change."

"So did they say why she's having seizures now?"

Mark fills me in on Diane and her sickness. I listen to him and still can't believe this is happening to her. It really makes you stop and put everything in perspective. Diane has never been my favorite person, but I wouldn't wish this on her or anyone else. Now that she's dying, I think back on our run-ins and realize how crazy and childish it all really was. Because of this, Mark and I wasted precious time together, and Mark and Tyler missed time they should've been spending bonding as father and son. This just makes you realize how precious life is and how at any minute your world as you know it can be turned upside down.

"Mark, I can't believe this is happening. So have you thought about what you're going to do about them staying alone?"

"I haven't. I guess I need to think of something fast. She may be coming home in a couple days."

"Okay. I need you to hear me out before you say no."

"No, Holly, absolutely not," he says apparently reading my mind.

"I didn't even say anything."

"But I know what you're about to say, and it's not going to work. I don't think that's a good idea at all."

"Mark, what other option do we have? Unless you plan on going to stay with them," I say, knowing that'll never happen because I'll never allow it.

"Hell no, I'm not going to stay with them, and they're not coming to stay with us. I don't mind Tyler, you know that, but how would that look for us to have Diane staying with us?"

"Mark, the woman is dying. I hardly think she's in any condition to try and cause trouble for us."

"Holly, there has to be another way."

"Okay, well you tell me. We can't afford to hire anyone to stay with them."

"Why does this have to be our problem? Diane can afford to hire someone. Yes, she's dying, but she's not dead yet. She's still the same Diane, just a little weaker."

"Well, if she's the same Diane, then you should know she's not about to hire anyone to come stay in her house."

"And you really think she'll willingly come and stay here?"

"She will if she feels she's doing it for Tyler."

"What do you mean?"

"All we have to do is make her believe by staying here she'll help to make Tyler's transition that much easier, which, now that I say it, isn't such a bad idea."

Mark sits with a far-away look on his face. I can tell he's thinking about my idea. "

"Well?" I finally ask.

Well, after all these years of marriage, I still can't believe how wonderful you are. You are truly one of a kind. I don't know any other woman who would open up her house to the woman her husband cheated with. I'm speechless. I don't even know what to say."

"Just say yes so I we can move on and I can tell you what happened today after you left."

"If you're sure this is what you want to do, then fine, but you know I have to convince Diane first."

"In her condition, I don't think she'll be up for much of a fight. Anyway, how about this for news? You remember Erica, my coworker who stopped by the hospital to drop off the fruit basket? Well, she came by today. "

"Oh that was nice of her." he says yawning.

"I know you're tired so I'll cut to the chase. She said my dad is her dad."

"Wait what?" he asks, now wide awake.

"You heard me right."

"Are you being serious?"

"Do I look like I'm playing?" I say staring him dead in the eyes.

"Surely you don't believe her, do you? You don't know that woman. How do you know she's not lying?"

"Why would she lie about something like this, Mark? What would she have to gain? It's not like we're filthy rich or anything. Anyway, she has a picture of him that she carries around in her wallet. She said her mom gave it to her."

"Holly, I would still be careful. Did you talk to your dad about it?"

"No. I was too angry to speak to him."

"How about this? How about you talk to your dad before you convict him of something he may or may not be guilty of doing."

"I'm trying not to get too worked up, but it's hard. You didn't see her—how devastated she was when she saw him. It took a while just to get her to talk because she was so shaken up. I just don't believe she was putting on. I think that was the real deal, but you're right. I'm going to lay this to rest, right now anyway, and I'll discuss it with my dad tomorrow."

Mark and I get into bed and hold each other. I can tell by the tightness of his grip that he needs me just as much as I need him right now. Through all these years it's nice to know we still have each other to lean on. Mark's arms have always been my safe place. I guess some things never change.

Chapter 39

"You know, Holly, I've always thought something wasn't quite right with you. Now I know for sure that I'm right. Something is truly wrong with you."

"Why? Because I have compassion?"

"No, because you obviously love trouble," Janelle says as she sits at my kitchen table drinking her coffee.

Janelle called this morning. She was out early so she asked if she could come by and have coffee with me. I was happy because I could really use the company. She has barely taken her first sip before I start telling her everything that happened on yesterday. I told everything from my dad's supposed infidelity to Diane's seizure. I even told her about my invitation to allow Diane to come and stay with us. That's the part I should've left out.

"I cannot believe you invited that woman to stay in your house. So you're just inviting trouble in, is that it? Haven't you been through enough with this woman? What is it, do you just enjoy being tortured?"

"Janelle, the woman is dying. Do you really believe she's concerned about Mark at this point?"

"I guess we'll find out soon enough, now want we?"

"Janelle you know how I am. She can barely take care of herself. How's she suppose to take care of Tyler too? She's in need, and I don't believe in turning my back on people in need."

"I'm sorry, when did that become your problem because I missed that newsflash?"

"She's in need," I try to explain to her again.

"Okay, Mother Theresa, well save the world, why don't you, and in the meantime Ms. Diane will have plenty of chances to get her hands back on your man."

"Whatever, Janelle." I say as an attempt to end this part of the conversation. "I noticed you didn't say anything about my father and Erica."

"Girl, please, she's lying and you know that."

"You know, for some reason that's exactly what I thought you'd say," I say, laughing.

"Good, then you really didn't need me to say it, now did you?"

"What if she's not lying?"

"But she is so next topic."

"Well, I've decided to take a different approach. I called my mom this morning and invited her to lunch."

"That's nice. You two need some mother-daughter time together."

"Please mother-daughter nothing. I want to pick her brain to see what she knows about this."

"Oh, Holly, I don't know if that's such a good idea. Don't you think you should talk to your dad before you bring your mom in this? What if it turns out not to be true and you've worked her nerves for nothing?"

"Janelle, everything in me tells me Erica is not lying. I'm going to my mom first because if she knows something I can trust her to be completely honest with me."

"And if she doesn't know?"

"I'm not going to tell her, if that's what you're wondering. I have a tactful way of handling this, trust me."

"Okay. I just hope you know what you're doing."

"I do."

"Well, with that said, I'm going to get out of here and go run a few errands before…" She stops midsentence and gives me a very devilish look, which tells me she's up to something.

"Before what?" I ask, knowing this can't possibly be too good.

"Are you ready for this?"

"Probably not, but tell me anyway."

"Before it's time for my appointment with my advisor."

"Advisor? What is this advisor advising you on?"

"Which classes I should take this semester," she practically sings.

"Classes? You're going back to school?" I say almost too excited to talk.

"Yep, I am. Can you believe it?"

"I must say, this is a very pleasant surprise."

"Now you know I'm a little dusty, so you're going to help me, right?"

"You know I am. Girl, you are going to do great. I can't even begin to tell you how proud I am of you. Do you know how many people opt out of going back? Believe me, they always have a good excuse why they can't do it. You have no idea how much courage it takes to make that commitment again. I can't say enough how proud I am of you," I say as I get up to hug her. "Finally, a good surprise."

"The first of many, I'm sure," she says as she walks to the door.

"Let's hope you're right."

"Don't hope—believe," she says with a tone that does make me believe. She sounds convinced that what she's saying is true.

I walk her to the door, and we say our good-byes. I look at the time and notice it's almost eleven o'clock, which means my mom and dad should be out of church soon. I didn't make it this morning. I guess I'm still recovering from the party and everything else that happened on yesterday. Mark and Shelia, his sister, decided to go ahead without me. To my surprise they wanted to take Kirsten with them. I happily got up and assisted with getting her dressed. Being able to have a peaceful few hours is well worth it. I'm sure Mark will take his sister out to eat before coming back here. I'm not sure what time Shelia is leaving so decide to leave her a note letting her know how much I appreciate her coming and sharing in the celebration with us. I'm sure I'll still be out with Mom when they get home.

I hurry and get dressed so I can arrive at Shoney's before my mom. She's always so punctual, and she hates to wait. I think that's her only pet peeve, having to wait. How can someone be patient and impatient? She's patient with people and she works well with children. I don't know if I've ever heard her raise her voice, even when people deserve it. She always says, "They don't know better, or they may just be having a bad day." However, if she's made to wait it's like her whole world is about to collapse. She'll fuss and fuss about so-and-so being late to this or that. My mom is funny, I must say.

I arrive at the restaurant about five minutes before she does. She's still dressed in her usher uniform, so I guess she dropped my dad off and came right over.

"Hey, beautiful," I say as I get up to hug her.

"Hello yourself. You didn't wear that to church, did you?" she asks as she looks at my sleeveless sundress. My mom is so old-fashioned. She's a firm believer that a woman should never wear sleeveless tops or dresses to church. "It just doesn't look right," she always says.

"No, Mother, I did not wear this to church. I didn't make it this morning. I was still pooped from yesterday."

"Holly James," she says in a tone that signifies her disappointment with my decision. My mother feels that if you're not in the hospital or jail, you should be in church on Sunday morning. I remember when I had the chicken pox and the doctor specifically said I was to stay at home in bed, but my mother refused to accept that. I was in church on Sunday morning, spots and all. She just made sure I sat away from everyone else.

After placing our drink and food orders, I decide to stop prolonging the inevitable.

"Mom, I asked you to come because I need some advice."

"Oh, baby, you didn't have to bring me here for advice. You know I'm always happy to advise you in any way," she says, patting my hand on the table.

"I know, but I thought this would be a nice outing for us. Besides, how often do I get to have you all to myself?" I say, smiling at her.

"You're still spoiled rotten, I see."

"And who's fault is that?"

"I don't know, must be your father's," she says, laughing. "But, anyway what kind of advice are you in need of, my dear?"

"Well, it's Mark."

"Mark? Is he okay?"

"Oh yeah, he's fine. It's just that I don't know if I can go on pretending that nothing happened in our marriage. He cheated for nine years. How am I suppose to just let that go?"

Her mood instantly changes. I watch as she ponders my question for a while longer. I'm sure she's probably trying to think of a way to handle this without giving too much information away.

"Holly, all I can tell you is you have to find a way to work through it. I'm sure it's hard, but the two of you can do it together."

"I don't know, Mom. I think this is one of those easier-said-than-done situations. You don't know how hard it is to deal with this day after day. I just don't know if I'm strong enough to do this, Mom."

"Well, since you don't know, I'll tell you. You're strong enough to do this. You just need to believe that your marriage and your family are worth it."

"So, you're saying you believe if Dad ever cheated on you, you'd be able to forgive him?" I wait for her answer. I'm sure this is where she'll tell me he did cheat or something to imply she's been down this road before.

"I believe I would be able to forgive him and move on," she says, then takes a sip of her iced tea. I see this conversation isn't going anywhere, so I'm just going to come out and ask. I know I told Janelle I wouldn't, but I have to know.

"Mom, I wasn't totally honest with you when I invited you to lunch."

"Oh, how were you dishonest?"

"I didn't need advice on my marriage. The truth is things are going great between Mark and me. I needed to talk to you because I heard something yesterday and I need to talk to you about it."

"Okay. What is it?"

"Well, this isn't easy so I'll just say it. There's a girl, well lady, who thinks Daddy is also her dad." I spit it out and watch for her shocked reaction. Surprisingly, it never comes.

"Erica, I assume."

"You know about Erica?" I ask very shocked.

"Of course I know about Erica."

"Well can you tell me why I've never heard of her?"

"Because we didn't think there was a need to tell you about that. It happened a long time ago, and once her mom found out she was pregnant she packed up and moved to California. Your father and I haven't heard from her since."

I'm sitting here listening, but still don't believe what I'm hearing.

"So you mean to tell me I have a sister and no one thought that would be information worth sharing?"

"Holly, we didn't keep it from you to hurt you. In fact, it was just the opposite. We wanted to protect you."

"Protect me from what?"

"From the feelings you're obviously having now. I can tell you're hurting, and this is just what your dad and I didn't want to happen. At the time you were too young to understand, and we didn't feel it was appropriate to discuss this with you."

"Okay, but that was then, Mom. What about now? I'm all grown up. You didn't think I could handle the news now either?"

"Holly, that was over twenty years ago. Believe it or not, it's not something we think about every day. After so long you just put it out of your mind."

"I just can't comprehend that. How do you put a child out of your mind?"

"How do you know about this anyway?" she asks, totally avoiding my question. I know it's because she has no answer that makes sense.

"Erica and I work together. When she came to the party yesterday she almost fainted when she saw Dad."

"Did he see her?"

"No. He was playing with Kirsten. Do you think he'd recognize her if he did see her?"

"Probably not. Like I said, her mom left when she found out she was pregnant."

"So, he's never seen her before?"

"We've seen pictures. Her mom sent them each year around Christmastime. After about five or six years the pictures just stopped coming."

"What is it, Mom? Why can't they just be happy with what they have at home?"

"Holly, I've learned over the years that men are going to be men, and it has nothing to do with us. Believe it or not, your dad and Mark are good men. When it comes down to it, they're good providers, good fathers, and even though it sounds crazy, they're really good husbands. We mess up because we expect perfection, and that's not going to happen. We have to remember they're human and they're going to make mistakes."

"I know what you're saying is right, but I really don't like that philosophy. Shouldn't we be able to trust our husbands?"

"Let me tell you something, and if you remember this, you won't have so many disappointments in life. God is the only one you can trust. Don't trust Mark, me, your dad, your daughter, or anyone else. Putting all your trust in humans is never a good idea. If you never remember anything I've taught you, always remember that.

My mom and I finish our lunch and talk some more. I'm shocked when I leave because I'm not nearly as angry I thought I'd be once this ugly rumor was confirmed. I'm so happy I talked to my mom first. She has a way of always making you see how a terrible situation isn't as bad as you may think it is. I thought I'd leave angry, ready to do bodily harm to my father for hurting my mother, but once again she was the voice of reason. Another thing she told me was no one really knows what goes on between a man and woman but that man and that woman. I guess that's true because all that drama was going on right under my nose and I had no idea. If anyone would've asked me Friday about their relationship, I would've summed it up in one word: *perfect.*

Chapter 40

I finish Diane's room as I hear Mark's car outside. I've been trying to get things together and clear out the room of all of our things. This isn't exactly how I planned to spend my spring break, but I have to do what's right. *Okay, Lord, I'm doing this because I believe it's the Christian thing to do. Please don't let this situation get the best of me. Please help me to keep my eyes open and allow me to clearly see if this is a bad idea.* I already felt uneasy, but Janelle didn't help the situation at all. Now I have all these images running through my head. I have to push those thoughts aside and do what I feel is right, and right now I feel the best thing to do is to open up my house to Diane and Tyler.

"Holly honey, we're here," Mark calls from the living room.

"I'm back here," I holler. "Okay, I guess it's showtime," I say to myself as I make my way to greet them. I pause before walking into the room because I see Mark helping Diane get situated on the couch. I don't know why this picture disturbs me so much because obviously if she's here he's going to help with taking care of her. I just really hope she doesn't get the wrong idea and take his niceness for something more than it is.

"Oh, hey, honey," Mark says as he looks up and sees me standing in the doorway.

"Hey," I say, trying to sound normal. Boy, it sure didn't take long for me to start having regrets about this whole living arrangement.

"Hello, Mrs. James," Diane says once I finally make my way over to them.

"Please call me Holly," I say, trying to lighten the mood a little for both of us.

"Holly, I can't thank you enough for what you're doing for Tyler and me."

"I just want to do what's best for Tyler. I don't think it's fair for him to have to take on that kind of responsibility."

"Mrs. Ja…Holly, I hope you know I would never put Tyler in that kind of position where he would have to take care of me, if that's the responsibility you're talking about."

"I know you would never do anything to intentionally put him in that situation, but I just feel that would happen if you two continued to stay alone," I try to explain because I can hear the defensive tone in her voice.

"Holly, I know you mean well, but please understand Tyler is my everything. I guess I just don't like to think I would do anything that would hurt him in any kind of way."

"Diane, I know you wouldn't. I didn't mean it that way. I guess I should just be quiet because obviously I don't know what to say."

"Holly, it's okay. This is a new situation and an adjustment for all of us. I'm sure Diane knows you didn't mean anything in a mean or hurtful way," Mark says.

"I think we're all a little on edge. I mean come on, it's not like this is your typical situation. We can all dance around it if we want, but it's not going to change the past," Diane chimes in.

"Diane, listen, I extended the invitation because I felt it would be best for Tyler. You're right, this isn't your typical situation, but it is what it is, and we just have to deal with it. Our main priority right now should be to make sure he's happy and living somewhat of a normal life."

"I don't know how normal that's going to be. I mean look at us. He's living under one roof with his mom, his dad, his dad's wife, and their daughter. Is it just me or is that just not normal?" she says, sounding very doubtful of her decision to come here.

"It sounds even worse when you say it," I have to admit.

"Well, I hate to break up this family bonding moment, but I'm going to pick up Tyler from his soccer game," Mark says.

"I'll come with you," Diane says, trying to push herself off the couch.

"Diane, why don't you just get some rest? They'll be back soon," I say, trying to convince her to stay here. Mainly because it's obvious she's in no condition to be moving around, and somewhat because I don't want her riding around thinking they're the happy little family. I'm trying hard to deal with this, but I must admit I'm a work in progress. I'm not totally comfortable yet.

"Yeah, Diane, you stay here with Holly and I'll go get Tyler. I promise I'll bring him right home to you." Mark assures her.

"So I see this is what I have to look forward to, you two treating me like a little baby."

"We're not trying to treat you like a baby, but you need to save your energy," I say.

Mark leaves to go get Tyler. Kirsten is still fast asleep, which means I have nothing to occupy my time. I know this situation will be difficult, but I didn't think it would be this uncomfortable. If I feel this way, I can only imagine what Diane's feeling right now.

"Okay, Mark's gone so you can finally tell me what's really on your mind," she says, interrupting my thoughts.

"What's on my mind?" I ask, confused by her statement.

"Look, Holly, I know there has to be a reason you're doing this. I'm not crazy enough to believe you would actually be okay with your husband's mistress living under the same roof as he is. So tell me what's really the deal. Why are you really doing this?"

"Diane, it's no secret you aren't my favorite person in the world. Each day I work hard to put that part of my life behind me. I try to forget what effect you've had on my marriage and on my life. I'm not going to lie and tell you this situation is an easy one. It's a really big pill to swallow."

"So again I ask why are you doing this?"

"Honestly?"

"Please."

"I'm doing this because you're dying. I'm doing this because over the past few years Mark's wanted nothing more than to have a real relationship with his son. I know this situation is very difficult for Tyler. I'm afraid if you don't stay here and help him to adjust he never will. He's so use to being with you he may regret having to all of a sudden come and live with us. I don't want Mark to have to experience being disappointed or rejected by the son he loves so much. So you ask why I'm doing this. The answer is simply because I love my husband."

"And here I thought it was because of me all the time," she says, smiling.

"Sorry to disappoint you," I say, smiling back at her.

"Well, whatever the reason, I still want to say thank you and I'm sorry. I did everything in my power to tear you and Mark apart. I know I made your life a living hell, and the sad part is that was my intent. I wanted you to be miserable. I did everything I could to hurt you, and here you are opening your house…" she says, starting to get a little choked up.

"Diane, it's okay. I know you regret what you did."

“Holly, that’s just it. It wasn’t until I found out I had a few months to live that I did finally start to regret my actions. It’s funny how dying will make you put things into perspective. You know what really makes me sad?”

“What?”

“It really makes me sad to know I’m not the type of person I would want my son to be. I don’t want him to ever settle for being second best to anyone. I played the fool for a long time. It was always obvious to me that Mark was never going to leave you, but I allowed myself to believe one day he would. I guess when reality really set in, that’s when I decided to take matters into my own hands. Mark once told me you’re a Christian woman. So do you think this is God’s way of punishing me for all the horrible things I’ve done?”

“No, I don’t. Death is a part of life, and one day we’re all going to die. That’s always been God’s plan for us.”

“I’ll have to take your word for it. No offense, but God and I don’t have a very good relationship with each other.”

“May I ask why?”

“I’ve just never felt he existed in my life. It’s kind of hard to believe in this bigger-than-life person when it seems you’ve spent your whole life suffering. For as long as I can remember, I’ve been suffering through something. I guess I shouldn’t be surprised by my final diagnosis. It’s not like anything has ever gone my way.”

“I’m so sorry you feel that way. I know this may not make you feel better, but I can assure you God never left you. He’s been right there with you throughout your suffering.”

“Well, you’re right. That doesn’t make me feel better. So you’re telling me the whole time I’ve been suffering, God who supposedly has the ability to do anything, decided not to help me? No that doesn’t make me feel better at all.”

“Okay. Well can I just say one more thing then I’ll leave it alone?”

“Go ahead.”

“Have you ever thought that maybe God has been waiting on you to turn to Him?” With that said, I decide to leave her alone to think about what I said.

Chapter 41

I did something today I hadn't been able to do in a long time. I sleep in. The past couple weeks since Diane's been here I hadn't been able to sleep much. Most of my time is consumed with taking care of her and Kirsten. We did end up hiring a nurse to be here with her during the day. Diane's health has really started deteriorating these past two weeks. She's lost a lot of weight due to her nonexistent appetite. She's too weak to get out the bed so I have to take care of all her personal hygiene, when the nurse isn't here. She had her last doctor's appointment last week. The doctor said in so many words there's nothing more they can do for her. They sent her home with us to die in peace. A part of me wishes they would've admitted her to the hospital because at least she would be there when she does die. I hate to admit it, but the thought of someone dying in my house isn't a very good thought for me. I don't know what I thought the outcome would be when I asked Diane and Tyler to move in. I guess I thought once she got to this point she would be in the hospital, not in my guest bedroom.

I lay in bed a while longer and finally decide to get up and check on everyone. Today's Saturday so I don't have to guess where Tyler is. I know, without doubt, he's in the room with his mom. He stays there so much that Mark and I decided to buy a futon to put in there so he'd have something to sleep on. He has his own room, but he doesn't seem too interested in it, and with good reason.

I hear Mark in the living room talking to Kirsten. I watch them from the hallway. My heart swells when I see the interaction between the two of them. Mark is such a great father to both his kids. He would do anything to make sure they're happy. I decide not to interrupt them. I pass by Diane's room and notice the door's close. I lightly knock on the door, then turn the knob slowly because I don't want to interrupt their moment either. When I crack the door I see Tyler sitting in a chair with his head at Diane's side. I hear what sounds like crying so I decide to go ahead and make my presence known. I walk over and he's totally oblivious to me being there.

"Tyler, what's wrong?" I ask as I turn my attention to Diane. I see that something is terribly wrong. She looks like she's sleeping, but her color is very pale. I touch her and do not expect the coldness that I feel. My heart drops to floor and all I can do is call for Mark.

"What's wrong?" he says, running into the room.

I look at him and say the words I've been dreading since Diane and Tyler have been here. "She's gone," is all I can get out.

"She's…" he says, stepping closer to the bed.

I nod to confirm he did hear my right.

"Tyler, why didn't you come get us?" I finally ask.

He looks up at me with tears streaming down his face. "She asked me not to," he says.

"When did this happen?" Mark asks.

"Last night," he says.

"Last night! Tyler, you should've…" Mark begins but stops when he notices the look on my face.

"I heard her coughing so I got up to check on her. She looked like she couldn't breathe so I told her I was going to get help. She grabbed my hand and shook her head no," he says as he starts to cry again.

I walk over to him and notice he's holding her hand. I can tell by the imprint he's been holding it for quite some time. "Tyler, we have to call the coroner to come get her," I try to explain.

"No! They're not taking my mommy," he says as he places his body on hers.

"Tyler, please don't do this. I know this is hard, but you have to let them come get her," I again try to explain. I turn around to look for Mark for help, but notice he's left the room. I'm sure he's gone to make the call.

I try to pry Tyler off his mom, but he's not budging. I decide it's best to let him stay there and hold her as long as he can. I know this is going to be extremely hard for him. He's so young to have to endure so much pain. I can't imagine not having my mom, so the thought of losing her so young is enough to choke me up.

"Holly," Mark says from the doorway. I walk over to him to see what's next.

"I called and they're sending someone out now. We're going to have to get him out of here."

"Mark, he's not going without a fight. I've already tried to move him. Why don't we just let him have this moment? We'll move him when the coroner comes."

"Holly, I just don't think we should let him stay in here. He shouldn't keep seeing her like this."

"Mark he's been with her like this all night. A few more minutes isn't going to hurt."

He reluctantly agrees to leave him alone. We watch from the door as he lies across her crying. The bond they share is unbreakable. This is probably going to be the hardest challenge in his life. This is truly going to be a day he'll never, ever forget.

Chapter 42

It's been over a year since I was hit with the realization that my dad isn't the perfect man I made him out to be. Seeing Erica again was very awkward at first. Neither one of us really knew what to say. She called one night and invited me out to dinner. She said she didn't like the way things were between us and we really needed to sit down and clear the air. I agreed to meet her, and we actually had a wonderful conversation. We talked about everything from our childhood to dating. I tried to avoid talking about my home life too much because I didn't know how that would make her feel. We've become really close since then. I can't say we have a sisterly relationship, but I feel we will develop one eventually.

I did talk to my dad about Erica, and he explained the situation to me. Even though nothing he said made it right, I had to take a long look at my situation and remember I really don't have room to criticize him. I guess the part that really upset me is when he tried to lecture me on marriage. I realize now he was so upset because he didn't want to see Mark and me go down the same path he did. In the end I understand everything he does is only to protect me. Being a parent, I can appreciate his need to want more for me than he and Mom had. I decided that wasn't a battle I really wanted to fight with my dad. We discussed it and it's over. Our relationship is stronger now than ever.

As for him and Erica, well that's a different story. He's tried to reach out to her on several occasions, but she wasn't very receptive. She still has a lot to sort out. I can't be mad with her because I don't know what she's feeling. I grew up with both my mom and dad living in the house with me. I can believe that void of not having a father isn't something she can just move on from. I expect that time will bring the two of them closer. I have to admit I have mixed emotions about their relationship. I'm not use to sharing my dad with another person besides my mom. The little girl in me really doesn't want to have to share him with her, but the adult in me wants them to patch things up and get to know each other the way I know each of them, as wonderful, loving, and caring individuals.

Janelle did enroll in college. She had a rocky start, but things are starting to smooth out for her. She just had to mentally prepare herself to get back into the groove of doing papers and studying for exams. Janelle is the type who's always looking for the easy way out. That's why she dates married men. It's a relationship of convenience, and she doesn't have to put in the time and effort to make it work. She can care less if it works or not because she has nothing invested. I'm praying hard she'll find someone to call hers and settle down and have the life she deserves. I keep telling her she's too good to be anybody's number two. I really believe that, now if I can just get her to believe it.

As for my family, well, things couldn't be better. Kirsten is the joy of our lives. She's your typical almost two-year-old. She's very hyper and energetic, and Mark and I both tease each other about being too old for this parenting thing. It's strange how life has a way of working out. Mark and I started off trying to have a child, with no luck, and now we have two children. Tyler's transition wasn't as easy as we'd hoped it would be, but with good reason. For so long it's been him and his mom. He took her death very hard. He still has days where he sits in his room crying. I try to comfort him as best I can, but I don't think I'm doing a very good job.
Mark's been great with him though. He does things to try to occupy his time like taking him fishing and signing him up for after-school sports. He seems to enjoy doing those things, and I believe time really does heal all wounds. Right now we just allow him to grieve however he sees fit. All we can do is be there for him and reassure him he's not alone. He has a family who loves him and cares for him and always will.

I've come to realize life is like one big classroom. Each day there's something new to learn. I learned my lessons the hard way. Mark and I have gone through a lot in our marriage, but in the end it strengthened our bond. I'm grateful Dexter is a thing of my past. After his mom passed, he moved back to Atlanta. Even though he's gone the thought of him coming back and revealing his true identity still haunts me. I know I should've come clean with Mark. I just felt he could handle my news better thinking the guy I slept with was thousands of miles away. I'll probably feel guilty for my actions forever. I can almost see why some dirty little secrets are best left in the mind of their keeper. I've always heard that there's life after the pain, I can honestly say there is, and if you live right you may find it's actually better than before.

As I sit here wrapped in my husband's arms I realize this is the man I want to spend the rest of my life with. He is all the man I need. No one said marriage would be easy. In fact, it's the hardest job I have; however, whether it's good, bad, or indifferent we are in it until the end, and that's a promise I never plan to break.

Meet the Author

L.A. Lewis is a free lance writer and educator. She's been writing for over fourteen years. She's a 2001 graduate of Southern University in Baton Rouge, LA., which is where she currently resides with her husband and two children. When she's not writing she enjoys spending time with her family, cooking, and reading.

Look for her next book, "The Gift of An Abundant Life" coming December 2009. This book is guaranteed to inspire and uplift. It challenges you to start living the life God designed for you to live.

www.ingramcontent.com/pod-product-compliance
Ingram Content Group UK Ltd.
Pitfield, Milton Keynes, MK11 3LW, UK
UKHW041948190726
13854UKWH00004B/1847